PLAYING

FOR

REAL

The debut novel of
R E Barringham

Also by R E Barringham

Stand By Me
Two Weeks In Corfu

Acknowledgements

I'd like to say a huge thank you to the following people for their help and support. Firstly to my two editors, Doug Watts of JBWB.co.uk and Michael LaRocca of CHINARICE.org for honestly criticising my work and finding fault in the right places. Also to Dean and Rachel for all their help and support and for putting up with me throughout the journey of writing this book.

<u>**Warning:**</u>

Prepare to be afraid

Chapter 1

Prologue

Neville Johnson threw open the door and ran from his upstairs study. Behind him thunder roared and lightning flashed, filling the room with bright pulsating colours.

"CATHALU!" the voice roared behind him. "ABADDEN I invoke you!"

There was no time to stop and look back. In fear for his life, Neville Johnson didn't even believe that he had time to run down the stairs so instead he jumped over the banister railing and dropped to the floor below.

Too late he realised what a long drop it was. He braced himself for a painful landing.

CRACK!

Neville wasn't sure if he actually heard the sound but he definitely felt it. Both his ankles broke simultaneously as soon as his feet hit the floor.

The agony made him fall onto his side and scream, but nothing could be heard above the din coming from the study. The pain shot up his thighs and into his groin.

With his mouth open wide he continued to scream, afraid to move because he knew that would make the pain worse, but also knowing that he had to escape his tormentor or be killed.

So much had happened recently and so many had died. Now he lay there feeling utterly helpless and he couldn't stop screaming.

Then the chanting began.

"Nema reve dna reverof, yrolg eht

Dna rewop eht, modgnik eht si eniht rof."

Neville knew the thing upstairs meant to kill him and was invoking and employing as many evil demons as it could to destroy him.

He needed help.

Why had he jumped over the upstairs railing? He shouldn't have allowed himself to panic the way he did. But he had been taken completely by surprise when the thing had suddenly manifested itself before him.

Now it towered over him, and he could see it was a wizard, at least seven feet tall. It wore a long, black, hooded robe, its face obscured by the blackness within the hood, except for a pair of red glowing eyes.

Neville Johnson had already seen the warning and knew that if he feared the wizard then he would die. But he couldn't help being afraid when it suddenly appeared right in front of him, and so he had fled.

Now he lay cursing himself for having reacted the way he did and not simply running straight down the stairs and carrying on out the front door.

But it was too late now for regrets. The front door might as well be a million miles away because he could never make it in time with the pain he was in.

His only hope of surviving was to reach the telephone that sat on a small table a few feet away. But would anyone be able to get there fast enough to help him? It didn't matter. It was his only chance and he had to try.

He put his palms flat on the floor and pushed himself up slightly. The excruciating pain in his legs made him scream even louder and higher.

As he began to move he heard footsteps on the landing and the dreaded voice sounded much closer.

"Live morf su reviled tub,

Noitatpmet otni ton su dael dna."

As Neville heard the words he knew exactly what the wizard was saying. It was reciting the Lord's Prayer in reverse. This was a common incantation but he knew that the wizard was powerful enough to use these simple words for great evil. Neville Johnson was scared. He was more afraid than he'd ever been in his whole life, and recently many things had made him afraid, but not like this one.

The pain from moving was great but his fear of dying was greater. He inched along the carpet, screaming all the time. His throat hurt and his open mouth ached, but his screams continued regardless.

"Su tsniaga ssapsert ohw esoht evigrof ew sa."

The wizard was getting closer to the top of the stairs. Neville continued screaming as he inched along, dragging his legs behind him. He wasn't sure if he was screaming from the pain or his partial loss of sanity, because he knew he couldn't stop screaming even if he wanted to, but right now, he didn't want to. Too much had already happened these last few weeks and his mind was struggling to cope with this new surreal situation he now found himself in.

Coloured lightning continued to pulsate and thunder clapped loudly and continuously, only now it was all around him.

He used his arms to pull himself along the floor. The pain made him feel nauseous and he came close to passing out. His progress was slow, almost nonexistent, but he had to keep trying because time was running out. The wizard was now at the top of the stairs and continued to chant.

"Sessapsert ruo su evigrof dna,

Daerb yliad ruo."

Neville turned briefly and glanced up the stairs. The wizard's head was turned and its eyes were upon him. Neville started to shake uncontrollably and heaved himself forward as fast as he could.

The pain from his ankles bolted all the way up to his chest and Neville screamed harshly, his throat already dry and sore.

He reached forward as far as possible and his fingers just managed to touch the telephone lead. He leaned a fraction further and yanked the wire towards himself. The telephone clattered onto the floor and the cordless receiver landed by his chest.

"YAD SIHT SU EVIG!"

Neville glanced up the stairs again and saw that the wizard had its arms raised and its hands pointing skywards.

Despite his fear and pain, Neville noticed that although the wizard's arms were vertical, its long loose sleeves still covered the full length of its arms and didn't slip back to its shoulders as anyone else's would have. It was a simple thing to notice and he wondered why, in amongst all this horror, his logical mind picked up on such a triviality. But he paid scant attention to these thoughts. There was no time left to think about anything but escaping this waking nightmare.

He picked up the receiver in his trembling hands and pressed the "talk" button. The red light illuminated to show that the receiver was connected and he could now dial 999. He wasn't sure what he would say or how he would speak because he was still screaming.

As though sensing it was running out of time, the wizard chanted faster.

"Nevaeh ni si ti sa htrae no

Enod eb lliw yht

Emoc modgnik yht

Eman yht eb dewollah

NEVAEH NI TRA OHW REHTAF RUO!"

It screamed the last sentence as loud as it could, just as Neville pressed 9 for the third time.

The sudden searing heat in the back of his head and down his spine told him that the incantation had worked. He'd fought so long and hard lately and defeated everything that had tried to destroy him. He'd beaten them right up until this last battle, but this personification of evil standing above him was his Waterloo.

The pain from his ankles now seemed to be spreading. It felt as though every bone in his body was breaking one by one. It was unbearable, more than any human could cope with. Neville felt his consciousness slipping away as the agony increased. It was as though he was leaving his body and the breaking bones now belonged to someone else.

His screaming abruptly ceased but his mouth stayed open. A low guttural sound began deep in his throat and gradually became louder before fading away.

Slowly he began to fall forward, until his face was pressed firmly into the carpet and his arms lay limply by his sides. The telephone lay nearby, useless and forgotten.

"Hello. Emergency services. Which service do you require?" came the voice from the telephone receiver.

"Hello? Is anyone there? Hello?"

But no one heard.

Neville Johnson was dead and the empty house was now quiet as a tomb.

Chapter 2

Josh Harrison sat in front of the computer on the small desk in his bedroom. The morning sun shone through the window, lighting up his ginger hair.

His bedroom was neat and tidy for a thirteen-year-old. His bed was in the far corner. A lamp and an electric alarm clock stood on a small neat chest of drawers beside it. On the wall by the door, built-in wardrobes ran the full length of the room. His mother had made the navy blue quilt cover and pillowcase on his bed and also the matching curtains at the window.

But Josh wasn't aware of any of these things right now; only the computer occupied his conscious thought. He had even forgotten that his mother was still standing by his side, waiting to see if the sight of the computer would cheer him up.

He raised his hand and pushed the "start" button. The computer whirred into life and on the screen came the words Journey to the Promised Land. Wow! Uncle Neville's special game.

He opened the CD drive and looked in. There sat the shiny disk with the words "Journey to the Promised Land" printed across it with the words "Travel to the Depths of Terror" in smaller print.

Josh was thoughtful for a moment. It was the last game his uncle had played.

Uncle Neville had been found dead at the bottom of his stairs. An accident, according to the coroner's report. But how could anyone die from only having broken ankles? There had been no cause of death found so the coroner had no choice but to record the death as accidental.

In Josh's mind the whole thing had been very suspicious. The police had found no sign of a break-in, nothing to indicate that anyone else had been involved and yet it had looked as though Uncle Neville had jumped from the upstairs landing and broken both his ankles as he landed. The whole thing just didn't make sense. Why would he do that?

Journey to the Promised Land must have been the last thing he'd been working on because the disk was still in his computer.

Uncle Neville had spent weeks working on his new game, even becoming somewhat fanatical about it. Seeing the disk in the drive meant he'd finished it and played it. So why panic and why didn't he call for help? He'd managed to reach the telephone but then for some reason his heart had stopped beating.

That had been three weeks ago.

"Don't you want it?" his mother asked. "I thought that you'd like to have his computer seeing as the two of you always spent so much time together on it."

"Yeah, I guess so," said Josh. "But Journey to the Promised Land was his most special game and he wouldn't even play it when I was there, let alone let me play it myself, and now it's mine. It just doesn't seem right." He let out a deep sigh and closed the CD drive.

His mother smiled. "You know, sometimes I think the only reason he made computer games for a living was because he liked playing them so much himself. He always was a big kid, as well as an eccentric old hippie."

"He was the smartest person I ever knew," said Josh defensively.

His mother stroked his hair. "I'm sorry. If it upsets you to have his things in your room we can always put them away for a while."

"No, having his things isn't the problem."

Josh couldn't say any more. His heart was still breaking.

Uncle Neville had been Josh's best friend, even though Josh was only thirteen years old. His uncle's skill and ability at creating computer games fascinated Josh. There was nothing that man didn't know about computers and their programs. Sometimes Josh was sure Uncle Neville knew more than the so-called computer experts.

He would tap away at the keyboard and input many intricate commands into his games and then he and Josh would observe the results. Sometimes the computer was confused about what it had to do and then all manner of strange things would happen within the games.

In one game Uncle Neville wanted to change the background colour to green. He typed the instructions into the game's system, but when he restarted the game it seemed that everything in the game had disappeared, except the background colour which was very green indeed.

Then when he tried to move the characters in the game they all kept taking a few steps and then falling over. The two of them had laughed until tears came to their eyes.

Uncle Neville was puzzled but soon realized that he'd changed not only the background colour to green, but also everything in the background too. So it all blended together into one big mass of green so all the digital characters on the screen were walking into rocks and other objects they couldn't see and falling over. Josh had often had funny moments like that with Uncle Neville.

He also loved his uncle's slow and meticulous way of working. Uncle Neville worked in his study and could spend hours absorbed on a particular program while surrounded by well-organised chaos.

He had been separated from Josh's Aunt Hazel for some years now. His mother said she didn't blame her sister one bit for leaving Neville because all he ever cared about was his computer and his games.

Josh couldn't see what the problem was. His uncle was a genius and quite rich from all the games he invented too, so what did it matter if he worked long hours? Aunt Hazel should have spent more time with him as Josh had done, then she could have been having lots of laughs too.

Josh couldn't understand how anyone could fault Uncle Neville. He was a handsome man and even his big nose and long wavy hair added to his charm. He was such an individual person and never cared what anyone else did or thought.

All the kids Josh knew spent their time trying to fit in with everyone else. They all talked the same, dressed the same and listened to the same kind of music. Anyone who didn't do these things was considered strange and uncool.

But Uncle Neville seemed to hardly ever notice the world going on around him and only ever aimed to please himself, and what pleased him the most was making computer games. His house was always untidy and cluttered but this just seemed like an extension of his well-organised but chaotic personality. He was always so efficient at his work, yet so disorganised in life.

Josh had been his guinea pig and would try out all the games his uncle made and then tell him what he liked and disliked. Uncle Neville would frown and consider Josh's opinions carefully; then he would suddenly smile and begin making notes and corrections and Josh could almost see the light bulb go on above his head as he did so.

Uncle Neville also allowed Josh to try already marketed games made by others and tell him what he thought would make them better. Uncle Neville would once again set to work and re-invent the games in a much-improved and well-disguised version. In Josh's opinion, Uncle Neville was brilliant. He would spend days or weeks working on a project, burning the midnight oil night after night until the game he was developing was perfect.

The only game he never allowed Josh to test for him was *Journey to the Promised Land*. He always insisted that it was his special project and that he didn't want Josh to see it before he'd perfected it. He told Josh that this game contained "X," his secret ingredient, never before tried but which could be dangerous in the wrong hands.

"Josh, this is the best idea I've ever come up with. If this works out the way I expect it to, this will be the most realistic game ever."

"You mean the things that happen in the game are just like things that happen in real life?"

"No, Josh, it will be much more than that." Neville rubbed his hands together thoughtfully as he spoke, then ran his large right hand through his long, auburn hair, drawing it away from his face. "You see, most game designers think that having 3D scenes in the game is the most important thing in making the game seem real. But I think there's more to it than that. I think it's far more important that everything looks, acts and sounds real."

Josh nodded, but plainly wasn't quite grasping what he was being told, so Uncle Neville carried on.

"For instance, I don't want a haunted house to look like it came from a fairground. I want it to look like an ordinary house, but dark and forbidding, so that the person playing the game can *feel* the danger lurking within, that way they become more a part of the game. And for that same reason I want to give the people in the game more personality so that the person playing can bond more and feel more involved in who they're playing with or against."

"So instead of the game being three dimensional, you want to take it further, to another dimension."

Uncle Neville smiled and slowly nodded. "Very good, Josh. Very good indeed. In fact I might even include that in the blurb on the CD cover."

Josh smiled and felt proud of himself.

"But this program is very long and complicated but I'm sure I can do it, if I can install 'X' in the right places."

"What exactly is 'X'?"

Uncle Neville tapped the side of his large nose with his index finger. "Top secret, I'm afraid. It's my own clever invention and I intend to keep it mine."

Josh didn't understand the need to keep it a secret from him. Who would he tell? He probably wouldn't be able to understand it anyway.

Over the next few weeks his uncle became more preoccupied with his new game. Josh would call around after school every day as usual, to find his uncle scrolling through a computer screen that looked to be filled with hieroglyphics.

Uncle Neville kept on scrolling and muttering and his table was littered with pieces of paper scrawled with hastily written notes. Every now and then he'd stop scrolling and rifle through the notes until he found the one he was looking for and then type in some more foreign-looking instructions. Josh marvelled at the way his uncle seemed to know exactly what everything was on the screen.

As the days turned into weeks, Uncle Neville became completely absorbed in perfecting *Journey to the Promised Land* and seemed to forget that Josh was there.

Then one day Josh entered the study as he was playing the game.

"Hi, Uncle Neville."

His uncle jumped and immediately switched off the game.

"Josh, what are you doing here so early?" he said, looking round the room nervously.

"It's not early. I've finished school."

"Well, look..." Uncle Neville seemed pre-occupied. "I'm really busy right now and I, um...I have to go out soon."

Josh felt hurt. He knew his uncle was lying. He wasn't busy because Josh had just seen him playing a game and as for going out, well, he didn't believe that either.

"OK then. I've a lot of homework to do anyway." Josh turned and quietly left.

After that day Uncle Neville never used the game while Josh was there.

"Will I be able to try your new game soon?" Josh asked him one day.

"No," was the only abrupt answer he received.

Uncle Neville didn't mention the new game again even though he kept the disk permanently in the computer's disk drive. Josh had to try out his games on the spare computer instead. It all seemed so strange but his uncle didn't offer to explain anything and Josh had the feeling that it was more than just his new computer game that was the problem. Even the neighbourhood seemed hushed and still without the usually blaring loud music and fast cars.

"I saw some bunches of flowers outside a house nearby as I came up the street. What are they for?"

"There was a death," Uncle Neville said without emotion.

"An old person?"

"No. Two teenage boys."

"Is that why there's no loud music anymore?"

"How am I supposed to know?" snapped Uncle Neville. "It doesn't matter anyway. It's none of my business."

Josh felt hurt again. He'd never seen his uncle like this before. His nerves seemed as taut as piano wires but Josh couldn't understand why.

It seemed that all Uncle Neville wanted to do was play Journey to the Promised Land. It was as though he was addicted to it. Several times Josh had heard the game switch off as he entered the house, but Uncle Neville always pretended he'd been immersed in another project when Josh came into the study. All this heightened Josh's curiosity about this special game.

Up until now he had been really looking forward to trying it one day. But now Uncle Neville was mysteriously dead and Josh didn't believe that he was the clumsy type of person to fall down the stairs, or the crazy type to jump. But still, nothing could explain his demise. Although he didn't know why, he felt that Uncle Neville's downfall had something to do with his unwholesome obsession with his new game.

Just then Josh's father, Roger, came into the room, put his arm around his mother's shoulders, and led her quietly out of the room.

Josh heard his parents go downstairs together in silence.

*

In the kitchen his mother sat at the table while Roger made coffee.

"Rachel, try not to worry about Josh too much. He needs to grieve and come to terms with it in his own time."

Rachel studied her hands. "But I'm worried he won't. He still seems to think that Neville's death was mysterious."

"If it makes him feel better to believe that then let him. Telling him he's wrong all the time will only make him feel worse."

"Always the psychologist, aren't you?"

"Yep. That's what I always tell my students. In fact, I always tell them I'm the best around and they believe it."

"That's because you're such a good psychologist that you can get into their heads and make those university students believe any old twaddle," Rachel said with a mischievous smile.

"You bet."

They both smiled at Roger's usual big-headedness.

"You just stop worrying so much about Josh," he told her.

"I can't. I'm his mother and it's my job to worry. I'm worried that he's lonely. He used to spend so much time with Neville, and he doesn't seem to have any friends his own age anymore. He used to hang around a lot with the Clarkson's' son until they emigrated. Josh would have been lonely if he didn't have his crazy uncle, but now he's gone too."

"Just because he doesn't invite anyone home, doesn't mean he has no friends. And besides, Josh is a bit of a loner anyway, but that doesn't mean he's lonely. Trust me. Josh will be fine."

But Rachel's brow remained furrowed.

*

Upstairs, Josh sat and stared at the computer. It wasn't a new machine; in fact it was quite a dinosaur compared to the slim, flat-screen models in the shops. But he knew that appearances were deceptive and inside the computer's old bulky exterior was the most powerful and precision-built motherboard there could possibly be. Uncle Neville knew everything there was to know about computers and he only built the best.

He'd always loved playing on this machine at Uncle Neville's, but here on the desk in his own bedroom it looked strangely out of place. Josh knew exactly how it felt. He too was used to being at Uncle Neville's. He knew his mother meant well by giving him the computer, but he wasn't completely sure if it was the best idea. It had been difficult for him to cope with Uncle Neville's passing, which was so unexpected it took everyone completely by surprise, especially Josh.

At first the news was difficult to take in. Aunt Hazel had been dancing with glee because she and Uncle Neville had never actually divorced and so she inherited everything of his.

She wasn't slow about things either and wasted no time in having the decorators in, throwing his things out and moving into his house with surprising alacrity. He must have left plenty of money too because she resigned from her job before he was even buried.

The funeral had been difficult for Josh. He'd never known such sadness in his whole life. His crying began during the funeral service and seemed to continue without stopping.

His parents kept him out of school while he grieved and it was the longest and loneliest three weeks of his life. His eyes had become sore and puffy and every fresh bout of tears made them worse. Today his parents had gone to visit Aunt Hazel in her 'new' home but Josh couldn't bring himself to go and his parents understood.

They had returned with the computer and brought it straight up to his bedroom. At first he thought seeing the computer again might make him cry, but it didn't. Perhaps he had no more tears to shed, which was just as well because he was going back to school on Monday. Today was Saturday so there was still time for his face to return to normal. He didn't want anyone at school to know he'd been crying.

School wasn't one of his favourite places. He'd endured years of teasing because of his short, thin body and ginger hair. He could never understand how he'd ended up with ginger hair because nearly everyone related to him had dark hair.

He'd obviously inherited his small stature from his mother because she was very petite and men whistled at her as she walked down the street. His father, by contrast, was a tall bear of a man with dark hair, a beard and moustache.

There were three bullies at school who were older than Josh and always gave him a hard time, but the school's anti-bullying policy meant that, thankfully, they couldn't harass him as much as they wanted to.

Luckily Josh was quite studious and loved to learn so his mind was always occupied with his lessons, instead of dwelling on any bad treatment he received from other children. However, his enthusiasm for education did little to endear him to his classmates.

Josh was always putting his hand up to ask questions during lessons and he wrote copious notes. He was also the student who handed his homework in on time and it was always completed correctly and with great attention to detail.

His teachers were impressed. His contemporaries weren't and so Josh spent most break times in the library by himself or sitting outside alone.

No, school was never a favourite of his because it was so socially isolating, but he did enjoy the lessons. He knew that over the past three weeks no one would have missed him, but he would be behind in his school work and have a lot of catching up to do.

Michael Clarkson used to be his best friend and they spent quite a lot of time together. Michael was more studious than Josh so the pair of them were a good match for each other. But Michael's parents had taken him to live in France, so Josh had compensated by spending more time with his uncle. But now he was gone too.

Josh sat and stared at the monitor. Curiosity about *Journey to the Promised Land* was already pricking at him, so he sat up straight, took a deep breath, moved the mouse and clicked the cursor over the words "New Game" at the bottom of the screen.

The computer tower whirred and clicked. On the screen appeared a scene of a man standing at the edge of what looked like a village. Josh gasped at the quality of the graphics. The picture seemed so real. No wonder this was Uncle Neville's pride and joy.

The man in the game was tall and slim yet muscular. He had shoulder-length mousy brown hair and his face was smooth and handsome. He was wearing what looked like a leather breastplate, tight dark trousers and knee-high black boots. Across his back he wore a drawstring bag. He looked so real that Josh could even see his chest move as he breathed and his hair was so life-like that every single hair must have been created separately.

The village looked startlingly authentic as all the people milled around, attending to their day-to-day chores. It was an old fashioned setting, a community of tiny cottages with thatched roofs and dirt roads. All the shops were small with people working outside doing carpentry, cooking, basket weaving and much more. It looked like a true-life scene from about three hundred years ago. He even saw a woman empty a chamber pot into the street.

He watched the goings-on in the village a while longer, fascinated by such intricate detail. He saw children picking their noses, someone cutting a pig's throat and people openly urinating in the street. It was like watching a history lesson called *The Disgusting Way We Used to Live.*

The people all spoke and interacted with each other as though they were alive and not digitally constructed computer graphics. Men flirted with the young women, children misbehaved and were openly chastised by their mothers and there were even two drunken men staggering around with tankards full of slopping ale.

Josh smiled as he watched it all, finding it more entertaining than watching television. The village people greeted each other with cheerful waves and loud hellos. Several times Josh was sure that they were looking and talking to him, but that just couldn't be, so he thought they must be greeting other people he couldn't see.

It was all so brilliant. He'd never seen a game like it before. If Uncle Neville had lived he could have made his fortune from graphics as good as this.

After a while, Josh reluctantly tore his gaze away from the village and turned his attention to playing the game.

There were options for the game at the bottom of the screen and he looked through them to try to discover how to play. It seemed that the man in the game was the hero and the object was for him was to travel to The Promised Land collecting weapons and objects along the way. He also needed to eat food to keep his strength up and to defeat any enemies he came across. There was a thick green line at the bottom of the screen showing how much energy the hero had and at the moment it was full. Josh knew that if the energy level sunk to zero then his hero would die. Energy was life in a game so it must be watched closely and not forgotten.

Apart from all the noise and conversations from the village, Josh was aware of strange background noises as well. They were quiet enough to be almost inaudible, gently picking at the edges of conscious recognition.

Josh leaned closer to hear them more clearly, but they remained elusive and secretive. At times Josh thought it sounded like monks chanting, then it sounded like sombre singing and then yet again he thought it was haunting music. Whatever it was, it added an eerie dimension to the village scene that was inexplicably disturbing.

Nonetheless, he thought it should be an interesting game because it had been Uncle Neville's secret project and Josh was dying to try it.

He had to give the hero an on-screen name, so he typed in "Salvador." He knew it was a corny name and that if anyone saw it they would laugh, but no one would see it because it was his game now and he wanted to keep it private just as Uncle Neville had done.

He liked the name Salvador because he was fascinated by works by the surrealist painter Salvador Dali. His weird paintings never ceased to amaze Josh who could study them for hours.

The game seemed quite basic. Salvador had to first go through the village collecting whatever he could. It appeared that the four arrow keys on the keyboard controlled Salvador's movements. If he pressed up then Salvador moved forward, down and he turned in the opposite direction, left for left and right for right. There were also other keys for making him pick things up, use his weapons and jump. So far it looked like a pretty ordinary game.

Josh began by pressing the upward arrow and Salvador walked forward into the village.

Immediately the villagers began to speak to him as he passed through.

"Good morning. I hope you find what you need here."

"Bugs! Bugs! This whole place is overrun with the damn things. Beware!"

"Hey, good-looking. If you seek fun and fulfilment you should go forth to Trixie Bell's."

"There's plenty of produce in the stores. More than you'll need."

"Come dine with us. We have plenty to share."

On outside tables and on the ground, Salvador found money, knives, swords, bows and arrows, a shield and food. He collected them all.

A beautiful woman, who looked like a gypsy, approached Salvador and held out a small knife with a beautiful jewel-encrusted handle. "Here, buy this. It will bring you luck because I've blessed it." Josh moved Salvador nearer to the woman, gave her a bag of coins, took the knife and stored it in his bag.

He walked Salvador into one of the village stores but most of the weapons there were similar to what he already had. However, there was one item that Salvador didn't have and that was an aerosol can. Josh thought it was out of context in such an old-fashioned village but he bought it anyway by trading one of his knives.

Once outside the store, Josh leaned forward for a closer look at the can. It was plain with no writing on it so he wasn't sure what it contained, but he stored it in Salvador's bag anyway.

He knew he shouldn't collect too many things because the heavier the bag became the more energy he needed to carry it. Fortunately though, at the moment, there was more than enough food around to keep up his strength. He even let Salvador store some food in his bag, just in case.

The food was what looked like lumps of white flakes. When he moved the cursor over the lumps the word "manna" appeared, which Josh knew was a reference to the food provided by God for the Israelites in the Old

Testament. He didn't know who provided the manna in the game and he didn't care as long as there was plenty of it.

Once through the village Salvador stood before a wide stretch of woods. The trees were close together and appeared to have few leaves despite the fact that they seemed to block most of the sun. The darkness within looked spooky and Josh felt as though Salvador would be swallowed up forever as soon as he entered. At first he thought of walking Salvador around the edge to see if there was another direction he could go in, but then he chastised himself for being afraid of a computer graphic.

It was only a game but he still had a feeling of trepidation as Salvador began his journey through the woods. The trees were close together, their trunks twisted into unnatural shapes. Some even looked as though the wood had taken on the image of screaming faces. But as Salvador passed by the misshapen masses, they morphed into less threatening, nondescript lumps of bark. The further he walked the creepier it became as dozens of irregularly shaped tree trunks squirmed and changed, like a Mexican wave of grotesqueness. Although it all looked sinister and the ever-present unearthly sounds continued, Salvador didn't appear to be in any physical danger. Yet.

He turned nervously at every sound and Josh constantly scanned the gaps between the trees for any sign of movement. How could a game make him so scared? He didn't even know what he was afraid of. There was just something about the woods that made him feel uneasy. The scary background noises were more audible in the quiet woods, adding to his unease.

He continued walking Salvador along the narrow path, but after a while it felt as though he was walking around in circles. He felt as though he was just passing by the same trees again and again. Was the game trying to trick him? He laughed at himself for even thinking such a thing. It was only a game and the woods weren't real. And how was it possible to tell one tree from the other? But still the nagging doubt remained.

He tried a different direction along another small path, and then another, but still the trees and the path all looked the same. Now he was lost, and he didn't know how to get out of the woods.

Josh thought it was a good time to check the memory section of the game, which he found to be empty. Strange. He'd expected to find at least one saved version from when Uncle Neville had played it. It was necessary throughout most computer games to 'save' the game at certain points while the hero was safe, then if something killed him further along, the player could return to where he'd saved the game and try again. It was sort of like putting a bookmark in a book so that if you lost your page you could just open it at your bookmarked page and start again from where you left off.

So that was what Josh did. He placed a virtual bookmark to save the game while Salvador was still safe in the woods.

The game was so realistic that Josh could hear the crunch of every footstep and snap of every twig. Salvador even wafted away all the flies and bugs that flew into his face and there was the sound of birdsong in the air.

Soon Josh thought he could hear another sound, a kind of whooshing, fluttering sound. Bird's wings? No it didn't sound feathery at all, more like paper.

As Salvador continued forward, the papery, fluttering noise became louder until eventually it could be heard above all the other noises. Soon it was loud enough to drown out everything else, and that was when he saw it. Up ahead was a group of large white-winged insects hovering in mid-air.

The creatures had the shape of mosquitoes, with their long thin bodies, sharp tongues, and long dangly legs, but they were much larger than normal. Some of them were as large as Salvador's hands or bigger. The quality of the picture on the screen and the realistic effects meant that Josh could also see the ugly, gargoyle-like heads of the creatures whenever they flew close to the screen. Josh knew it was only a game and that the creatures weren't real, but every time they flew close to the screen, he could have sworn they were looking right at him.

He moved Salvador a few paces back and positioned him behind a tree out of sight. He watched the mosquitoes whirl and fly, graceful in movement, yet ugly as sin. What he was seeing enthralled him. Up and down they flew and over and over each other.

Eventually, when he'd seen enough, he decided the best course of action was to try to find an alternative path away from the swarm. He turned and backtracked the way he'd come and veered off onto another track to the right.

Soon he could hear the fluttering sound again and up ahead he could see the big mosquitoes. He'd been sure he hadn't walked round in a circle, but he must have done.

He turned around again and took another path in the opposite direction but within seconds he could hear and see the mosquitoes again. There must have been more than one swarm or else they must be following him. Either way, he wasn't going to escape them.

He clicked the mouse over the insects and a description of them appeared on the screen:

Large poisonous mosquitoes. Swift in movement. Attack as a swarm.

Great! How was he supposed to defeat these? Mosquitoes were pesky insects at the best of times and they would always inevitably sting someone. So what was he to do?

Just as well these don't travel as a swarm in real life, thought Josh, *or they could kill someone.*

*

Outside Josh's bedroom window, a swarm of large white-winged creatures hovered unseen. Then silently, as one mass, they flew across the garden to the willow tree near the far end. Up into the high branches they flew, completely out of sight and unnoticed, except for one hungry bird sitting high up in the tree. It snatched at one of the insects with its beak and then instantly spat it out as though it tasted foul. The bird shook its head and flew away as the injured insect fluttered ungracefully to the ground and quietly died.

No other birds entered the tree and soon nothing moved there. The willow tree's new inhabitants sat patiently, waiting.

Chapter 3

Rachel Harrison was looking out of her kitchen window when she saw a small white object tumbling in the gentle breeze across her neatly mown back lawn. It turned lightly over and over until it was quite close to the house. She watched it with interest, not sure of what it was. A piece of paper? A tissue? A butterfly? No, it couldn't be a butterfly because it was much too big.

"What do you think it is, Tweety?" she asked the little caged canary behind her, without taking her eyes off the white object.

Curiosity got the better of her and she went outside to take a closer look. But even squatting down next to it, it was still hard to tell what it was.

She held back her wavy auburn hair with one hand and bent closer. She was unaware that anyone else was in the garden so the sudden voice from behind startled her.

"See anything interesting?"

"Oh Roger, you made me jump."

"I'm sorry but when my wife finds something more interesting than me to look at, I like to know what it is."

Rachel gestured for him to come closer. "It looks like a moth or something, but it's far too big...almost alien."

Roger knelt down and made a "hmm" noise in his throat, and then he stood up and pushed it with the toe of his shoe. It rolled over, exposing its spindly legs and undercarriage.

Carefully, with index finger and thumb, he picked it up by the tip of one wing.

"Yuck," said Rachel, wincing when she saw its face more clearly. "What the hell is it?"

Roger studied it closely for a few seconds in silent wonder. "It looks like a mutation of something that's escaped from a mad scientist's laboratory."

"It's huge."

"I know. Its body must be at least five inches long. I've never seen an insect this big before."

"Are you sure it's an insect?"

"Well, it's got six legs."

Rachel shuddered. "But look at its face. It's flat just like a human's, with two eyes, a nose and lips. But it's all twisted and scowling. That's not an insect. It looks more like something out of a horror movie. Oh God, Roger, put it down. What if it's not dead?"

"Well if it's not dead it's doing a pretty good imitation."

Roger turned the creature around and studied it. Rachel shifted uneasily from one leg to the other, hoping and praying that the creature wasn't going to suddenly wake up. She couldn't bear the thought of it opening its beady eyes, or worse, flapping its wings in her face.

"It just looks too weird with that freaky face."

"You're right. Insects shouldn't have faces like that or be so large." Roger gently placed the insect back on the grass and went into the garage. A few minutes later he re-emerged wearing his thick gardening gloves and carrying a large glass jar. He grasped the insect in his gloved hand and pushed it headfirst into the jar.

As he screwed the lid back on, Rachel said, "I was saving those jars to make more fruit jam this summer."

"It's all right, you can have it back when I've finished," joked Roger.

"Oh gross. No thanks," said Rachel with a grimace. "What are you going to do with it anyway?"

"There's an entomologist at the university so I'll take it with me to work on Monday and see if he knows what it is."

"Well, leave it in the garage until then, will you? I really don't want it in the house."

"Scaredy cat."

"When it comes to that thing, you bet I am."

*

Josh decided to take a break from playing the game. He didn't have a clue how to defeat the mosquitoes and he couldn't be bothered to think anymore. Having to fight over-sized insects didn't exactly make the game exciting. He'd expected something more dangerous and scary to jump out. Insects were just boring.

He saved the game, switched off the computer and went downstairs to watch television for a while. But that was boring too because there were no kids' programs on. So after lunch he returned to his room and once more attempted to play. Maybe the game would get better soon, but he needed to get past the over-sized mosquitoes first.

He turned on the computer and clicked on "resume game." On the screen Salvador was once more standing in front of the mosquitoes. He clicked the cursor over the small image of the bag on Salvador's back, and the contents were instantly displayed at the bottom of the screen. He chose the large knife as a weapon. It appeared in Salvador's hand and he began swinging it at the mosquitoes. But they were very fast and agile and all managed to dodge the swinging blade.

Salvador had to back away repeatedly as the mosquitoes slowly advanced.

Then without warning they were upon him. Josh pressed the "Enter" key on the keyboard repeatedly to keep Salvador's knife swinging. The more rapidly he pressed the faster Salvador swung the blade. But it was futile. Salvador fell to the ground screaming amidst the flapping, feasting insects. Josh couldn't see what was happening but he could hear sounds of tearing and chewing. He hoped it was only Salvador's clothes they were attacking but he could see Salvador's energy line at the bottom of the screen ebbing away until it was gone and Salvador lay still.

The mosquitoes flew back and disappeared into the trees again, blending into their surroundings until they could no longer be seen amongst the leaves.

Salvador lay on the ground, bitten and bleeding, the graphics so real that it looked like an actual person laying there, his body ravaged. Pieces of torn flesh seemed to be hanging from every wound.

"How could mosquitoes be so vicious?" Josh said to himself. They usually only stabbed a needle-sharp tongue through a person's skin, but these creatures appeared to have bitten and ripped the skin wide open.

Outside the window to his right, movement caught his attention. He stood up and went to the window, grateful for any distraction.

He saw a squirrel jumping from branch to branch in an old tree. The branches shook every time the squirrel landed, sending leaves cascading to the ground. As he watched, the squirrel raced down the trunk and tumbled about on the lawn as though enjoying its own private game. Josh watched it for a while; its antics making him smile.

The squirrel seemed to be a permanent resident in their garden and could usually be found in one tree or another. But Josh was not a fan of the squirrel and wished it would go and live somewhere else. He didn't used to mind it, until last summer when he'd been playing with his basketball in the garden and went beneath the big willow tree to bounce the ball off the trunk.

It was fun because the wide trunk had a very uneven surface and so the ball never bounced back in the same direction twice. But as Josh amused himself by diving left or right to catch the ball, the squirrel fell out of the tree directly onto the top of his head. Both Josh and the squirrel got a terrible shock and the squirrel bounced onto Josh's left shoulder. As it landed, it dug its claws into his skin to try to stop falling further and gave Josh's shoulder a nasty bite as well.

Josh screamed and shook the squirrel loose and ran inside. At the same time the squirrel hit the ground running in the opposite direction.

His mother had tried everything to stop the bleeding but nothing worked. In the end she'd taken him to the hospital and they'd had to wait nearly two hours to see a doctor, with Josh's shoulder bleeding the whole time. The doctor had ordered Josh's wound to be stitched up and he'd had to have a tetanus injection as well. All in all, it had not been one of his better days.

The rotten creature, Josh thought. He knew it was just an accident that the squirrel had fallen on him, but it didn't have to bite like that.

He looked back at the computer monitor and was surprised to see that one of the mosquitoes was hovering in mid-air right up against the screen and was looking directly at him with its grotesquely twisted face and black eyes. He jumped and then laughed at himself. It was silly. The mosquito was only a computer graphic and couldn't possibly see him. But then again, he'd previously been sure that the entire swarm had flown into the trees and none had been left behind. So where had that lone creature come from?

As he watched, the mosquito turned and disappeared into the trees too. Josh decided he'd had enough of playing the game for one day so he closed the computer down.

*

Later that evening, just as darkness was descending and the neighbourhood was quiet, the squirrel scampered across the lawn. It stood on its rear legs and sniffed the air. Something was wrong. It sniffed again. There was danger in the air.

A loud bark and a sudden bang against the wooden fence behind sent the squirrel scurrying to the base of the willow tree. It stopped and looked back towards the fence, but there was nothing to be seen.

It relaxed instead of ascending the trunk and sniffed the air again. Dog. That's what it could smell. It was the dog that was always at the other side of the fence and was just waiting to sink its teeth into the squirrel one day.

But the squirrel was smart and knew that it was safe as long as it stayed out of the dog's territory.

It ventured cautiously out onto the lawn again, sniffing the air as it went. There was definitely a smell of dog in the air, but there was something else as well. Without moving its head, the squirrel looked all around with its dark little eyes and that's when it saw the danger. A ginger cat had secreted itself under the dense foliage of a small bush and sat silently watching its intended prey.

The squirrel's tail flicked rapidly from left to right as it anticipated its next move. It needed to get out of there fast to somewhere the cat couldn't easily follow. Without giving any advance warning, it turned and ran up the willow tree's trunk, higher and higher until its acute sense of danger told it that there was more to fear up ahead than down below.

Stopping abruptly, the squirrel twitched its nose then kept perfectly still while it scanned the dark inner recesses of the tree. Too late it saw and heard its approaching foe.

The large white mosquitoes emerged from their resting places amongst the branches. In one quick movement the squirrel about-turned and bolted back down the tree.

But the swarm of mosquitoes flew swiftly out of the tree and were upon the squirrel as soon as it reached the ground. The poor animal had no chance of escape as all the mosquitoes attacked it at once, tearing at its flesh and injecting their poison.

The squirrel threw itself to the ground where it thrashed and twisted, unable to shake the insects loose. Over and over it rolled, desperately trying to crush the alien creatures. But the mosquitoes were very large and as they bit into the squirrel's soft flesh, it only took one small shake of their heads to tear the skin loose before they gorged on some of the meaty flesh below and finally injected their deadly poison.

The poison rapidly worked its way through the squirrel's body and soon it couldn't move anymore. The paralysis numbed the pain of the feasting mosquitoes, leaving the squirrel feeling unnaturally calm and peaceful.

The mosquitoes left their dying, bleeding victim and retreated back up into the branches of the willow tree.

As the small, twisted and ragged body lay on the grass behind the tree, its eyes took on a glassy appearance and then its foot gave one last twitch before its life was extinguished.

Chapter 4

The following Sunday morning dawned bright and sunny. It was the kind of warm summer's morning that promises to turn into a gloriously hot day.

Josh and his parents ate a leisurely breakfast outside on the patio. In the kitchen, the canary sang happily in its cage, its spirits lifted by the beautiful weather.

The warm morning also lifted Josh's spirits. Since Uncle Neville's death he'd begun to believe that his sadness would never go away, but now he felt positive that eventually he'd be able to think about his uncle without feeling burdened with grief.

His father finished his coffee and leaned back in his chair. "So Josh, what are your plans for today?"

Josh shrugged. "Dunno. I hadn't thought about it really."

"I don't believe it. It's a beautiful warm and sunny day, your last day before going back to school and you don't know what to do with yourself?"

"I don't make plans. I just do whatever I feel like doing."

His father leaned forward and crossed his arms on the table. "And what do you feel like doing?"

Josh shrugged again. "Dunno really. Thought I might have another go at the computer and see if I can figure out the game."

His parents both frowned. His mother opened her mouth to speak but his father cut her off. "You're going to waste beautiful weather like this and sit in your bedroom all day?"

"Not *all* day. I just said I want to have a look at it. Anyway, what are you going to do?"

"I, my boy, have a whole stack of essays to mark."

"Ha! So you're going to be inside and *waste all this beautiful weather*," said Josh, imitating his father.

"No, I'm going to sit right here marking essays so I'll be *enjoying* the weather not wasting it."

"Well, I would join you but the computer plug won't reach this far."

"In that case you can join me out here when you've finished, sarcastic little devil that you are," said his father with a grin.

"Maybe," Josh said as he stood up and carried his plate and cup into the kitchen. He didn't want to sit and discuss his non-existent plans for the day anymore so he went straight up to his bedroom. He really didn't understand adults and their obsession with having to be outside on a warm day. To his mind everyone should do whatever they wanted at the weekend. He knew his parents would soon get tired of sitting in the sun anyway because his father always got too sweaty and his mother liked to spend hours in her sewing room.

Josh himself was just looking forward to exploring his new computer and trying out his new game and hopefully finding out more about Uncle Neville's secret ingredient.

Because it was such a nice day he opened his bedroom window wide before sitting down in front of the computer.

The computer tower was under the desk so he leaned down and pressed the "start" button. The tower whirred and clicked and within seconds *Journey to the Promised Land* appeared on the screen. Josh frowned. On any normal computer a disk wouldn't start up without the person using the computer instructing it to do so.

At the moment he wanted to see what else was on the computer hard drive so he leaned down and pressed the "eject" button to remove the disk from the drive. The disk drive, however, was unresponsive. He pressed it again and again but still nothing happened. He knew of no other way to remove a disk from the drive. He pressed the "escape" key on the keyboard to try to end the game, but it too was equally unresponsive.

At the same time Josh's eyes were drawn to the somewhat unnerving lifelike graphics on the screen.

His hero, Salvador, was back at the saved version of the game where he was lost in the woods. Before he went any further, Josh clicked the mouse over Salvador's bag to see if there was anything useful in there to kill the mosquitoes.

He saw the spray can that he'd collected earlier. Could that be bug spray? No, surely it wasn't that simple to defeat those deadly creatures. But not being able to see anything else more suitable, Josh clicked the mouse over the spray can and it appeared in Salvador's hand. Then onward he went until he saw the mosquitoes. As they swarmed towards him, Salvador held up the spray can. A large vaporous cloud issued from the nozzle when he pressed it, enveloping the whole swarm. All the mosquitoes stopped advancing and as the cloud thinned Josh could see them falling one by one to the floor where they squirmed and fluttered.

Once they were all on the ground Josh walked Salvador forward. His feet trod on the still-writhing insects. They shuddered and jerked as their bones cracked and they issued tiny little squeals of pain that seemed so real that Josh felt the hairs stand up on the back of his neck. He momentarily thought of keeping Salvador still to end the creatures' agony, but he reminded himself that it was only a game and the mosquitoes didn't really exist and they weren't really suffering, although part of his conscience remained unconvinced.

To get it over and done with quickly, he marched Salvador around and around over the pile of insects until they were still and silent. It wasn't pleasant to listen to, but it was quick. Josh saved the game there so that they would remain dead. He took a few moments to overcome his guilt at annihilating the mosquito swarm.

He slumped back in his chair. Was that it? Was it really that simple to defeat his first enemy? Although it had been a gruesome affair it had still been very easy. If the game continued being that simple then it would soon become very boring indeed. He wondered why his Uncle Neville had thought this game was so special.

*

Outside in the garden, the dead squirrel, hidden from sight behind the willow tree, was now the only evidence that the mosquitoes had ever existed. The tree was filled with birdsong once more and everything was as it should be again.

*

On the computer screen Salvador was still in the woods with the mosquito creatures squashed under his boots. Using the arrow keys, Josh walked him forward. But parts of the mosquitoes were still stuck to his soles and with every step he took there were squelching sounds and mosquito debris was left in his wake until every bit had been walked off. This added touch of reality was unsettling and Josh unconsciously squirmed in his seat.

He walked Salvador down several different paths looking for an end to the woods. Every path still looked like all the others and all the tree trunks turned and morphed as he passed by.

After several minutes of perseverance, Salvador emerged into a very large overgrown field. The grass and weeds came up to the top of Salvador's knee-high boots. There were small green bushes here and there and a few wild flowers but none were higher than the grass. In the middle of the field stood an old, ramshackle, timber house. Three unpainted and warped steps led up to the weathered veranda that ran the full length across the front. The windows were dark and dusty and webs hung from every corner.

As Salvador made his way across the field, the house took on an evil appearance, as though frowning at his approach.

The two top windows, with their gothic arches, became like watchful eyes. Josh was nervous. As Salvador neared the house, it seemed as though it took a deep breath. He could have almost sworn that the sides of the house expanded as it took in air and held it, waiting to exhale if its front door was opened and the air escaped. The closer Salvador became, the more sinister the house seemed to be.

A sudden long creaking sound issued from the house. Josh felt his heart beating against his ribs. He began to feel afraid for Salvador and was glad that he didn't have to enter the house himself. Damn this game. How could it make everything on the screen so alive and so real? Josh sometimes felt as though he was looking through a window into another world rather than playing a game of fiction on a screen.

As Salvador mounted the creaky steps and neared the worn and shabby front door, a door with loud, rusty hinges could be heard slowing opening from inside. An involuntary shudder travelled the length of Josh's spine.

He saved the game at this point, afraid that once through the door there would be no going back. It was as though entering the house would be more like being swallowed up and left to the mercy of whatever lay inside. The door was stiff and hard to open at first. Salvador had to lean his shoulder against it to force it to move and as he entered the house, the door slammed shut behind him, cutting off all the outdoor noises. The sudden silence made Josh jump.

Soon other strange noises began. Josh had never heard anything like it before. The sounds were barely audible, but they were there. The house was dim inside and covered in dust and webs. The scene looked so real that Josh was almost sure he could smell the mustiness.

The noise continued, a kind of soft, scratchy sound. He moved Salvador into the centre of the room and then scanned around 360 degrees.

He was standing in a large room with a staircase to his left. The staircase had open spindles but it was impossible to see what lurked in the upstairs darkness. The room he was standing in had two overstuffed dusty armchairs and a small coffee table in front of an unlit fireplace with a black cast-iron surround. A tall bookcase stood beside the fireplace and a door in the far right corner led into the next room. There was an oval hearthrug in front of the fireplace but apart from this one small covering, the dusty floor was bare.

The almost inaudible noises still persisted but still there was nothing to be seen. He edged Salvador further inside, always mindful of any hidden danger like a trap door.

The floor beneath his feet remained solid, but the walls and ceiling began to move. At first it was no more than a feeling that they were moving, but then he began to see what was happening. The walls and ceiling were undulating in places, moving as though the house had a pulse.

As Josh watched, the pulsating areas began to expand further and further until they were bulging inwards and stretched to the limit. The pressure caused resounding rips, long slashes appeared all around and above Salvador, and then something dark began to ooze from the gaps.

At first they looked like worms, hundreds of hairy worms. Josh moved the cursor over some of them and words appeared on the screen.

Spiders. Large. Poisonous. Fast.

It wasn't worms that he was seeing, but spiders' legs. Hundreds of them, forcing the rips wider as they pushed their way into the room.

By the time he had read the words, Josh realized it was too late for Salvador to escape. He was completely surrounded.

The spiders covered every inch of the walls and ceiling and they advanced quickly, some simply falling onto him from above. In the blinking of an eye Salvador was completely obscured by the web-spinning predatory creatures. They enveloped him so thickly that they moved as one heaving mass, with their soulless black eyes lacking any emotion and their venomous pincers aiming at Salvador's flesh with loathsome clicking sounds.

Josh felt completely defenceless as he sat and watched the unfolding horror before him.

*

Outside Josh's bedroom, the six-foot-high, solid wooden fence at the bottom of the garden began to shake. Only lightly at first, but soon becoming more pronounced until every piece of wood rattled. It started at one end and continued to spread until the whole fence was moving.

Then out from the tufts of grass below, dozens of large, hairy spiders' legs became visible, squirming and pushing up out of the ground as though rising from premature graves. The fence shuddered as the legs reached up and caught the bottom of it. They used the fence as leverage to haul themselves out, kicking loose tufts of grass in their efforts to free themselves.

Unseen and unheard they began to advance slowly across the garden.

Chapter 5

After lunch Josh's father reversed his car out of the garage onto the front drive and commenced to give it a thorough cleaning inside and out. Josh stayed in the kitchen and helped his mother with the dishes. It wasn't a job that he loved nor did he volunteer to do it, but helping with simple chores around the house was part of the proviso for getting his pocket money every week. His mother washed while he dried the dishes and put them away. They chatted amicably together as they worked and the little canary sang happily in their company.

"The canary's in fine voice today," said his mother. "I'll open the window more so that he can hear the other birds in the garden." She leaned forward over the sink and pushed the window wide open.

The canary's cage was hanging from a hook in the low ceiling and was near the open window. The bird instantly began to chirp louder.

Josh's mother smiled. "See, he loves fresh air and the company of other birds' song."

"For someone who lives alone he sure is cheerful," said Josh.

"He's not alone. He's the fourth member of our family."

"How long do canaries live?"

"Forever," his mother said quickly.

Josh laughed. "No he won't, Mum. He probably won't live very long at all. Canaries don't, you know."

"He's never going to die," she answered swiftly. "That bird will live forever and so will we all. No one else in this family is going to die, ever."

Josh smiled at his mother. She had always loved her family dearly and couldn't bear the thought of them having to part, but he sometimes wondered if she said these things in fear or if she was joking.

Josh could remember having a brother and sister who had both been stillborn and his mother went into some kind of depression after the second one. Even though he was very young at the time he could still remember her sadness. She sometimes visited their graves, but she always went alone. Her grief seemed to be a very private thing. She never mentioned it and so neither did he or his father. Obviously his mother wasn't going to try to have any more children so Josh was to remain an only child. He sometimes wondered what it would have been like to have a brother and sister.

Josh now knew how she felt about grief. His sadness over losing his uncle had been deep and he too had shouldered his grief alone. It just wasn't an emotion for sharing, and talking about it would only make it take longer to heal.

"He'll be a very old bird if he lives forever," said Josh.

"Then we'll have an elevator installed up to his perch so that he won't have to climb the ladder anymore."

Josh could well believe that she would. The cage was big enough for several canaries and looked quite fancy the way it was modelled on a Buddhist temple, and it contained every available luxury a bird could want.

But his mother was the same about everything. Their house was large and filled with many of his mother's personal touches. All their furniture was old and solid and lovingly restored and reupholstered by his mother. She had also made all their curtains and hand embroidered all their tablecloths and place mats.

She was also an excellent seamstress and made many clothes for all three of them. And when she wasn't sewing or working on things for the house, she was in the kitchen preserving and pickling fruit and vegetables from the garden or from wherever she had been out gathering fruits and berries from fields and riverbanks.

Yes, his mother was certainly a homebody and she made sure they all ate well and lived comfortably, including the canary.

Once the dishes were done Josh went into the living room to watch television and his mother retreated to her sewing room.

Unfortunately both of them had forgotten that the kitchen window was wide open and didn't see the neighbours' ginger tomcat watching the canary from the garden.

*

The cat had been hiding nearby, listening to the little bird sing. It couldn't believe its luck when the window was thrown open to provide easy access to the bird. The cat bided its time, waiting until it was sure the people were gone and not likely to come back. When it felt that it was safe to proceed, it deftly jumped up onto the kitchen windowsill and peered cautiously inside to make sure no one was there and then turned its attention to the canary's cage.

The cautious feline silently crept onto the worktop next to the sink and sat watching the canary. The tip of the cat's tail moved slowly from side to side in anticipation of the kill.

But it would wait until the time was absolutely right. There was no room for mistakes.

The canary, sensing the danger, ceased its song. But Josh with the TV on, and his mother with her radio on, did not notice the canary's sudden silence.

After a few minutes the cat began to pace up and down, its eyes still riveted on the cage that hung only a few feet out of reach. The bird froze, its eyes never leaving the cat as it stalked. Up and down the cat continued to walk, trying to decide the best angle to attack the bird from and wondering if it could pull its helpless victim through the narrow bars quickly enough before it was disturbed. The people were sure to interfere if they knew the cat was enjoying the kill. For some unknown reason this always upset them, but it had taught the cat to always be quick if it wanted to keep its prey.

Now it was time. The cat knew which was the best position to leap from, and was sure it could snatch the bird, pull it through the narrow bars and be out of there before anyone noticed. It positioned itself carefully, gave a slight wiggle of its abdomen for added projection and then leapt at the cage.

It landed very fortuitously with one paw on top of the cage and one on the door, which sprang open immediately. Moving with lightning speed, the cat let go of the cage door and used its now free paw to swipe at the canary. Again it struck lucky and its claws brought the stunned canary swiftly to its mouth. Then without pausing for even a heartbeat, the cat let itself fall to the floor then immediately jumped through the open window and fled into the garden.

The canary was still in the cat's mouth and was too shocked to even make a noise.

Once it was at a safe enough distance the cat stopped and looked back at the house. No one was coming. It lowered the bird to the ground and held it firmly under one paw before releasing it from its tight jaws. It looked down at the comatose little creature. This was going to be an experience to savour.

The cat extended its claws around the bird and threw it up into its mouth. The bird didn't try to struggle or try to escape. The cat dropped the bird back onto the grass and batted it with its paw. The bird limply tumbled to one side. Quick as a flash the cat scooped it up again, tossed it high in the air and then slapped it back down, pinning it under its paw. It tossed the bird repeatedly, leaping on it the moment it hit the ground as though it was a difficult enemy doing all it could to escape.

The bird, however, had already died of fright, but the cat didn't care either way and continued to amuse itself with the tiny lifeless body.

*

Josh had been feeling restless so he thought watching TV might help him relax. He pressed the remote control and channel-hopped until he found a suitable cartoon to watch. But his restless state of mind soon got the better of him and he began sitting and then slumping in all manner of positions until finally he hung upside down with his feet hanging over the top of the sofa and his head almost touching the floor.

He discovered, however, that watching TV wasn't easy in this position and soon he was unsure as to what he was seeing. So he channel-hopped again to find something more familiar to watch. He came across an old episode of *The Simpsons* which he'd already seen several times so he hung there and watched it.

After twenty minutes he realized his blood had filled his head and he could feel his pulse throbbing loudly in his ears.

He turned himself the right way up and sat quietly for a few seconds, light-headed, while his blood rushed back to the lower parts of his body. He felt rather light-headed and made a mental note never to hang upside down for that long ever again.

As soon as he felt almost normal again, he turned off the TV and went into the kitchen to make a cup of coffee. Most of his friends thought it was strange that he preferred coffee instead of the fizzy sugary drinks they all liked. Even their mothers were impressed that he liked to sit and have a hot drink. But to Josh, a cup of coffee was what he'd always preferred so it didn't seem strange at all.

As he picked up the kettle he shouted, "Mum do you want a cup of coff…" but his words were cut short when he saw a yellow feather in the sink. He turned and looked up at the empty cage. Then turning to look out the open window he saw the ginger cat lying on its back in the garden, all four feet in the air clawing madly at the limp little bundle of yellow feathers.

He felt an overwhelming sense of guilt for leaving the window open but at the same time he was angry at the cat for harming their defenceless little bird.

He went outside and clapped his hands loudly. The cat, which was unaware of his presence, immediately leapt to its feet in fright.

"Shoo, you rotten bastard." The cat quickly fled across the garden and over the fence. Josh went back inside to find something to pick up the canary with. He knew that he should just carry it with his bare hands but he couldn't stand the thought of touching the ragged, and probably still warm, body.

He looked through the kitchen drawers until he saw the neat pile of cleaned and ironed yellow dusters. He took one outside, draped it over his hand and carefully picked up the bird. The cat must have been playing with it for some time because it was in quite a bad state. Most of its feathers were on the ground and its body was ripped and bloody.

Luckily its head was mostly untouched and fully feathered so Josh wrapped it so that was visible. He didn't want his mother to be too upset and he thought she might be if she saw the state of the whole bird.

He went inside and called his mother into the kitchen.

"I'm sorry," was all he said when she came in.

His mother looked from the bird in Josh's hand to the empty cage. "What happened?"

"It was next door's cat. I'm sorry, Mum, it must have come in the open window and somehow managed to open the cage. I found it out in the garden."

He saw the look of hurt on his mother's face and at that moment he would have done anything to make things right again. He felt he'd had enough death and upset in his life recently.

"Well it's pretty warm today so we'd best bury him straight away," was her only reply.

Together they went to the back of the garden and buried the bird under a bush. Josh then quickly set about the task of cleaning out the birdcage. He took it outside and thoroughly washed and dried it before storing it on a shelf in the garage.

When he came back in he went straight upstairs and his mother retreated once more to her sewing room. Neither of them spoke the whole time.

Up in his bedroom, Josh slumped down heavily into the chair and turned on the computer.

Damn! He couldn't believe the cat had killed the canary. He wouldn't have been so upset if the cat had eaten it, but to torture it for fun was deplorable.

A lone tear appeared in his left eye but he brushed it away immediately. He was too old to cry over a dead bird. He'd cleaned out the cage straight away because it hurt too much to see it hanging there empty. The kitchen had already seemed empty enough without the canary's song.

How he hated that cat. It was always chasing birds in the garden and unfortunately it quite often caught them too. To Josh's mind the cat was nothing more than a serial killer.

To help him forget what had happened, he turned his attention back to the screen and immersed himself in the game again. The scene was where he'd last saved it and Salvador was waiting once more to enter the old spooky house. He walked Salvador through the front door again, only this time he would try to do a lot better because now he was aware of the spiders so they wouldn't take him by surprise again. Forewarned was supposed to be forearmed, wasn't it? He also forearmed him with a large knife.

All the walls and the ceiling started moving again, spiders stretching the smooth surfaces as they fought their way out. As soon as the spiders' legs began to appear through the walls, he made Salvador swing constantly at them with his knife.

At first this tactic was successful and he managed to swiftly separate most of the spiders from their limbs. But eventually there were too many of them. Those dropping from the ceiling made it especially difficult for him as Salvador didn't seem capable of swinging the blade directly above his head. Soon he was completely cocooned in spiders' webs and hanging upside down from the ceiling.

Again and again Josh reverted to the saved version of the game, repeatedly tried to defeat the spiders but he couldn't do it and it always ended up the same way. He wondered why Salvador was in the house anyway. What was he supposed to achieve by being in there? If the aim of the game was to journey and collect helpful objects then there should be something there of vital use to him.

Perhaps he should be concentrating more on collecting what he needed instead of exhausting his supply of energy on fending off the multitude of deadly arachnids. He sat and thought about it for a while, trying to come up with a better strategy. He needed to enter the house and take what he needed as fast as possible before the spiders had the chance to attack and overwhelm him. Maybe there was something in the house that he could use to kill the spiders. But the question wasn't where it was, but how he could find something to kill the spiders while being attacked by hordes of them. There was no time to do anything once he entered the house.

Time! That's what he needed! Why hadn't he thought of it before?

The spiders hadn't killed Salvador but rather had wrapped him up to save him for later, and then they had left.

Josh walked Salvador into the old house again only this time he didn't fight the spiders. Again the spiders pushed their way through the walls and ceiling and completely wrapped Salvador in webs and hung him upside down. Once the spiders retreated, Josh used this time to scan Salvador's digital environment instead of ending the game and trying again. He was looking for something useful to defeat the spiders but there was nothing there. On a table towards the rear of the room was some food and what looked like a pile of grain. Josh couldn't see how grain would help him - after all you couldn't kill something by feeding it grain - but he decided he'd take it anyway because it might become vitally important later on in the game. So, he reasoned that because there was nothing in the room to help him defeat the spiders, his only defence would be prevention. He needed to avoid the spiders rather than confronting them. The question though was how to pick up the food and grain and run out of the house before the spiders attacked again.

Josh replayed the game several times more, making Salvador dash in as fast as he could and head straight for the table at the back of the room. But every time he picked up the food and grain and placed them in his bag, he didn't have enough time left to make it out of the door to safety.

In the end he gave up and turned the game off.

*

Out in the garden the back fence once again began to shake. One by one, more spiders emerged and made their way across the lawn to join the others already in the willow tree. No one saw their journey despite the spiders being twice the size of tarantulas. They moved slowly and effortlessly between bushes until they were hidden under the willow tree's branches which hung to the ground. Then on they went to the tree's trunk where they ascended to the lower horizontal branches.

Several birds in the tree took flight and no others arrived, as though they all sensed the threat of danger. There the spiders patiently waited for several hours, without moving, except for their round abdomens, which stirred rhythmically with every small spider breath.

Later in the evening, the neighbours' ginger cat ventured once more into the garden. It went immediately to where it had left its prey, but apart from a faint scent there was nothing there, not even one yellow feather.

A sudden noise from under the willow tree caught the cat's attention. It turned and stared at the darkness beneath the low-hanging branches. It could just make out something small on the grass. A bird? A mouse? Something even more powerless? Anticipation of a swift kill was over whelming. Stealthily, it stalked to the tree, ready to pounce on whatever it found.

The cat lowered its head to peer under the hanging leaves, but it was too dark to see clearly and its keen nose couldn't pick up any scent. Once through the hanging branches its eyes immediately adjusted to the dark gloom and it saw a frog sitting at the bottom of the tree trunk. The cat sat down to watch it to see what it would do, but the frog didn't move at all. The cat began to inch closer until it was within striking distance but the frog remained still. Slowly the cat raised its front paw and struck the frog squarely on top of its head. The frog showed no reaction whatsoever and didn't even blink.

The cat raised its paw again and battered the frog on the head several times. This time it got a reaction, although not the one that it expected. The frog simply inflated its chest to bulbous proportions and so the hammering of the cat's paw made it fall over. Most intrigued, the cat stretched out on the ground and began rolling the frog back and forth between its front paws.

The cat was totally absorbed in its cruel torment when suddenly three large creatures seemed to appear from nowhere and land on the cat's back. Instinctively the cat jumped to its feet and shook itself vigorously in an effort to dislodge the unwelcome intruders. But the spiders hung on with their large pincers. The cat hissed and spat and bolted up the tree trunk hoping that the spiders would fall off once vertical. But too late it realized it was running headlong into more of them. Without stopping, the cat leapt over them and kept on running, its claws piercing the bark with every step thus allowing it to continue on its course against gravity.

As soon as the cat felt it was high enough to be out of immediate danger from the other spiders, it leapt onto a wide horizontal branch and turned into a snarling hissing ball of fury as it again tried to dislodge its unwanted passengers. But the spiders had no desire to leave their host so they hung on even tighter, their large pincers cutting deeply into the cat's skin.

The exhausted cat paused, growling deep in its throat. The pain in its back was immense but its most worrying concern was that dozens of other spiders were fast approaching from below. The terrified feline attempted to climb higher but it was becoming physically weak and found climbing to be slow and difficult as the poison from the spiders on its back worked its way through the cat's body, slowly paralysing it.

Within seconds the other spiders had reached the cat and climbed all over it as they began to engulf their prey in sticky webs. The cat was desperate to remove itself from this nightmare situation but its now permanent paralysis held it powerless while its forbidding captors worked with precision, cocooning all the cat's limbs and head separately before drawing them all together and wrapping them up tight.

The cat could do nothing but lie there and wait. It was very afraid and traumatised and desperately wanted to move and fight its way out, but its body remained uncooperative and motionless. It lay on its back, its legs, tail and head held tightly together, pointed skywards.

Once they'd finished, the spiders moved away. Minutes ticked by with nothing happening, and then the cat felt itself turning over. The spiders were behind it, pushing it out of the tree.

The sticky webs stayed glued to the branch until the cat was stuck to the underside, and all it could see through the tangle of webs over its face was the ground far below.

Then the weight of the cat caused the sticky webs to come unstuck from the branch inch by inch until the cat plunged to the ground with a thud. Its bones cracked as it hit the ground, but thanks to the paralysing poison, it didn't feel a thing.

As the cat lay dying the frog hopped near.

"Ribbit," the frog said, and then confidently hopped away.

The cat watched it disappear from view and its dying thought was of wanting to torment the retreating frog.

Chapter 6

Josh woke up on Monday morning and saw that the weather was as good as the Sunday before. It felt strange to be going back to school after three weeks away. But it also felt good to be getting out of the house again.

His mother fussed over him before he left.

"Are you sure you'll be all right at school?"

"Of course I'll be all right," Josh answered impatiently. "There's nothing you could do if I wasn't, anyway."

"I know but I'm worried about you. You've been off for quite a while now."

"Yeah, and I've got loads to catch up on. That's why I need to get back. I'm going now. I'll see you later."

"Bye." He had the feeling that his mother wanted to bend down and kiss his cheek, even though it had been a few years since she'd done that.

He left before she had a chance.

*

Rachel was enjoying a well-earned mid-morning cup of coffee when the shrill ringing of the telephone interrupted her reverie.

"Hello?"

"Hi, it's me."

"Hi, Roger, what's up? You sound worried."

"I am a bit. Listen, Rachel, I'm on my way home. I gave that weird mosquito creature to Frank Cartwright this morning. You remember Frank at the university, don't you?"

"Sure."

"Well, he was very interested in the thing and said that he'd never seen one before or knew of anything like it. He was really keen to find out more so he took it to his lab and he's just got back to me now and said that he's looked it up and spoken to many other entomologists and as far as they're all concerned this creature doesn't exist."

Rachel found that absurd. "Of course it exists. We found one, didn't we?"

"Exactly. That's one of the reasons he was worried. This could be an undiscovered species that we know nothing about. But the other reason he's worried is worse."

"Go on then, tell me the really bad news."

"He examined the thing and found that it's loaded with poison. In fact he said it was carrying enough venom to kill several people. He's had to report it to the authorities and they're sending out a search team to our house immediately to see if there are any more or if there's some sort of nest."

Rachel suddenly felt cold despite the warm day. "Roger, you're scaring me. When are they coming?"

"That's why I'm ringing. Frank said they'd be coming ASAP so I've cancelled my classes for the rest of today and I'll be home soon. Just do me a favour, will you? Close all the windows and doors so that if there are any more out there, they can't get into the house."

"But I haven't seen any more of them. Have you?" Rachel began to shift nervously from one foot to the other.

"No, but I don't want to take any chances. If there's one then it can be assumed that it at least has parents somewhere. Just close up the house and I'll see you soon. All right?"

Rachel felt uneasy as she replaced the receiver. She went to the kitchen window and looked outside. Surely if there were big poisonous insects outside, there'd be other signs of them like dead birds that'd eaten them. But then again maybe the birds had a natural instinct to leave poisonous insects alone.

She did as instructed and closed all the windows, which seemed a shame on such a warm summer's day. As she went upstairs to close the bedroom windows she nervously scanned the ceilings for any signs of insects.

Soon Roger arrived home and they sat in the kitchen and had a cup of coffee.

Within half an hour there was a knock at the door. She went to the door with Roger. There on the doorstep was an officious-looking little man in a pinstriped suit.

"Mr and Mrs Harrison? I'm Mr Roberts from the Environmental Health Agency." He strode passed them into the house, speaking so quickly that Rachel and Roger unconsciously leaned towards him to hear what he was saying.

He stopped in the hallway and Rachel walked ahead of him into the kitchen and motioned for him to sit at the table. Mr Roberts sat down and put his briefcase on the table, a briefcase too large for such a small person, Rachel thought. He extracted a lined pad and pen and placed them neatly together on the table. He closed his briefcase and placed it neatly by his chair.

"So, what can either of you tell me about this insect?"

Rachel glanced at Roger, prompting him to speak. "There really isn't anything we can tell you. We only found the one mosquito in the back garden yesterday."

"What makes you think it's a mosquito?" snapped the little man quickly.

"It just looks like a giant mosquito except that it's white and has an ugly face."

"Where was it?"

"What, its face? It was on the front of its head," said Roger sarcastically, obviously knowing what the little man meant but irritated with his pompous attitude.

Rachel gave Roger a smile to show that she was enjoying his joke.

The little man gave a swift sigh of impatience as though he was dealing with two impudent children.

"Now, let's be adult, Mr Harrison. We both know I meant where the insect was when you found it."

"Oh, no sense of humour appreciated, I see. In that case we found it in the middle of the lawn in the back garden and yes it was already dead and no we haven't seen any others or a nest or anything else to indicate that there are more of them."

Mr Roberts opened his mouth to speak but before he could say anything there was a loud knock at the door.

"Ah, that will be my men," said the little man striding importantly from the room.

Rachel and Roger looked at each other and silently sniggered.

*

Josh's first day back at school passed quickly, uneventfully and mundanely. His mind wasn't on his schoolwork as much as usual and he asked no questions during lessons. His teachers glanced at him often with concerned expressions but said nothing directly to him. At break times he stayed in his classroom. Usually being found in a classroom during breaks was considered one of the worst offences a student could commit and was treated as being punishable by death.

But today Josh stayed inside and looked over his work to see what he'd missed these last three weeks, and no one who saw him told him to leave.

When the last lesson of the day was over, Josh reluctantly left the classroom and walked out of the building with slow, heavy footsteps and an even heavier heart. He'd been missing Uncle Neville terribly but now that his life was back in its normal routine, without his uncle to visit after school every day, he felt sad all over again and his heart felt as though it would break once more.

As he trudged to the school gates he was surprised when he saw his mother waiting for him.

"Hi, Babe," she greeted him cheerfully, but Josh knew something was bothering her and it must be something big to make her meet him like this.

"Mum, I've told you before, I'm too old to be picked up from school," he joked with her.

She smiled at him briefly then her face grew concerned. "Oh Josh. All hell is breaking out at home. I didn't want you to walk in alone in the middle of it all so I thought I'd try and explain it to you first. That way you won't get a shock when you see the men in white protective suits swarming everywhere."

"So hell is full of men in white protective suits?" Josh was confused and intrigued.

"No, but our home is. You see, your dad and I found a really strange looking white mosquito-type of bug a couple of days ago. It was already dead so Dad took it to work to show it to an entomologist at the university and he said he'd never seen one before. But he did say that it's very poisonous so it had to be reported and now there are loads of people in protective suits at our house looking for any more bugs or a nest or something."

"So the men are all in the garden?"

"Yes. They were all in the house at first. They've searched every nook and cranny but they're in the garden now. But listen, sweetie, we have to keep all the windows shut for the time being just in case there are some more out there because we don't want them flying in. So no matter how warm you feel upstairs, don't open your window."

"OK." Josh knew his mother was worried. She was trying to keep the fear out of her voice, but it was there just the same. He briefly became worried himself. Large white mosquitoes? Just like in his game? But what could be the connection, unless the creatures had leapt out of the game and into reality? But that was silly. What on earth made him even think of that?

Jeez, Josh, get a grip, he chastised himself.

When they arrived home the sight that greeted them amazed Josh. There were two large vans parked outside and two men in white plastic-looking protective overalls with insect mesh helmets and large white rubber boots were searching the front garden with lots of serious-looking equipment. They carried backpacks full of some sort of liquid that flowed through a thin pipe to long-barrelled guns they held in their hands. They reminded Josh of the characters in *Ghost Busters* and looked very out of place and UFO-ish. He and his mother walked past them and went into the house.

His parents hugged each other, and then his father turned his attention to Josh.

"How was your first day back at school?"

"Quite boring compared to your day at home, I think. How come you're home so early, Dad?"

"I didn't want to leave your mother to cope with all this," he said making a sweeping gesture with one arm. "The insect we found was quite large and very white. It was the weirdest-looking thing we've ever seen. Have you seen anything like that around here the last few days, or ever at all?"

Josh was thoughtful for a moment. "Well...I've seen that exact same insect on the computer game of Uncle Neville's I've been playing but I don't think I've seen one in real life."

"Believe me, if you had seen one you'd know you had. They even look as though they could be out of a game and not really real."

"Is that what that game's about then, insects?" This was from his mother.

"No, it's about a man journeying through a strange land and defeating different enemies along the way. But his first one was a swarm of big white mosquito creatures with almost human faces but they were all twisted and ugly. They were real creepy."

"So are these," his father said. He and his mother looked at each other questioningly then quickly looked down. Josh saw their exchange and knew exactly what they were thinking as he'd had the same thought earlier.

"Come on," said his mother. "Let's go see what the Ghost Busters are doing in the back garden." Josh smiled at his mother's description of the men. All three of them went into the kitchen and looked out the window. There were four more people in protective suits in the garden and they were all at the back of the willow tree.

Josh's father spoke but he sounded grim. "It looks like they've found something else."

As they watched, the men brought out two small objects from behind the tree and placed them on the lawn in front of the kitchen window. One was a dead squirrel with festering sores that the bluebottles couldn't leave alone. The other object was larger and thickly cocooned in spiders' webs.

Josh's mother shivered and folded her arms across her chest as she watched the scene unfolding before them and his father put his arm protectively around her.

Two of the men outside began to cut through the webs and soon Josh and his parents could see that inside was the neighbours' ginger tomcat.

Josh had seen enough. Too many things in his life had died recently. "I'll be in my room," he said and went upstairs to change out of his school uniform. He didn't want to see what was going on in the garden anymore so he closed his curtains before turning on the computer.

The spooky house in the game looked and sounded even more eerie than usual in the darkened room. Josh knew that he needed a new strategy to outsmart the spiders but he wasn't sure what. When he thought of the spiders an image of the dead cat briefly passed through his mind but the image was so fleeting that he made no connection with what he was seeing on the screen.

He decided that the large knife that Salvador was using was the wrong weapon, but when he looked in his bag he couldn't see anything else more suitable. He chose the small knife instead of the large one. But what good was that? A small knife could only cut small things and the spiders were too large and too many. Then a brilliant plan began to form in his mind. Maybe he could use the small knife to cut something small, like webs. That was the answer. He needed to cut open the webs before he became completely wrapped in too many of them.

He walked Salvador into the house once more and made him run as fast as he could to the table at the back. Salvador reached the grain and the food and Josh clicked the cursor over them and they disappeared into Salvador's bag. Then he turned and tried to leave. But the spiders were immediately upon him and began spinning their webs. Salvador used the knife to slash open the webs and the spiders while edging back towards the door.

The fight was long and not at all as easy as he thought it would be. He continued to make Salvador hack whatever was in front of him with the small knife. Every movement of the blade sliced through webs or one or two spiders that screamed as they fell to the floor, thick liquid oozing from the slits in their bulbous bodies.

The spiders were relentless in their persistence but soon Salvador was able to take a chance and leave the house during a split second when there were no spiders on him. The timing was so tight that as the door slammed shut behind Salvador, many of the spiders' legs were already halfway out and so were amputated when the door closed tight. The ear-piercing screams made Josh wince. All the legs outside fell on the veranda floor and jerked and twisted in a macabre dance before their nerve endings finally died. Josh saved the game there.

*

Down in the garden, one of the men swore that he had heard something up in the willow tree. A ladder was brought and positioned against the trunk under the dense hanging branches. The four men, professional as always, played Scissors-Paper-Rock to decide who was going to be the unfortunate one to climb the tree.

Up the ladder went the loser, muttering that paper covers rock and wins and rock *never* bashes paper.

Up high in the tree he heard a rustling noise to his left. He turned his head quickly and tried to see what it was, but it was dim inside the branches and the leaves were dense up there. He reached over with his left hand, stretching as far as he could to part the leaves, but he wasn't quite high enough.

He heard the noise again, saw some of the leaves moving near his finger tips and withdrew his hand quickly. He stared at the leaves, expecting them to move again at any minute, but they remained still. Again he stretched as far as he could to the leaves but they remained annoyingly just out of his reach. He was already standing on the second-highest rung and didn't want to go any higher because he always felt unsafe at the top. He would have climbed onto the branches to go higher, but strict health and safety regulations being what they were meant that he wasn't allowed to stand on anything high up unless it had been tested for safety, so he had to stay on the ladder.

Reluctant as he was to stand on the very top rung of the ladder, he knew that he had to. Looking down, he checked that someone was still holding the bottom.

The rustling came again.

"Hurry up, Kev!" someone shouted from below.

Well, it was too bad if they were kept waiting. He'd never wanted to come up here looking for poisonous bugs in the first place and he had no equipment with him, so even if he found something one of the others would have to come up and get it.

He took a step higher to the top rung of the ladder. The rustling came again and somehow sounded louder. He looked at the leaves to his left but this time there was not movement. As he reached across he could have sworn he saw something in amongst the foliage. He drew back his hand momentarily but then told himself not to be stupid because there was nothing there. But he knew that he had seen something and what he'd seen looked like an over-sized spider's hairy leg. Of course spiders that big didn't exist. He knew that and tried to laugh at his own over-imagination of what he'd seen. But he couldn't laugh because he knew what it was that he'd glimpsed. Again he tried to tell himself that spiders that large didn't exist.

But something that can spin a big web killed that cat, his rational mind reasoned with him.

He leaned over again. The leaves shook. His heart was beating fast and he was nervous, but he had to see what was in there. As his gloved hand touched the leaves they became suddenly still. This made him jump. He looked at the gap where he thought he'd seen the spider's leg, but it was just an empty gap. Slowly he put his hand up, acutely conscious of every movement he made and ready to withdraw his hand at the slightest hint that anything other than leave was in front of him. He parted the leaves. There was definitely nothing there.

He must have been mistaken.

*

Back in the game, Salvador was trying to walk away from the house. He walked away down one path but after twisting and turning several times, it led back to the house. He tried another path, but again the path twisted and turned in several directions and eventually Salvador arrived back at the house again. He tried the third and final path, but again the same thing happened and once more Salvador was back in front of the old house.

Perhaps his task there wasn't finished yet. But he'd seen nothing else in the room that could have been of any use to him and surely there weren't other enemies to defeat in amongst all those spiders?

Maybe he had to do something outside the house. The game kept forcing Salvador to be outside the house so there was a chance that this was where he was meant to be. He walked Salvador around the outside of the house to see if he could see a clue of any sort as to what he was supposed to do next.

As he walked along the back of the house there was a loud CRACK and Salvador fell through an overgrown skylight into the basement and he landed with a loud thud and made an "ooof" noise as though he'd had his breath knocked out of him.

The basement was dark because the small hole above that he'd fallen through provided the only light, but Josh was aware that something was moving down there. At first he couldn't see anything, only blackness. It was so dark that he could only just see Salvador. Soon the sounds seemed closer and the blackness in front of Salvador's feet seemed to move. Josh's eyes were glued to the screen, eager to see what was there, but he didn't have to wait long. The darkness at first seemed to be rippling in a strange, eerie way. As Josh watched the moving sheet of darkness seemed to part into hundreds of small black pieces. Josh leaned closer to the screen and realised that the pieces were actually rats that were either waking or coming to life, so many of them that they formed a dark carpet over the basement floor.

He backed Salvador away as far as he could but he kept coming up against walls.

The rats continued to march towards him. They were the size of normal rats and each one had a glossy black coat, but it was their eyes that were different. Their eyes were black and had an empty, soulless appearance as though the rats were void of either thought or emotion, and moved merely as robots under instruction.

Josh tried to think of a useful weapon to use against them but could think of nothing.

"Josh."

His name was whispered very quietly but it made him jump and his heart began to hammer in his chest. He paused the game and looked around his bedroom suspiciously. Everything was as it should be yet he had a creepy feeling as though he wasn't alone anymore. He scanned the room carefully taking note of every piece of furniture to see if there was anything unusual, but again he saw that everything in his room was right where he'd seen it last time he looked.

Was he mistaken then? Had he actually heard someone whisper his name or had he just imagined it? Maybe the game was making him jumpy. His heart continued its unnatural thudding in his chest.

Trying to be brave, and not admit that he was scared, he opened his curtains with trembling hands, telling himself that it was just too dim in the room with them closed and that was what was making him edgy. All he needed was a bit of daylight and he'd be fine.

He saw that the men were still in the garden, only now all six of them were out back, carefully checking every tree and bush and even the garage. Josh thought that it was lucky for them that there were no aggressive rats out there too. Thankfully they only existed in the game.

*

At the base of the willow tree, where the roots grew into the ground, there was a gap, a small void that the men had already prodded and probed during their earlier search of the garden, but found to be empty.

However, from within there now came a shuffling sound, the sound of movement. Then there came the squeak of a rodent.

But no one heard these barely audible sounds.

Chapter 7

By early evening the men had packed everything away and left. Apart from the squirrel and the cat, they had found nothing and so had no reason to return. They did, however, give Josh's parents an emergency number to ring if they saw anything else unusual.

The family sat down to a later-than-usual dinner. Not much was said during the meal, as no one knew quite what to think about the day's events. It had certainly been no ordinary day.

As soon as the dishes were done Josh escaped back upstairs. It had been warm with all the windows closed all afternoon and so he couldn't wait to hit the shower. The water felt refreshing and the clean, sweat-free feeling he had afterwards felt like heaven. It was still a warm evening but being able to open the windows made all the difference as a slight breeze stirred the curtains and the air.

As he combed his clean, wet hair he heard a dog frantically barking.

Through the window he saw it was the dog that lived in the garden at the bottom of theirs and it was standing near the other side of the fence. At first he couldn't see why it was barking so anxiously, and then he saw a tabby cat in a tree. He thought someone from the dog's house should come and tell it to be quiet but no one did. It wasn't surprising though because that dog never seemed to be disciplined and was always left outside alone every day and he'd never seen anyone ever take it for a walk.

It wasn't a very nice dog but it was hardly the unfortunate animal's fault if it wasn't taught how to behave, although Josh still didn't like it. Not long ago, when Josh was playing with his football in the garden, he accidentally kicked it over into the neighbour's yard. When he pulled himself up to the top of the fence to have a look at where his ball had gone, the dog suddenly leapt up and bit his hand.

Josh had got such a fright that he instantly let go of the fence and fell back into his own garden, landing squarely on his rump. The fall jarred his spine and his back was sore for the next few days. His fingers had been bitten, but thankfully not hard enough to break skin.

Now as he watched the dog he saw it jump up and throw itself repeatedly at the tree where the cat was cowering. The poor cat looked frightened each time the tree shook with the dog's efforts.

As Josh watched, the cat took a chance to go for the safety of the fence and leapt across. The dog immediately turned its attention to the fence, leaping up and applying its full bodyweight to try to dislodge the frightened feline. The cat took a few wobbly steps along the top of the fence before the huge leap from the dog sent the cat tumbling off the fence and out of sight.

There was a tremendous racket of growling, spitting and fighting. Josh felt sick at the thought of the cat being ripped to pieces by the dog, but within seconds the cat appeared on top of the fence again and swiftly leapt away into the safety of their garden and in one smooth motion, ran up the willow tree and out of sight.

The dog continued to bark its threats but the fleeing cat was long gone. Josh was relieved. He stayed at the window looking outside for a while, quietly observing the neighbourhood, and then he sat down and switched on the computer.

On the screen Salvador was once again outside the derelict old house. He was reluctant to send Salvador back down into the rat-filled basement. He couldn't understand why he had to go back down because he couldn't see that there was anything to collect there. But he did understand that until he defeated the rats he couldn't move forward in the game. So, because he couldn't think of anything else to do, he plunged Salvador back into the basement.

Again the rats emerged from the dark recesses. They didn't move very fast but there were certainly a lot of them. He made Salvador kick out at them and jump on those nearest. The sounds of the rats screaming and their bones breaking seemed so real that Josh felt cruel for attacking them. Their blood was pooling out onto the floor as the rats writhed around in the throes of death.

Josh watched the scene with a sickening fascination. The rats reacted realistically, as though they were really hurt and dying and not just computer simulations.

Salvador grunted every time he brought his foot down, making it sound as though he really was putting in hard effort. The whole scene was difficult to watch, but Josh knew he must defeat the rats or Salvador would die. So as loath as he was to continue, he determined to carry on.

But his momentary lapse in concentration was his downfall. The rats were at once upon Salvador, tearing off pieces of his flesh with their teeth. Salvador screamed, thrashing and rolling on the floor to try to dislodge them but it was no use.

All too quickly, his skin was torn from his body and the rats began to feast on the gelatinous flesh underneath. The rats became so great in number that Salvador was no longer visible beneath them, but his dying cries lingered mournfully above the noise of the fighting, gorging rats.

Josh grimaced at the sound of tearing flesh and the chewing sounds of the rats. This game was too lifelike for comfort. He could tell that Salvador was still twitching and squirming under the feasting rats even though his screams and cries had ceased.

He pressed "Escape" on the keyboard, the screen went blank and he turned the computer off.

He felt uneasy, as though he had just witnessed someone actually being eaten alive. How did Uncle Neville put such realism into the game? Or a better question was, why? He had never known such a realistic game as this one, and at the moment he wished he still hadn't.

*

Late that night, the neighbourhood was silent. There were no lights on in any of the houses and the streets were deserted of traffic and pedestrians.

The neighbours' dog was the only thing stirring as it left its kennel and urinated on the lawn. It then padded down to the bottom of the garden and sniffed over the ground where it had fought the cat earlier, enjoying the memory.

A strange sound began at the other side of the fence. The dog cocked his head to one side to listen. Was it the cat? Something was approaching the fence from the other side, so he hoped it was the cat.

The dog sniffed at the bottom of the fence and gave a low growl. He could smell something but was unsure of what it was. Then the noise began. Something was happening at the bottom of the fence. It sounded like something was eating the fence. The dog was confused. The fence wasn't food so why was something eating it?

The dog was feeling insecure. He took two steps backwards and sat down to watch. The wood was gradually eaten away in two places and two small noses poked through.

The dog got up and sniffed at one of the noses. Razor-sharp teeth sunk into the soft pulpy flesh around his nostril making him yelp and stumble backwards. He stayed where he was, afraid to explore the creatures again.

The holes in the fence grew bigger until they were large enough for the rats to pass through. The dog stood up and growled at the first two but two more immediately followed then two more and two more. Normally he would attack rats, but he'd already been bitten once which made him cautious, and soon there were just too many of them. He was also uneasy about how brazenly they were approaching him instead of running in the opposite direction like he'd expect them to.

This whole situation was wrong. The dog walked slowly backwards without taking his eyes off the rats as they increased in number. As the rats moved forward the dog kept retreating until he was close enough to turn and run into his kennel.

The rats continued to march across the lawn. Dozens more poured through the holes in the fence. The dog could only watch in mute fear.

They kept marching forward, noses constantly sniffing the air. Then they entered the dog's kennel. The dog snapped at them and tried to move back as far as he could, but the kennel was not big. The rats bit into his paws. The dog tried to yelp but was too busy biting at the rats that clung onto his toes.

The rats filled the kennel, climbed all over the dog and tore at his flesh.

The dog panicked as the rats ran up his legs and up his back. There were so many that he didn't know which one to try to remove first. They bit deep into his flesh, shaking their heads to tear the skin loose.

The dog twisted this way and that, snapping at the rats, but no sooner did he pull one off than another would bite into him. Each rat he removed took a mouthful of his flesh with it as he tore it loose. He was losing the fight.

Now they were on his head and trying to chew his ears off. He shook his head but it only made the rats bite harder to hold on.

Two of them were on his chest and one reached up and bit his neck. Blood began to gush down his fur. More of them came to the new wound and began to eat. The dog was confused, afraid and in pain, but the rats were relentless.

Sleep. The dog was getting sleepy. He fought the urge to lie down and give in, but the tiredness was overwhelming. The pain from the rats' bites had subsided. He could feel them ripping his flesh and chewing it but it didn't hurt anymore. He felt a rat walk along the side of his face and rip at his lip. How was the rat managing to walk sideways? Then he realized that *he* was lying down. He didn't remember doing so but he was just too sleepy now to think about it.

As he closed his eyes for the final time in his life, a rat latched its teeth onto his eyelid and ate it.

By the time the dog's bones were picked clean the rats' bellies were full. One by one they started the journey back across the lawn and through the fence. One of the rats spat out a small piece of dog fur as it went but this would never be found in the long grass, which was well overdue for a trim.

Soon all the rats were back under the base of the willow tree, out of sight and completely unnoticed by all the sleeping families nearby.

Chapter 8

"Come on Josh, get a move on," his mother called up the stairs. Josh hadn't realized it was so late. He was busy watching what was going on in the neighbouring garden at the back. His view was partially blocked by the willow tree but he could see the family standing near the dog kennel and Mrs Spencer was crying. There was a policeman and a policewoman there too. Mr Spencer was talking to them and shaking his head the whole time.

Josh noticed that their dog was nowhere to be seen and coupled with the fact that they were all near its kennel and they all kept peeking in now and again, made him think that something must have happened to it. And it must be bad if the police were there.

He didn't like to see it chasing cats and he was afraid to look over the fence in case it bit him again, but it wasn't the dog's fault that it was the way it was.

Whenever anyone came out of the house the dog would jump up and get really excited to see them, but all they would ever say was "get down, you bad dog." They never seemed to care about it.

Josh tore his gaze away from the window, went downstairs, hugged his mother goodbye and set off for school. When he reached the end of the street another boy came up to him as he crossed the road.

He'd seen the boy on the way to school many times before but they had never spoken to each other before so Josh was curious as to what he wanted now, and also a bit suspicious.

"Did you hear about the Spencer's dog?"

Josh was relieved that the dog was all he wanted to talk about. He was also intrigued because he was dying to know what was going on. "I saw something had happened. They were all in the back garden with the police."

"You can see into their back garden?" The boy obviously thought this was excellent news.

"Sure, we live right at the back of their house. I can see their garden from my bedroom window."

"Cool."

"Where do you live?"

"Across the road from them. We saw the police car and Mum went across to see what was up."

"And...what happened?"

"Well, it's really extreme and most amazing. You won't believe it."

"What? WHAT?" Josh thought he would burst if he didn't find out soon.

"Someone ate their dog." The boy waited for Josh's reaction.

Josh couldn't comprehend what he was hearing. "You mean their dog's gone?"

"No, it's been eaten. They came out to feed it and all they found was its skeleton in the kennel. My mum had a look and when she was telling us she was sick. You should've seen it. She spewed up her breakfast all over the carpet. It was gross."

Josh was stunned. "So someone ate the dog and threw the bones back into the kennel?"

"Well, my mum said they must have eaten it in the kennel because there was loads of blood in it and the bones were all laid out as though the dog was laid down asleep. My mum said it looked more like the dog's flesh had disintegrated while it slept. She said there were all smears in the blood as though mice or something had been walking through it. I think they probably ate it."

The boy was relishing all the gory details but Josh felt disturbed by the news. He thought about playing Journey to the Promised Land and Salvador being eaten alive by rats. That had been gross to watch and even worse to listen to, even though it was only a computer game. But for it to happen in real life seemed just too evil.

What torture that poor dog had gone through was anyone's guess. The most worrying thing though, was that this was the third weird animal death this week, and it was only Tuesday. There was already the dead squirrel and the dead cat and now the dog too.

All the talk that day at school was about the dog. Quite a few kids had searched him out at break times to ask about the squirrel and cat. Today he seemed to be the centre of attention, which didn't please him at all as he preferred to blend into the background unnoticed.

Except by Leonora.

Now she was someone who he wished would always notice him and come and talk, but she never did. He doubted that she was even aware that he existed. He wasn't sure what it was about her that attracted him but he was smitten all the same. She was in the same year as Josh but was in another class. She'd only started at the school the previous year and the only reason he knew her name was because he'd heard her two friends call her.

Her two friends seemed like bitches, but they and Leonora had quickly become an inseparable trio who always passed him by without a second glance. But he was always hopeful that one day she'd notice him and he'd get to know her.

By the time school was over Josh was extra glad to be home and by himself after so much attention and so many questions, so he spent the rest of the afternoon sprawled in front of the TV.

His mother came and tried to talk to him about the neighbours' dog, but Josh had already had enough of that conversation for one day. She told Josh that she wanted him to be careful, but careful of what, he wasn't sure.

During dinner his parents talked about it non-stop. Josh disappeared up to his room as soon as he could. He sat down to play the game but the thought of the man-eating rats made him uneasy. He didn't want to have to see that again.

He switched on the game and before entering the basement again he checked Salvador's bag for a suitable weapon and saw the grain that he'd taken from the house. He wasn't sure what good it could do, but rats ate grain, didn't they? Perhaps he could use it to distract them for a while. What he would do while they were eating, he wasn't sure. But it was the only plan he had so he chose the grain and Salvador carried it with him into the basement.

Once again the rats emerged from the dark recesses and they all surrounded Salvador. He threw down the sack of grain, which spilled across the floor. The rats stopped moving forward and instead sniffed the air. Then they all swarmed over the grain and began to eat.

It seemed strange that these computer-produced images could act in such a lifelike way. Chewing noises could be heard while they ate, as well as several squeaks when tiny rat arguments broke out over certain grains. But all the while their eyes remained bleak and empty, which made them look lifeless.

As he watched, some of the rats twitched and squeaked, then more and more began to do it and soon they were all writhing and twisting as though in agony.

Rat poison! The grain must have actually been rat poison. Thank goodness.

He moved Salvador around past the dying rats to look for a way out. The basement appeared to be completely empty. In the darkness Salvador bumped into nothing but solid stone walls. So with no weapons or food to collect, Josh couldn't understand why Salvador had been compelled to go down there. His only reason seemed to be to find the rats and kill them.

As Salvador walked, the blackness became even blacker and Josh had to crane forward to see him in the gloom.

Thud! Salvador walked into something but it wasn't a wall. Josh squinted hard to see what it was. It seemed that the ceiling was much lower here and Salvador had hit his head. Josh bent him down and continued walking. Further along he saw a square patch in the ceiling. He moved Salvador beneath it and straightened him up.

The square lifted and daylight pierced the darkness. Josh jumped Salvador up through the trapdoor and he landed back outside the house. The rats dying screams could still be heard from inside so he closed the trap door to block out the sound.

He saved the game at that point to make sure that the rats stayed dead and he didn't have to make Salvador go in there again. This certainly seemed like a day for rats. His mother had told him that rat trails had been found in the dog kennel that morning and it looked like they'd been running round the lawn too. Two holes had been found in the fence although no evidence of rats was found in their garden.

It just seemed like a very big coincidence that the rats had appeared in the game last night and eaten his hero and they'd also appeared in real life and eaten a dog. But was it really a coincidence?

Josh sat bolt upright in his chair, suddenly unsure. No! It had to be a coincidence. But then what about the poisonous spiders in the game and the cat found cocooned in webs?

He felt his heart beating and it seemed much louder than usual. What about the first enemies in the game, the mosquitoes? His parents had found what they said was a strange-looking mosquito and it was poisonous too. So poisonous that people had come to their house the same day to try to track down more. Finding a poisonous mosquito must have created an emergency situation because the response by the authorities couldn't have been any faster if they'd dialled 999.

Josh sat and pondered the situation some more, desperately trying to think of something that could reassure him that it really was a horrible and unfortunate coincidence. But deep down he knew it wasn't.

The squirrel, the cat and the dog were all animals he'd seen recently AND he'd thought bad things about them. Was his own anger driving the enemies in the game to kill?

He gave a nervous laugh when he realized how ludicrous that thought was. But then he wondered, had he thought bad things about the animals before or after they were attacked?

Before, it was always before. Each one of them was alive and kicking the first time he saw them and then dead the next.

He looked at the screen again. Salvador was still standing outside the house. No wonder the game looked so real; it was real.

But it's impossible, his rational mind told him.

But what if I'm right? his intuitive mind argued.

Josh decided there was only one thing to do to ease his conscience. He'd turn the game off and not play it at all and then when something else happened he'd know for sure that it was nothing to do with him or the game.

"I won't play with you anymore. I won't be responsible for any more deaths," he told the computer as he closed down the game and switched everything off. But as the game disappeared from the screen, he could have sworn that Salvador turned his head and glared at him.

Josh flinched. He didn't want to be unnerved by the game anymore so if he kept it switched off then it couldn't bother him. He stood up, stretched, and took his bathrobe off the hook on the back of the bedroom door before he left the room.

He went into the bathroom and had a shower, thinking that perhaps he'd feel better if he was clean, sort of wash all the bad things away, so to speak. The cascading hot water drummed pleasantly on his skin and as he relaxed and worked up a soapy lather over himself, he momentarily forgot about how much the game had frightened him.

All too soon the showering was finished and Josh reluctantly turned the water off, stepped out of the shower cubicle and dried himself. He put on his bathrobe and brushed his teeth thoroughly but although he was moving his mind wasn't on what he was doing. The events of the last few days played over and over in his mind along with the events in the game.

Salvador was killed by poisonous mosquitoes. His parents had found a poisonous mosquito. Salvador had been attacked by spiders. A cat had been found cocooned in webs. Salvador had been eaten by rats. A dog had been eaten by rats. Worst of all it was Josh himself who'd had bad thoughts about the animals only hours before they died.

He clenched his hands and stamped one foot. Damn it! He had to stop thinking about it. There was no logical conclusion to it all, only an illogical one.

THE GAME'S NOT REAL! he screamed inside his head, but the words were empty of meaning. There was no getting away with it. The game was real.

No it isn't, he screamed silently again. It was so frustrating to not want to believe something that he knew was true.

Well, he would just have to prove it one way or the other by leaving the computer off and waiting to see if anything else happened. If it did then he'd know it wasn't the game that had caused it. But if nothing happened, well...he would have to wait and see.

When he re-entered his bedroom he felt his blood run cold and his heart sink down into the pit of his stomach. He knew for certain he'd turned the game and computer off but there on the screen was Salvador standing outside the old house, just where he'd been left. He was looking around from left to right as though trying to decide which way to go.

Goose pimples popped out over the whole surface of Josh's skin and he shuddered.

There must be a glitch in the computer, his rational mind told him. Or maybe I just didn't turn it off properly. But he knew neither of these statements were true.

The urge to turn and run overwhelmed him. He stood, breathing hard to overcome it. After what seemed like an hour, but in reality was probably only a minute, Josh went to his chest of drawers and took out some underwear, shorts and a T-shirt and quickly dressed, without taking his eyes off the screen. He'd felt somehow more vulnerable while he was wearing only a bathrobe.

With great trepidation Josh seated himself in front of the computer, half expecting something to jump out and kill Salvador, but nothing happened. He put his hand to the keyboard and pressed the "Escape" key to turn the game off but nothing happened. In frustration he pressed it again and again but it was futile. He then tried pressing every key on the keyboard, but there was no response to any of them. He pressed them all individually and then tried slamming his palms down on several keys at once. Salvador remained where he was and continued to look around. Not even the arrow keys worked.

Josh desperately pressed the "Off" button on the computer tower repeatedly, but still nothing happened. The game remained stubbornly on the screen.

Salvador began to pace backwards and forwards impatiently. Josh kept pressing everything he could, but the game still remained on the screen. He wondered if it was trying to force him to play. But that was ridiculous wasn't it? Computer games couldn't control humans.

Could they?

Chapter 9

Josh was nervous. He sat in his chair and watched the computer screen helplessly. In the game Salvador seemed to have found a path close to the house that Josh had not seen before and began to walk along it, away from the house.

Josh was very afraid. He had his hands in his lap and wasn't moving. The game was playing on its own.

Salvador continued his solo journey through the field behind the house. The field eventually led to some woods. Salvador stopped and looked nervous. Josh put his hand on the mouse and Salvador seemed to immediately relax. It was unnerving enough that the game could play on its own, but it was even worse when the character in the game was scared to be alone and knew instantly when Josh was about to step in and help him.

He clicked on the word "Save."

As soon as the game was saved at the point outside the woods, Salvador took a deep breath and continued unaided into the woods, the trees surrounding him as though trying to cage him. He maintained his slow pace without interruption, turning his head nervously at every sound. Josh sat wide-eyed and spellbound.

The woods were now dark and dense and strange noises echoed around chillingly. As Josh continued watching, he kept glimpsing things between the trees, but every time he looked straight at them they disappeared, making him wonder if they were ever really there at all.

He shifted uncomfortably in his seat, his hands unconsciously gripping the edge of the chair.

A strange being appeared in front of Salvador. The words *Goblin: fierce creature that dwells in chinks or cracks* appeared momentarily at the bottom of the screen.

Josh knew the game was trying to torment him into playing and even though he was more than tempted to put his fingers on the arrow keys and take control of Salvador, he resisted and remained an observer.

"I don't care what you do. I won't play anymore," he told the screen with false bravado. The goblin turned its head and smirked at him.

It was a small creature, no bigger than a young child, but Josh knew from playing other games that goblins were extremely evil and capable of the vilest savagery. It was a grotesque looking little thing. Its skin was grey and wrinkled and it reminded him of Gollum from *Lord of the Rings* except the goblin was completely hairless and did not stoop. It stood arrogantly upright.

Salvador took out a long sword and began swinging it at the goblin, but the goblin was very nimble and easily dodged out of the way of every stroke of the sword. So Salvador moved faster, but so did the goblin. He walked forward swinging the sword as fast as he could. The goblin laughed, ducking and diving as though everything was a joke. Then as it dodged low to avoid the next swing of the sword, it made an unexpected move and stuck out its leg, tripping Salvador over. Then it produced a small knife out of nowhere.

It moved so fast that Josh wasn't immediately sure of what he was seeing. The goblin held the knife on the ground with the blade pointing skywards. It had managed to place the knife so quickly that it had it in position before Salvador had finished falling, so that his chest fell directly onto the blade.

Salvador went sprawling to the ground with an "OOF!" and his sword slipped from his hands and clattered away. The goblin laughed out loud and looked Josh straight in the eyes. Josh recoiled in surprise and the goblin sniggered.

Then it danced gleefully around Salvador's squirming body, singing a song that could hardly be heard.

Josh's mind raced. What did all this mean? Was somebody else going to die? And if so who?

Suddenly the goblin ran toward the inside of the computer screen until its face was up close to the glass. Josh jumped back in his chair in shock and almost tipped it over. The chair balanced precariously on its two back legs. Josh could have leaned forward to right it again but was afraid to move closer to the goblin. So instead, after hesitating for only a split second, he let the chair fall backwards and he tumbled with it.

As soon as his back hit the floor he bounded back up and looked at the goblin, afraid to take his eyes off it for even a second.

The goblin threw its head back and laughed until tears came into its eyes, then the laughter abruptly ceased.

It stared at Josh momentarily and smirked, before turning and walking back towards Salvador's now lifeless body. After every few steps it turned and looked back at Josh over its shoulder as though making sure he was still watching.

Once it reached Salvador it kicked him over onto his back. With its foot on his chest it pressed down hard and at the same time grasped the knife and twisted it to pull it free.

Josh heard the wet sucking sound as the metal blade came free from the flesh that was holding it. Blood seeped from Salvador's corpse, soaking the ground around him, and his energy line disappeared from the screen. The goblin looked up at Josh impassively, before using the small knife to slash open Salvador's abdomen.

Throwing the knife to one side it threw its head back and laughed excitedly and plunged its hands into the wide, gaping wound and pulling out reams of intestines and spreading them all around. On and on it played, laughing all the time, until Josh wrenched his mind free of his dumbstruck state of horror and pressed the "Escape" key.

The game disappeared from the screen. Josh's shoulders slumped in relief, but his mind still reeled as he tried to comprehend what he had just witnessed.

The sounds and the graphics of Salvador's death and mutilation had been disturbingly real. Josh almost felt as though he'd seen a friend being murdered. But what was most upsetting was the goblin's arrogance, as though it enjoyed every minute of performing its gruesome deeds and seeing Josh's revulsion.

He also had to concede that he was confused as to why everything had happened. Up until now Josh had played the game himself and every time he'd had bad thoughts about something, Salvador had been killed in the game and likewise the animal he'd been thinking about died too.

But this time he hadn't played the game himself nor had he been angry at anything or anyone, except the game. Nevertheless the game had played on and Salvador had been killed again, only this time it was worse than before. The game hadn't chosen insects or rats, but an evil goblin capable of mind-numbing, horrific deeds.

Josh could only conclude that the game had chosen its own victim and as Salvador represented Josh in the game, Josh himself must be the next victim.

His hands began to tremble and there was nothing he could do to make them stop. Josh couldn't remember ever being so afraid in his life. How he hated the computer game. Only now he was afraid that the computer game hated him too.

That night Josh slept with his light on.

*

In the early hours of Wednesday morning all was quiet in Josh's street.

Just after 2 a.m. Gerald Radcliff walked down the road. He was on his way home after an evening at his local pub with Stuart and an Indian takeaway, which they'd taken back to Stuart's place and washed down with several more beers.

Stuart was a great mate. Always ready for a night out and always kept plenty of cold beers in his fridge for later. A great guy.

They had done a lot of talking throughout the evening, mostly politics, religion, women and great guys. They had discussed many of their friends and work colleagues and both had agreed that most of them were great guys, except Don Spencer who, they agreed, was a bit of a prat and deserved to have his dog eaten.

Gerald had told Stuart what a great guy he was and how he loved him. Yep, Stuart was a great guy and he loved him a lot. Usually it was only drunks who said things like that but that couldn't be true because Gerald hadn't had that much to drink but he'd said it anyway.

Suddenly he tripped over something that wasn't even there and it made him stagger to one side. Oops, carefully does it. If anyone saw that, they might think that he *was* drunk.

He staggered across the grass verge and leaned against one of the trees that lined the street. Gerald looked at the long line of trees on both sides of the road and thought how pretty they looked. Yep, the trees sure made the street look pretty.

Then his rambling thoughts abruptly halted.

What was that noise?

He looked up and down the street but couldn't see anything. Nobody was about. He was all alone.

But there it was again, a noise that he couldn't make out, but it seemed to be coming from one of the trees. Maybe it was just a cat or something.

He turned to continue his journey home but thought he glimpsed something as it ducked behind one of the trees. Then he saw it again behind another tree, and then another.

But every time he looked at it, it disappeared. He thought, from what he'd glimpsed, that it looked a bit like a small child. But what would a small child be doing out at this time of night? And why would it be hiding behind trees?

Gerald felt slightly unnerved, and as adrenaline started to pump through his body, sobriety tried desperately to return to his beer-soaked brain. He decided that it would be better to walk down the middle of the road, away from the trees. Not that he was scared or anything. God, what a baby he'd be if he was scared of a little noise and a few trees. No, he just felt like walking somewhere more open and less claustrophobic, that was all. No big deal.

He moved as steadily as he could to the centre of the road, and with his head held high he began to walk. But still he thought he saw a child up ahead amongst the trees. He started to feel scared and he could hear his blood rushing around his brain.

Now just calm down. This is no time to get hysterical. There's no one there, especially not a young child. But despite his logical thoughts Gerald failed to persuade himself that they were true. Maybe there wasn't a child out there, but Gerald knew he'd seen something and God only knew what.

He turned and looked up and down the street. There was no one around and the darkened windows in all the houses told him that all the residents of Myrtle Street were slumbering soundly in their beds. Gerald wished now that he'd not had a drink and that he had someone to turn to right now, but there was no one. But there was, however, *something* out there with him.

Alone and frightened, with his heart now racing, Gerald began to run. He didn't care how un-macho or un-cool he looked; he just wanted to get the hell out of there and to the safety of his own house. After only a few steps he saw, too late, that something was hiding close by in the trees ahead and it suddenly ran out towards him. Gerald was so startled that he tripped over nothing again and went sprawling onto the road.

The thing moved with lightning speed. Before Gerald connected with the ground it produced a small knife, as if from nowhere, squatted down and held the small knife, blade up, in the exact place where Gerald's chest would fall.

As he hit the tarmac, Gerald felt two sensations of pain. First the impact with the hard surface broke two of his ribs and made it difficult for him to breathe. At the same time the knife sent a searing hot pain into his chest as it plunged in deeply.

He could see the creature was dancing around him as he lay there in extreme agony, and his fear heightened. He wanted to scream and yell so that someone might see him and come to his rescue but he couldn't make a sound. He was wracked by pain and wanted to scream, but screaming would only make it worse, if that were possible.

The creature pushed its foot against Gerald's shoulder and turned him over onto his back. The agony of moving was excruciating but Gerald was powerless to resist. He thought it had been better facing the road because at least he couldn't see the horrible face of the thing above him.

Now it leaned close to his face and sniffed him. He could feel the beads of sweat literally pop out on his face as his fear intensified. He felt amazingly sober now and despite all the drinking he'd done, his throat was parched.

The thing smelled revolting, like meat that had been left a long time and was festering and rotting. It grinned at him, exposing its needle-sharp teeth. Its gleaming eyes were penetrating, like something he'd seen in a horror movie, and its skin, including its bald head, was a dirty grey-green colour. If this creature was a child, it sure was an ugly little bastard.

Gerald wished that what was happening to him was just a drunken dream. He was living his worst nightmare. In fact it was worse than that because he had never imagined that something as abominable as this could ever happen to him. And what the hell was the thing that had stabbed him?

Surely such a thing didn't exist? But whether he believed in its existence or not was irrelevant. It was here and it seemed intent on hurting him.

The creature began to laugh quietly to itself as it put its hand around the knife handle. Then in one swift movement it twisted the knife and pulled the blade out of his chest.

Oh God! The pain! Dear God, how much more can I endure? Gerald thought he would pass out. The pain was too much and for a few seconds he couldn't move or breathe. But the goblin wasn't finished with him yet.

As Gerald felt the warm blood soak his T-shirt, the goblin began to slash at his abdomen with the knife.

Oh Dear God, when will this nightmare end? The beads of sweat now ran down the sides of Gerald's face in rivulets. He wasn't sure which felt worse, the pain in his chest or the frenzied attack on his abdomen. He prayed for death, which was preferable to this living hell.

The goblin then began to pull what looked like thick spaghetti into the air. Gerald wanted to lift his head to get a better look at what was happening to him but his chest was a hot mass of agonising pain much like his abdomen and so he couldn't move at all.

Is that my intestine he's messing with? Gerald watched in abject horror as the grinning goblin gleefully pulled and stretched Gerald's intestines every which way.

The whole situation was more than Gerald's mind and body could take and he mercifully passed out.

A few minutes later the death he prayed for arrived.

The goblin cocked its head and sniffed at Gerald's corpse. Its hands released his intestines and it stood up and laughed.

Then turning, it walked slowly back in between the trees with the bloody knife in its hand, and as it walked between the trees it melted into the darkness and disappeared.

Chapter 10

George Potter had lived next door to Josh and his parents for more than 10 years. Someone once told him that once you hit forty you start to develop lots of niggling health problems. George found that after fifty it got considerably worse. He now thought that he must have a prostate problem because lately he needed to urinate two or three times every night.

So here it was, three fifteen in the morning and he was off to the bathroom for the second time that night. The trouble with getting up more than once a night was that it became progressively harder to get back to sleep.

He quietly padded across the hall to the bathroom, hoping that when he returned he could go back to sleep until it was time to get up in the morning.

But when he was back in bed, he heard the sound of laughter from outside. He got out of bed and went to the window, wondering who would be in the street so late at night.

At first there didn't seem to be anyone out there, but then George thought he saw what looked like a bald-headed child between two of the trees further along the road. He craned his neck closer to the window but saw that there was actually nothing there. *It must have been a trick of the shadows,* he told himself.

But then he realized that he could see something out there. Although his view was partly obscured by the trees, he could see that there was a man lying in the middle of the road with something spread all around him.

Thinking that the guy must be drunk and needed moving before he became a hit-and-run victim, George knew he had to do something. But he didn't want to go out there alone because you never knew. The guy might not be drunk at all. He might be some nutcase lying in wait of an unsuspecting Good Samaritan.

He picked up the receiver of the telephone beside his bed and dialled 999.

"Hello. Which emergency service do you require?" asked the operator.

"Ambulance please," George told her.

He replaced the receiver after the call.

"What's up?" his wife asked sleepily

"There's some guy laid in the road outside. I'm going out to wait for the ambulance."

George put on his dressing gown and slippers and went outside. His wife did likewise but only went as far as the front doorway where she watched George go out into the street to where the man lay.

George was curious to see what the lumpy substance was that the guy was lying in. But when he was close enough to see what it was he wished he hadn't.

I'm going to be sick, thought George. But before he'd even finished the thought, he vomited.

*

Wednesday morning dawned bright and sunny but the residents of Myrtle Street didn't notice the fine weather.

Their attention was totally absorbed in the activities in the middle of the road.

Roger and Rachel Harrison had been up since 5 a.m., unable to sleep any longer because of all the voices outside. A small white marquee had been erected in the street and people in protective white body suits were going in and out.

None of the neighbours seemed to know what was in there but they all agreed that it must be gruesome because some people were coming out and vomiting.

Police prohibited residents from venturing beyond their property boundaries unless absolutely necessary. Many police were bent double or down on their knees searching in all the grass verges and putting everything they found into plastic bags and labelling them.

Josh awoke at 7 a.m. and was immediately aware of some sort of commotion outside. He got out of bed and looked out of the front landing window.

Wow! It was like a whole different world out there. There was a small white marquee in the middle of the road and the people in white body suits going in and out looked like an all-too-familiar sight.

There were police cars and ambulances parked all over the place and the police were meticulously combing the street on their hands and knees.

Josh felt a sinking feeling in the pit of his stomach. Without even knowing what had happened, he already knew what had caused it. He didn't need to see anymore and went to shower and dress and then joined his parents outside.

A policeman was talking to them and handing them a business card.

"If you recall anything at all, no matter how small or insignificant it seems, please give us a ring."

Josh's father held the card as though it was something nasty. "It's like we said, we wish we could help, but we didn't hear anything until 5, and then all we heard was you guys."

"Thanks for your time anyway. There'll be door-to-door enquiries later," said the young policeman. Then looking at Josh he asked, "Is this your son?"

"Yes," his mother said. "This is Josh."

"Well, Josh, as you can see there's a lot going on here today. Did you hear anything strange last night?"

"Someone's dead, aren't they?" Josh said without emotion.

"How do you know that?" asked the young constable.

Josh shrugged. "I've seen police shows on TV. Is it someone we know?" He was dreading the answer.

"No," his mother reassured him. "It was a stranger passing by."

"How did he die?" But before anyone could speak, Josh saw a man in a white protective suit come out of the marquee and vomit. Immediately he knew the answer.

"He was murdered," his mother said.

Josh knew he could describe exactly what was in the canvas, right down to the last twelve inches of intestine on the floor. But he kept this information to himself. He felt guilty, sad, confused and mentally over-burdened. Too many emotions were crowding his mind.

He knew that the game was now controlling him and would force him to play even if he didn't want to. It was using his anger to choose its victims and choosing victims at random if he wouldn't co-operate.

What was he supposed to do now? If he became angry with someone they would die and if he didn't then someone he didn't know would die. It was a total and complete *Catch*

22. His only consolation was that the game had to end sometime, didn't it?

"Come on, breakfast." His mother's words brought him out of his deep thoughts and back to the present. Having breakfast was a good idea. Right now he needed to do something normal in this abnormal morning. They said goodbye to the policeman and went inside.

Josh was thoughtful while he ate. Twice his mother asked him what was wrong. "I've never seen you this quiet."

"I'm fine," he reassured her with a smile, but his mind was whirling with the problem he was facing. One thing was for sure, he couldn't trust the game to play alone. It would always allow the enemy to win. He would just have to play and he would have to make sure that he defeated the goblin.

After breakfast he packed up his lunch and took his bag upstairs to his room to choose which books he needed for the day.

As he neared his bedroom he heard the strange noises from the game. He felt a heavy dread in the pit of his stomach. What was going to happen now? He didn't want to go into his room, but he had to. He couldn't just stay away from his bedroom forever, or not even for one day. He needed some books for school. Taking a deep breath he entered his room.

The game was already on and his hero was back at the beginning of the woods before he had seen the goblin. Josh kept one eye on the screen as he packed his bag. Salvador seemed to be marking time and looking from left to right, but he didn't move forward. As he watched, Salvador turned to the screen and watched Josh. He was waiting. He was waiting for Josh to play the game again and the expression on his face looked impatient.

Josh sat down with a sigh. He really didn't want to play but the computer was obviously giving him no choice.

"Josh. Hurry up or you'll be late for school," his mother shouted up the stairs making him jump and he could have almost sworn that Salvador winced too.

"Coming," he called back and the game blinked off.

He stared in disbelief. The game was obviously more aware of what was going on than he had ever imagined. It even knew that he had to go to school. Josh stood up hurriedly, nearly knocking the chair over in his haste. He needed to get out of there. He clumsily reached for his bag and dropped it twice before finally getting a firm hold of it and leaving the room.

He went despondently to school.

Chapter 11

Josh mistakenly thought that school would provide a sanctuary of normality in his troubled and already complicated day. But it didn't.

Just getting there had been like trying to manoeuvre through an obstacle course. He'd needed a police escort to pass the crime scene in his street and then he'd been confronted by a barrage of TV and newspaper reporters. They walked in front of him, trying to block his exit while pelting him with questions about what was happening in the street.

Josh began to panic and turned to head back home. One of the police constables at the end of Myrtle Street, standing at the barrier holding everyone back, saw Josh's dilemma and came to his rescue.

Taking Josh gently by the elbow he guided him back through the reporters.

"Just let the boy through," he gruffly instructed them. "He's just trying to get to school and he hasn't seen anything. Now, come on, all of you stand back and let him through."

The reporters reluctantly parted and allowed Josh and his chaperone through. Once through them all Josh heaved an audible sigh of relief and he and the policeman both smiled at each other. But by this time the reporters had lost interest in them anyway as they swarmed all over their next unfortunate victim attempting to leave.

"There, you should be OK from here," said the constable as he let go of Josh's elbow.

"Thanks."

"No problem." The policeman turned and pushed his way back through the crowd.

Josh carried on, stepping carefully over the many electrical wires on the ground and weaving his way through the reporters' vans.

He met up with lots of other children on the way to school and they had no other conversation except last night's murder. Josh didn't particularly want to talk about it, but because he actually lived on Myrtle Street he was the centre of attention. All the children were bursting with questions.

"Were his guts really out all over the road?"

"Was there pieces of him strewn about everywhere?"

"Did they actually find his head hanging from a tree?"

Josh couldn't believe the stupid questions he was being asked. These kids really had no idea of the terrifying reality of this grizzly situation. He felt like screaming at them all "For goodness sake! You are all so ignorant! You know nothing at all and yet you are so arrogant that you think you know everything! Your morbid fascination is so juvenile! You don't have the slightest clue about what you're saying so just shut the hell up!"

But he daren't say anything for fear he would give too much away, yet he felt that if he didn't tell someone soon, he would burst. This whole burden of the secret he carried was becoming too much to keep in...but he must hold his silence. Even if he told them the truth they would laugh in his face. A computer game committing murder? It sounded so ludicrous yet Josh knew that it was very frighteningly real.

In frustration he snapped at them all. "Don't be so ridiculous. You've all been watching too many horror movies. Just get a grip, will you! There was nothing at all to see in the street this morning and the police had covered the body up."

"But I heard..." began one boy eagerly.

"I don't care WHAT you heard," Josh shouted, cutting him off. "I was there so I know what I'm talking about."

"God, you're always such a boring bastard," the boy spat back at him. "Even when the most exciting thing ever happens, you make it sound so boring." He stormed off in a huff and the other boys followed him.

Josh was relieved that the pressure to provide gory details was off him.

In school the lessons proceeded as normal but at break times all the talk was about the murder. At lunchtime Josh sat on a bench under a tree to eat his sandwiches on his own. He pulled a book out of his bag and read as he ate.

"Hello."

He hadn't been aware of anyone approaching him and so was surprised and delighted to see it was Leonora. She sat on the bench beside him. Josh had just bitten into his sandwich so he chewed and swallowed as quickly as he could.

"It's been a really gossipy sort of day today, hasn't it, with everyone talking non-stop about that guy being murdered? I heard that it happened in your street."

She was a very confident person, a quality that Josh admired but sadly lacked. He felt himself becoming incredibly bashful in her company and could feel his face burning as he blushed.

"Yeah," was all he could say, and he became annoyed with himself for being so shy. He never felt this way when he was with anyone else, so why did it have to happen with her? He could also feel the beginning of an erection, so he put his book down in his lap to cover it and tried not to think about it because he didn't want to make it any worse.

"So you must know the truth," she said, unaware of all the feelings and emotions pulsating through his mind and body due to her physical closeness. "You know everyone's saying so many different things I don't know what to believe."

"I wouldn't believe any of them if I was you." Josh was relieved that he'd found his voice again. "I've heard most of what they're saying."

"So what is the truth?"

Josh shrugged. "Nothing exciting, I'm afraid." He chose his words carefully so that he didn't give anything away. "A man was stabbed and died. The police had the body covered in a sort of tent while they examined it and they were searching the grass verges for any clues. There isn't anything more I can tell you other than that."

"So he wasn't gutted or decapitated?"

"I don't know. Everyone was asking me about it this morning and I told them that there was nothing to tell but they wouldn't believe me. They just thought their own made-up stories of blood and gore were much more interesting."

Leonora was thoughtful for a moment and then she smiled. "Yeah, they're right. Their made-up stuff *is* much more interesting."

Josh smiled too. "Yeah, but you wanted to know the boring truth."

"Yeah, I did, didn't I? Well, thanks anyway. See you."

She stood and walked across the yard back to where her two friends were waiting. Josh couldn't take his eyes off her and watched admiringly, until something else caught his eye.

Standing only a few feet away from Leonora and her friends were Carl Thurston, Lee Williams and Adrian Sparks, the three bullies whose biggest thrill in life seemed to be to tease Josh.

His heart sank at the sight of them. They must have seen the lovesick way he'd been acting with Leonora and now they were smirking at him. They were fifteen, two years older than Josh, and were always together, which only served to make them more confident and therefore more aggressive.

He didn't want another confrontation with them so he began to pack his things away. Then he had a sudden thought. Surely if they saw him quickly pack up and leave, they would know that he was running away.

He stopped for just a split second and smiled at how ridiculous that thought was. What did it matter what they thought? They wouldn't pick on him any less if he didn't try to escape them.

He finished putting his things away, zipped up his bag, slung it over one shoulder and quickly made his way towards the school gates without even looking up to see if they were coming after him. He didn't know where he was going to go once he got out of the school, but even walking the streets was preferable to facing the three bullies again, especially in front of Leonora.

But it didn't matter where he thought he was going to go because as he approached the gates he saw all three of them had headed him off and were waiting for him. He was too close to change direction and head somewhere else and he didn't want to turn his back to them so he just stood still where he was.

The three of them walked slowly towards him.

"Well, well, well," said Carl Thurston, who always seemed to be the more dominant of the three. "What do we have here then? Seems we have a ginger-headed geek who's in love." He pronounced the word 'lurve' and the other two sniggered through their noses.

"Does she LURVE you too, geek?"

"She was just asking about the murder," Josh told him honestly.

"Ooh, indeed."

There was more sniggering from the other two.

"So why would anyone come to you for information? Is that little ginger pea-brained head of yours full of knowledge then?" As he spoke he flicked the side of Josh's head.

Josh said nothing. He felt totally defenceless and humiliated. He wished that this was one of those marvellous moments that you see in movies where he could throw down his bag and perform swift karate moves on all three of them, knocking them all to the ground and rendering all them all unconscious. But unfortunately this was real life and Josh was not, and never would be, a black belt in karate.

"I asked you a question, geek boy. Are you an expert in murder investigations?"

Josh took a deep breath before answering. He knew Carl Thurston was looking for an emotional reaction. He wanted Josh to sound afraid and intimidated, but Josh didn't want to give him the satisfaction so he kept his voice as even as he could.

"No, but I live on the street where it happened."

"And this makes you more knowledgeable?" Again he flicked the side of Josh's head.

"I said no." Keeping his anger in check was getting harder. How he'd love to grab Carl Thurston's arm next time he raised it and break it in two.

"Then why would any female want to talk to you?"

"For the same reason that they DON'T want to talk to you." Josh immediately regretted his words, but it was too late.

"Perhaps you'd like to explain yourself before I kick your head in."

"What's there to explain?" Josh looked from left to right. "I don't see any girls clamouring for your attention. Seems they prefer more intelligent conversation than that."

Carl Thurston's face flushed red with anger. "Why you…"

"Oh go on. You can do whatever you want to me but you can't change facts. And the fact is that you're jealous."

"Me jealous of you? Don't make me laugh."

Josh knew he had hit a nerve by Carl Thurston's back-pedalling. One minute he was going to hit him but now he was trying to make light of what Josh was saying. He wasn't sure what nerve he'd hit but he decided to carry on anyway.

"You're jealous of Leonora talking to me and not you."

The other two took a step closer, suddenly very interested in whatever Josh had to say.

Carl Thurston noticed them move and began to talk faster.

"What, that slut?"

"Slut?"

"Yeah, you heard. She's nothing but a dirty slut. She'll talk to anyone, she will and that's not all she'll do."

"So why are you always watching her all the time?"

Carl Thurston raised his eyebrows questioningly. Josh wasn't sure if he didn't have a clue what he was talking about or whether he was wondering how much Josh knew, so Josh carried on.

"I'm not stupid. I've seen you looking at her all the time. But I notice she doesn't want to talk to you."

The other two began to snigger again but this time it wasn't at Josh.

Carl Thurston moved so fast that he took Josh completely by surprise. He grabbed Josh by the front of his shirt, swung him around and pinned him up against the front wall next to the gate. Josh's feet were almost off the ground and he was scared. He knew he'd gone too far but he hadn't been able to stop himself and now Carl Thurston was raging.

"Right, you mouthy little motherfu…"

"Mr Thurston! Take your hands off that boy immediately!"

They all turned at the sound of the voice and saw that Mr Johnson, the deputy head, had walked in through the gates without being noticed.

Carl Thurston still held onto Josh and looked back at him as though he was undecided as to whether he should still hit him at least once.

"NOW, Mr Thurston!" bellowed Mr Johnson.

Carl Thurston let go of Josh reluctantly. "I'll still get you," he hissed.

"The three of you go to my office and wait outside until I get there."

They all stood looking at each other.

"NOW!" Mr Johnson shouted, making all four of them jump.

The three bullies all slowly turned and walked away. Carl Thurston looked at Josh as he turned and threw him the most threatening look he could manage.

It worked. Josh felt threatened.

"Are you all right, boy?" Mr Johnson placed a fatherly hand on Josh's shoulder.

"Yeah, I think so. They're always picking on someone. It was just my unfortunate day to be picked on."

"Good lad. Leave them to me. I'll deal with them and I'll make sure there are no repercussions on you because of this."

"Thanks," said Josh, but he knew that there would be repercussions no matter how hard Mr Johnson tried to help. The three bullies would be punished and they would then be hell bent on taking it out on Josh sooner or later.

Josh was shaking and tried to hide his trembling hands out of sight. He wasn't only scared because of what had happened, he was also afraid of how this would affect things next time he played the game. He was frightened and angry and the game would know.

As Mr Johnson walked away, Josh saw that a small crowd had gathered and he felt embarrassed. Once more he was the centre of attention and once more he hated it.

As he walked home from school that day he felt exhausted. It had been a very trying day. First with the murder and then the bullies confronting him and now he felt sure that the game would be waiting for him to play when he got home. He tried to walk slowly but he knew he was only prolonging the inevitable.

A sudden voice from behind startled him.

"You may think you're clever, geek, but you'll be sorry."

Josh turned quickly to see Carl Thurston, his face like thunder.

"You might be safe for now but time is on my side and you WILL pay for getting me into so much trouble."

"It's your own fault. You shouldn't be so jealous." Josh spoke bravely but inside he was very afraid.

Carl Thurston clenched and unclenched his fists and looked as though he wanted to say something else. But then he turned and walked abruptly away without another word.

Josh let his shoulders drop in relief but he knew that his safety was only temporary and he ran the rest of the way home.

He was amazed when he turned into Myrtle Street to see that everything was back to normal. Such a difference from that morning. Bunches of flowers were laid on the side of the road near where the body had been, but everything else was back to how it had been before.

When he got home his mother was in the kitchen.

"Hi, Mum," he greeted her.

She turned and smiled. "Hi, Josh. How was school today?"

"Oh, you know, the usual."

"Well, it's not been usual around here, I can tell you. It's been all over the news today, even the national news. But that's not surprising considering the amount of news people hanging around."

"Yeah, I know. I couldn't even get away from them this morning," Josh laughed.

His mother looked concerned. "Oh no. They weren't bothering you too, were they? Honestly, you'd think they'd leave children alone."

"It wasn't too bad because a policeman made them get out of my way."

"I had the same problem and I was only going to the shop for some milk. And there's been helicopters circling and hovering for most of the day."

"Well it's all amazingly quiet out there now."

"I know." His mother smiled. "It was all 'here one minute, gone the next'. I'd have thought the police would have been here for days but apparently, apart from the poor victim, there was no other evidence of the crime being committed whatsoever."

This surprised Josh. He'd been dreading the police finding evidence of a strange alien creature and asking too many questions. But it seemed somehow logical that if the goblin didn't really exist, then there could be no trace of it.

But then again, the goblin must have existed for a short time last night, otherwise how could it have killed the man? This train of thought was too deep and confusing and Josh couldn't cope with it right now.

"So do they have any suspects for the murder?" he asked.

His mother's brow wrinkled as she tried to explain the perplexing circumstances. "Well, that's what's weird. It seems that although the man's body was ripped open, there's no sign that he's been murdered. The policeman told us that it's as though it just happened spontaneously. But it's impossible for that to happen, so it must be murder although there's no sign of anyone else being there."

Josh smiled despite the seriousness of the subject. "So it's as though a murderer dropped from above and murdered this guy without a weapon?"

"I guess so." His mother's brow was still furrowed. "They've taken the body to do more tests on it but at the moment it all seems so strange."

She busied herself as she spoke by getting out cups and putting the kettle on.

"The man's wife came here today to see where it all happened," she told him as her face lost its confused look. "I felt so sorry for her.

"Apparently it was George Potter who found the man just after three this morning, but he was so traumatised that he hasn't been out of the house all day and I saw a doctor there this afternoon so I can't imagine what it was that he saw."

I can, thought Josh miserably.

His mother made him a cup of coffee and gave him a piece of a cake that she'd baked that day. As Josh sat and ate he told her about what all the kids were saying at school. She grimaced as he spoke.

When he'd finished his coffee and cake his mother placed his cup and plate in the sink and then took pots and pans from the cupboards to start preparing dinner. She took out some potatoes and peeled them.

Josh stayed at the table, trying to pluck up enough courage to go to his room.

"Aren't you going to change out of your uniform?" his mother eventually asked him.

"Yeah," he told her and reluctantly made his way upstairs, knowing that he was on his way to sign Carl Thurston's death warrant.

As soon as he approached his room he could hear the computer humming. The game was already up and running. There was nothing Josh could do except sit down and play and try as hard as he could to defeat the goblin.

He entered his bedroom with his heart thumping and sat down in front of the computer. Nothing he had ever done in his life mattered as much as this and he was intensely afraid.

On the screen Salvador was about to re-enter the woods. At least this time Josh knew what enemy to expect, but how he was going to defeat it, he had no idea.

Firstly he looked in Salvador's bag to choose a weapon. He scanned the contents. Think! Think! But it was so hard to think when the choice he made was literally a life or death decision.

Eventually he chose a bow and arrow, thinking that his best chance was to shoot the goblin before it had a chance to come near. Once the goblin got hold of Salvador he knew he'd have no chance of surviving the vicious attack, so it was vital to kill it first. He was determined to win.

He let Salvador enter the woods slowly, shooting nervously and erratically at every noise he heard. Arrows flew from the bow and disappeared between the trees, but none seemed to be hitting anything.

He walked Salvador deeper into the woods, shooting several times at things he thought he saw in the shadows.

Then suddenly the goblin leapt out from the trees and onto the path directly in front of Salvador. In its hand it held one of the discarded arrows and it swiftly dealt Salvador a blow to the side of his head with it. Salvador fell heavily onto his back and even though Josh tried immediately to get him to stand up again, he wasn't fast enough.

The goblin leapt astride Salvador and clawed at his face. Salvador let out an agonising scream. Josh frantically pressed every key he could but didn't know how to manoeuvre Salvador to pull the goblin's hands away.

As Josh pressed the keys, Salvador kicked, punched and jumped but every movement was futile and did nothing to dislodge the manic goblin.

Then Salvador let out a long piercing cry. Josh was unsure what had happened. The goblin was moving so fast, but as it held up its hand in the air, Josh craned forward and saw that it held both of Salvador's eyeballs.

The goblin stood up, stepped away from Salvador and while still holding the eyeballs aloft, it skipped around and chuckled to itself.

Meanwhile, Salvador remained on the ground, screaming and thrashing with blood pouring from his empty eye sockets.

Josh sat open-mouthed. He'd felt so positive that he could win yet he'd been defeated so easily, quickly and horrifically.

He pressed the "Escape" key to take the game back to the saved version where Salvador was just about to enter the woods again. The game didn't respond. The goblin continued to dance around with the bloodied eye balls.

Josh kept tapping the "Escape" key. Still nothing happened.

In desperation he tried to switch off the computer tower, but still there was no response.

Then, laughing, the goblin ran closer to the inside of the screen, held up the two bloody eyeballs and looked triumphantly at Josh, who could only look back in horror.

Then the computer turned itself off and the screen went blank, leaving the sound of Salvador's screams still ringing in Josh's ears. Or was it, in reality, Carl Thurston's screams he was hearing?

Josh felt a doom-laden chill ripple up his spine.

Chapter 12

Carl Thurston went to bed just before midnight on that Wednesday evening.

It had not been a good day. He'd been hauled to the deputy head's office and had to endure standing there and being yelled at for ages. Who cared if he'd given the geek boy a hard time? He deserved a good slap anyway. And who did the prick of a deputy head think he was, going on about it so much?

The worst thing was that his parents had to go to school tomorrow to see the headmaster and discuss the school's zero tolerance policy towards bullying. His parents had a complete mental fit at him after the deputy head had rung.

"For God's sake, Carl," his father had thundered at him. "Why can't you just leave other kids alone? If they want to be geeky that's their business not yours."

"Oh that's rich coming from you, isn't it?" he'd sneered back. "Who was it that came home from the pub last week with a split lip after fighting with that little guy who you said was a dickhead and deserved a good smacking?"

"That was completely different. I'd had too much to drink at the time."

"Ha! So you're angry because I wasn't drunk like you?" He could see his father bristling with fury at having his behaviour questioned and his authority ignored.

"Stop it, both of you," his mother interjected. "Carl, it doesn't matter what your father does. What matters is that we both have to take time off work tomorrow because of what you've done. God knows we can't afford to lose money."

Carl's younger brother smirked. Although he was standing in the background he was in Carl's line of vision.

"Shut your face, you little prick!" Carl shouted at him.

"I haven't said anything," his brother protested innocently. "Honest," he added as his parents both turned to look at him.

"Don't take it out on your brother," his father warned him, turning back.

"You're in enough trouble as it is," his mother added.

"Just get off my back, will you?" He was tired of the whole thing but his father wasn't finished yet.

"We've put up with a lot from you. You're always getting into trouble. What's wrong with you? Your brother never does things like this."

That was enough. Carl didn't want to hear anymore. He'd heard it all before anyway, especially the speech about what a wonderful son his brother was. He found it hard to stomach the way they always fawned and fussed over his brother, thinking he was so perfect yet never knowing how sneaky and deceitful he was.

Right now he just wanted to go away from his family and put some distance between himself and them, so he headed for the front door.

"Don't you turn your back on me, you arrogant little shit," his father roared, but Carl kept on walking.

"You're part of this family and it's time you started acting like it. You never think of anyone but yourself and think you can do as you please. Well you can't. Things are going to change around h..." The slamming of the door cut off his words.

"Stupid old fool," Carl muttered to himself as he stormed down the path and out the front gate without knowing exactly where he was going.

He wanted to go to Lee Williams' house or Adrian Sparks', but he figured their parents would be freaking out at them about now too. So he just hung out around the town centre for a while.

The next three hours dragged by until Carl felt it was safe to return home. No doubt his father would be out at the pub now because that's where he was most nights and hopefully his mother would have saved his dinner for him because he was starving.

But as soon as he got home his mother began to lecture him and say that he couldn't have anything to eat because he didn't deserve it. He fled to his room hungry rather than listen to her anymore.

There wasn't much to do so he lay on his bed and watched TV for a while and leafed through a few magazines to pass the time then he reluctantly showered for bed.

The shower felt good on such a warm, humid evening, but the heat made him need to shower more than he cared to. Being clean wasn't a thing he normally fussed about but he hated to be sweaty, so showering every evening had become a necessity.

After the shower he dried himself and put on a clean pair of boxer shorts and once back in his bedroom he picked up all the magazines and put them away in his cupboard. Then he climbed into bed. He was undecided as to whether or not he wanted to watch TV. But a quick flick through the channels with the remote control proved that there was nothing on that he wanted to watch anyway, so he turned off the TV and the room went dark.

Carl stretched and turned onto his left side away from the TV. He didn't like to see the TV screen in the dark (although he would never admit it publicly). He was always spooked by the way it glowed for a while after he turned it off.

For quite some time he couldn't sleep. The room was so hot and his stomach was so empty. But mostly it was his thoughts that kept him awake as his mind re-ran all the events of the day. It had not been one of his better days.

Firstly he'd had to endure endless teasing this morning from his two mates after they'd caught him staring at the cool chick. He wasn't sure what expression he'd had on his face at the time but it must have been drippy because the other two had gone on and on about it for ages.

Of course he'd had to endure it without complaint because if he'd gotten angry at them he'd never have lived it down.

But then he'd seen the cool chick go and talk to the geek kid and they were smiling and laughing together and that had made him real angry.

He wasn't quite sure what it was that made him angry but he was livid just the same. So he'd tried to pressure the geek kid to put him off ever speaking to her again.

But the geek kid seemed to know what was going on. But how could he? Maybe it was just a guess. Well, it was a damn good guess if it was.

It might have been Carl himself who gave the game away because the geek kid had taken him by surprise and Carl knew that it had shown on his face.

Damn that geek kid. He'd always hated him. He was just one of those annoying people who rubbed him up the wrong way. He wasn't sure if it was his ginger hair, skinny body, goody-two-shoes attitude or his constant meticulous neatness that bothered him the most. It was probably all those things put together that made him one irritating little geeky shit.

Carl smiled to himself in the darkness. It wasn't over yet with the geek. All the trouble that had happened the rest of the day was his fault.

He'd get him. Yep, he'd give him the biggest hiding of his life.

And with that pleasant thought, he felt himself beginning to drift into sleep.

SHHLLP.

The sudden noise startled him and he opened his eyes. The sound had only been soft, but it was quite audible in such a quiet room. However, he was tired, so he told himself he must have heard it through the open window, and then he began to drift off again.

SSHHHH.

There it was again. It sounded like something soft being dragged across the floor. He continued to listen for a few more minutes until his tired eyes began to close once more.

THUD.

His bed shook with the bump.

Carl immediately sat up and turned on his bedside lamp. Looking around the room he saw that everything looked so normal with the light on, yet in the darkness he'd been terrified. His pulse was racing. He needed to reassure himself that there was no one in the room with him. The noises had come from the floor and his shaking bed worried him that someone was under it.

How childish was that? Thinking that there was someone under the bed was what little kids did. He wanted to laugh at himself for being so childish, but he was too afraid to smile. Children only *thought* things were under their beds; he unfortunately, *knew* something, or someone, was under there because he'd both heard and felt it.

Slowly he leaned over the side of his bed and looked at the floor. Nothing. Then he rolled over and looked down over the other side. Nothing.

So what was the bump? He concluded that he must have shaken the bed himself and not realized it. He looked around the room once more before switching off the lamp and turning over again on to his side. This time he WAS able to smile at his own childishness at thinking that someone was under the bed.

SSSHHHLLPP.

His eyes shot wide open. There was no mistaking it this time. Something really weird was happening and he didn't like it one bit. Flashbacks of every horror movie he'd ever seen, where something evil lurked in the darkness, went through his mind.

He rolled over onto his back and listened as carefully as he could but all he could hear was his own rapid breaths. He tried to close his mouth and slow down his breathing but it was impossible because he was more frightened than he thought he could ever possibly be.

The darkness of the room, which was usually his friend and helped him sleep, was now his terrifying enemy. His heavy window curtains made it doubly impossible to see properly.

Slowly, as he leaned forward and reached for the lamp to the left of his bed, he glimpsed a small, naked child standing to his right.

But just as he snapped his head to the right to take a better look, the child leapt up and thrust its head forward very sharply. Their foreheads came together with an almighty "clack" and Carl instantly had a blinding headache.

He was thrown back on the bed from the impact. What the hell was that thing? It was not a child like he had ever known before.

The child-thing instantly jumped on top of him and sat astride his shoulders, its sour-smelling crotch pushed firmly under his chin. It quickly placed its thumbs on his closed eyelids and pushed as hard as it could.

Carl had been too surprised by the presence of the thing to be afraid or be able to react fast enough. Everything was happening in microseconds. The pain in his head was bad but the pressure on his eyeballs caused more pain than his mind could cope with. He wanted to scream but there was no time. Before he had a chance to even open his mouth, he passed out.

The goblin released its tight hold and smiled down wickedly at the unconscious boy as blood pulsed out from under his closed eyelids. Then it swung its leg back over him, jumped down onto its belly on the floor and shuffled its way back under the bed.

Chapter 13

The next morning was bright and sunny and Josh ate his breakfast on the patio with his parents.

He took his empty dishes back into the kitchen when he'd finished and was just in time to hear the end of a local news bulletin on the radio.

"The teenage boy was taken to hospital and was said to be heavily sedated and comfortable. We'll bring you more on that story later."

Josh momentarily stopped moving as he listened. Could that be Carl Thurston? No. The boy in hospital was still alive. Surely if he'd been attacked by the goblin and had his eyes ripped out he'd be dead, wouldn't he? Josh thought so but he couldn't be completely sure.

"Another glorious day," said his mother, striding cheerfully inside.

"Just a pity it's a work day," his father said as he followed close behind.

"Never mind, it'll soon be the weekend and the weather forecast is still good. Josh? Are you OK?"

Josh came out of his reverie and realized that he was still holding his plate and cup.

"Yeah, I'm fine. I was just listening to a news report that said a teenage boy's been taken to hospital."

His parents shared a worried look.

"Weird, huh?" he asked, trying to sound as though he wasn't concerned.

"There are too many weird things happening around here," said his mother. "Let's hope this time it's just an unfortunate accident or something equally innocent."

"Too right," agreed his father.

Josh didn't say anything but he hoped they were right, for everyone's sake.

Later, throughout the school morning, he kept watch to see if Carl Thurston was around but he didn't see him anywhere. He didn't see Carl's two friends either, but he wasn't sure if that was just a coincidence.

At lunchtime though, he glimpsed Lee Williams and Adrian Sparks from a distance, but Carl Thurston wasn't with them. This was bad. It was possible that Carl Thurston was somewhere else at the moment, alive and well, but it wasn't very likely.

But just as he began to dwell on it, Leonora came and sat down beside him again.

"Hi," she greeted him cheerfully.

"Hi." He could feel himself beginning to blush again but it wasn't as bad as the previous day because now he had more worries on his mind.

"Have you heard about your friend?"

"Which one? I have so many," he joked.

"Carl Thurston."

Josh felt his face drop. "No."

"Well, last night someone came into his bedroom and tried to poke his eyes out."

Josh didn't know what to say.

"Was it you?" she asked.

Now he was dumbfounded. How could she possibly think he was capable of that? "Why would I?"

"Because I saw him picking on you yesterday and so I just wondered...you know." She didn't look at him as she spoke and instead stared at her legs as she swung them backwards and forwards, scuffing the sole of her shoes on the ground as she did so.

"Do you really think I'm that bad?" he asked her.

"Well, I don't know you, do I?"

"What exactly happened to him?" Josh was desperate to know but he tried not to sound too eager.

"All I know is that they took him away in an ambulance early this morning and his mother says his eyes are badly damaged and he probably will never be able to see again and so he won't be coming to school here anymore, will he?"

"I guess not." Josh felt ill at the thought of what the goblin must have done to him. But Carl Thurston was still alive and he probably saw the goblin which meant he would tell the police, and then what would happen?

"Do they know who did it?" he asked her.

"No. Apparently, apart from his injuries, there's no sign that anyone else was in his room, and he's being kept under sedation because of the pain and the fact that he can't stop screaming. It seems he woke his folks up screaming and wouldn't stop."

"How do you know all this?"

"One of my friends lives next door to him and their mothers are quite chummy."

"Leonora, are you coming or what!" someone shouted.

"Godda go. See ya."

Josh watched her walk over to her two friends and the three of them disappeared giggling around the corner of one of the buildings.

For the rest of the day he heard snippets of other kids' conversations about Carl Thurston. Some said he deserved it, others said it was the same attacker who killed the man in the street. Some believed he was blinded with a chemical spray and all of them knew that the other two bullies had sworn murderous revenge on whoever had hurt their mate.

When he arrived home he went into the kitchen to say hello to his mother.

She looked apprehensive as he entered.

"Hi, Mum. What's up?"

"I heard about what happened to the boy from your school today. I just don't understand what's happening around here anymore and now that poor boy wasn't even safe in his own bed."

Josh didn't know what to say and so stayed quiet and busied himself by getting a carton of orange juice out of the fridge and pouring himself a glass.

"Josh, are you OK?"

"Yeah, I'm fine." He hesitated briefly before continuing. "It's just that everyone's been talking about nothing else today at school and it's just so horrible."

"Did the police come to talk to anyone at school?"

"I've got no idea," Josh told her honestly. "He's two years older than me so I don't really know him, but I do know that not many people like him." Josh drank his juice in one go and put his empty glass in the sink. "I'm going upstairs to get changed."

"Don't you want anything to eat?"

"No, thanks. It's too warm and I'm not hungry."

Although Josh hadn't lied about not being hungry, it wasn't the warm weather that dulled his appetite. It was the fear about what he knew he had to do next.

He felt panic rising in his chest as he mounted the stairs. But when he entered his bedroom he was shocked to see that the computer was switched off. That was somehow scarier than seeing it switched on. He was so certain that the game would be on that he physically jumped when he saw the blank screen.

He was confused. Carl Thurston was badly injured but still alive. After how angry he had been at him the day before, the game would surely want him dead. Wouldn't it?

Apprehensively he approached the computer and sat in the chair and although he really didn't want to, he pressed the "start" button.

There was no response.

He pressed it again and again.

Still nothing.

The game didn't want to play, that was for sure. But why not? He sat for a while, wondering what was going to happen next.

He knew beyond a doubt that the game would kill Carl Thurston, but it certainly wasn't going to be now. Maybe the game wanted his suffering to be endured even longer or maybe the game was finished. No, that couldn't be it. The game was called *Journey to the Promised Land* and Josh had a feeling that he would be forced to endure the whole journey and all the battles it entailed.

So why had it stopped now? Carl Thurston was injured and in hospital but still alive in hospital. Yes, that must be it. Josh felt somewhat consoled by this new reasoning. Carl Thurston was safe because he was in hospital and surrounded by other people so the game couldn't hurt him there.

He was safe for the time being.

Josh felt confident about that.

Chapter 14

Carl Thurston lay in his hospital bed in intensive care. Heavy bandages covered his eyes, or what was left of them. He was in agony despite all the painkillers the nurses assured him he'd been given.

Would he ever see again? Who knew? He certainly didn't. He only had vague recollections of what had happened. He remembered being extremely afraid and his heart pounding. Then his memory was blank until he woke up screaming. He hadn't been able to stop screaming. The pain! Oh God, the pain! His eyes had been burning, aching and blind. He'd also been confused. Where was he? What was happening to him? It was like being in the middle of your worst nightmare and unable to wake up.

He could remember his mother crying and his father being angry and talking about "finding the bastard who did this." Was his brother there too? He couldn't remember and he was too tired to think about it.

He lay there in a blissful semi-doze, too sedated to remember the true horror of what had happened. Perhaps it was best if he didn't think about it right now anyway. But damn, he wished he could see. He wished he could pull off the bandages and look around the room.

He wasn't even sure if it was day or night or light or dark. He knew it was probably night because of the silence around him. He also had a vague recollection of his mother asking a nurse or doctor if Carl had eaten any dinner. The nurse or doctor had said no, he'd not been hungry and it was more important that he rested, so it must now be after dinner. Mustn't it? Maybe he'd heard that conversation hours ago, or days ago?

The next thing he remembered was a woman fussing with his sheets and saying good night. Was that the same day? Was it his mother? A nurse? He couldn't remember, but it was so quiet right now that it must still be night time and with the bandages being over his eyes he bet the nurses hadn't felt any need to leave a light on for him.

The thought of being alone and blind in a dark room in the middle of the night sent a shiver up his spine. He told himself not to be such a baby but in his present circumstances, keeping up a macho image didn't seem important anymore. His priorities in life had suddenly changed. All that was important now was getting better and being able to see again.

Oh God, if you can make my eyes all right again I promise not to take my eyesight for granted ever again, he silently vowed.

SSHHLLLP.

The noise startled him. Was it a nurse in the room?

SSSHHH.

No, it wasn't a nurse. He'd heard that noise before but he couldn't remember quite what it was. He tried to think. He knew he'd heard it recently. He also knew that the sound made him nervous. It actually made him more than nervous. He felt his heart rate increase. But what was the sound and why did it alarm him?

Then he could smell a sudden vile stench, which abruptly triggered in his mind where he'd heard those noises before. He took a sharp intake of breath and stiffened. He'd smelled that foul odour just after he'd been afraid; just before something had happened to his eyes. Someone had been in his bedroom. Someone had sat on his chest and...

His fear returned and crash-landed in his chest with an audible thump, making his heart pound and his mind race. He didn't think he could cope with the return of his assailant, who he knew was capable of unimaginable sadism. He felt as though he was going to pass out, which at that moment was preferable to this terrifying reality

But the putrid breath in his face brought him back to full consciousness and the full horror of his situation. He was alone, blind and sedated and someone who wanted to harm him was leaning right over his face.

Then the breath disappeared.

Footsteps. He heard soft footsteps hurrying around to the other side of the bed. It sounded like the person was barefoot. He held his breath and strained his ears to hear every sound. He wanted to press the buzzer to call for the nurse, but he wasn't sure where the buzzer was. He knew it was hanging over the railing round the bed somewhere but he daren't lift a hand to find it.

Then he heard a more familiar noise, the sound of a chair was being either pushed or dragged to his bedside.

Then there was silence. The quietness was more terrifying than anything he'd heard so far because now he didn't know where the person was or what was happening. He waited, and listened to the only sound in the room which was his own rapid breathing.

A grunt. He heard a small grunt. The chair make a wobbling sound on the floor as though one of its legs was slightly shorter than the others and so it rocked when it was sat on. He'd heard someone get onto the chair but it sounded like a lot of effort, like a small child makes when they're too small to simply bend their knees and sit down, and so they climb up and turn round.

Then he heard short sharp quiet breaths coming from the direction of the chair, but they seemed to be higher up. Was someone standing on the chair?

He waited, afraid to breathe or move. Why was this happening to him? Who was this person? Why had no one stopped them from coming near him? Where were all the nurses? This was hardly *intensive care* if no one *cared* what was happening to him.

Bugs. He could feel bugs crawling on his hair on the top of his head. Reaching up quickly to swat them away, his hand brushed lightly against another. It wasn't bugs at all. It was someone tormenting him by lightly touching the ends of his hair.

He leaned further away from his tormentor. What was happening? Why was this guy doing this to him?

Because of the bandages and eye injuries he couldn't see the scalpel in the goblin's other hand.

Carl Thurston felt something small move lightly across his throat from one side to the other and then he felt warm liquid oozing over his skin. He was confused but not in pain. His fear, however, was immense.

But before he had a chance to react at all he felt the palm of a small hand press down hard on his forehead, tipping his head back and exposing his throat. Then he felt more warm thick liquid gushing from his throat and he now knew it was his own blood.

Carl Thurston lost control of his bladder.

As the urine soaked into his hospital gown and bed sheets, he felt another hand reach inside his throat and grasp his trachea extremely tightly.

With his breath cut off so abruptly, his body jolted. Then with one hard wrench his trachea was removed and he passed out seconds before his blood-starved heart stopped beating.

Further down the corridor, in a room just off the reception station, Nurse Whittaker heard one of the patients' emergency buzzers. She hadn't been sitting down long as she'd only recently finished her last patient check. She was the only one who wasn't busy as the other nurses were stocking up supplies and sterilising equipment.

Nurse Whittaker put down her cup of tea and went out to see who was buzzing. It was the room that was furthest away. Typical. Why couldn't it have been the nearest one? She guessed it was what they called "Sod's Law" or was it more polite to call it "Murphy's Law"?

She hurried to the room only to find that the patient's hand had fallen onto the buzzer while he slept. She entered the semi-dark room, removed his hand and hung the buzzer over the bed rail.

As she strolled back down the corridor she looked into each room as she passed. All seemed well. Monitors were working and patients were sleeping. The last room she looked in was that of the young boy who'd had his eyes poked out. It was a horrible thing to have happen to him. She shuddered.

As she passed his room she saw that a chair had been pulled up beside his bed and he looked as though he'd been covered in a dark blanket. But the hospital didn't have any dark blankets, and how could he have gotten one anyway? He was blind and sedated.

As she opened the door to his room she thought she heard a shuffling sound from under the bed. She glanced down and could have sworn she saw the soles of two small feet disappear into the darkness beneath it. A child? No, it couldn't be. What would a small child be doing in his room?

But her attention was quickly diverted to the dripping blanket. As her eyes adjusted to the gloom she saw the shiny dark blood that covered the bed and dripped onto the floor and chair. The blood, she noticed, had also splashed up the wall. The boy lay splayed out on the bed, his head tipped back and a large fleshy mass protruding from his throat. The smell was offensive.

Nurse Whittaker put her hand over her nose as she staggered from the room. The other nurses in the supply room turned as she entered and from the look on her face they knew that something was horribly wrong.

Chapter 15

Josh came awake slowly the next morning. He lay there, half dozing, listening to the birdsong, but it soon became apparent that the birdsong sounded strange.

He brought himself to full consciousness, opened his eyes and listened more carefully. It wasn't just birdsong he could hear; there was something else as well. It was a familiar noise. Was it the bin wagon? No, it couldn't be. Today was Friday and bin-emptying day wasn't until Monday. Then with a feeling of alarm he remembered what the noise was.

It was the computer fan whirring as it cooled the motherboard in the tower. He sat up quickly, got out of bed and looked at the screen. The game had been playing on its own. The scene on the monitor was an abomination. Slowly he crossed the room and surveyed the carnage.

Salvador was dead. He lay on the ground in a pool of blood with his throat butchered. The goblin leaned over him. As Josh watched, the goblin looked up with a triumphant smirk and held up two eyeballs in one hand and something long and blood-soaked in the other.

Josh quickly struck the "Escape" key and the scene once more reverted back to where the game was last saved so Salvador was alive and had yet to enter the woods. He felt a sudden rush of relief as well as surprise that the game was now responding but he was also shocked that the game had played while he slept. But the most troubling thought he had right now was that someone else must have died and it must have been Carl Thurston as the goblin still had his eyeballs.

Before he went to bed, Josh had been convinced that the hospital was a safe place to be, a sort of sanctuary. He felt as though he'd been doubly cheated. The game had played on its own before but this time it had done it without his knowledge *and* when he thought Carl Thurston was safe. The game was playing dirty tricks. He now had to kill the goblin otherwise it might kill someone else while he was at school. He was being backed into a corner. If he didn't play then the game would play on its own, in which case the hero always died. At least if he played himself then he had a chance of winning, even if it was only a small chance.

He sat down and mentally braced himself for the challenge ahead.

After a moment's hesitation and a few deep breaths, Josh put his hand to the keyboard. First he looked in Salvador's bag. It was difficult to concentrate but Josh tried his hardest. He rubbed the crusty sleep from the corners of his eyes and ran his hand through his hair, desperately trying to think clearly and keep his mind focused on the task in front of him.

"Shit, shit, shit," he whispered repeatedly under his breath as he gazed at the contents of the bag, but could see nothing that sparked any ideas.

The problem with the goblin was that it was a tricky creature and could hide in the chinks and darkness between the trees and jump out without any warning. Therefore, Josh reasoned, it would be necessary to kill it before it had a chance to leap out. But how? Obviously the bow and arrows weren't the answer because that had been like sending the goblin a weapon to use against him.

Instead Josh chose a very long knife, long enough for Salvador to poke between the trees. Then, taking a deep breath, he walked Salvador into the woods.

Before long the woods became denser and the large number of trees began to block the daylight, making everywhere look dark and dangerous. As the gaps between the trees narrowed, Josh moved Salvador's arm so that the long knife stabbed into every dark space. He kept thinking he glimpsed the goblin between the trees, but every time he looked, the goblin seemed to appear somewhere else.

It reminded him of an optical illusion he'd once seen with a page full of small black squares. There always seemed to be a pale grey dot between the corners of the squares but every time you looked at the dots, they disappeared and could only be seen when you weren't looking directly at them.

That suddenly gave Josh a brilliant idea. Perhaps the answer was to stab at the goblin in the place where he *wasn't* looking rather than where he was, because obviously the goblin was playing the same kind of optical trick.

He stopped Salvador and turned him to face one of the trees. When Josh looked past Salvador and straight at the tree, the goblin seemed to be in both dark spaces at either side. If he looked to the right, the goblin was to the left, but when he looked to the left, the goblin was to the right.

Feeling suddenly very hopeful, he looked again to the right of the tree and stabbed the long knife in the gap to the left.

The sudden scream was so startling that even Salvador took a step backward. The goblin leaned its hand on a tree for support as it staggered into the open with the knife thrust deeply into its throat and protruding from the other side.

It made a strange choking sound and Josh wasn't sure if it was gasping for breath or trying to speak. It fell to its knees and clutched the knife handle in a feeble attempt to remove it. A few moments later it fell forwards to the ground, the protruding weapon making it roll onto its side. It lay still, and blood from the wound pooled around its corpse.

Josh quickly saved the game there. He didn't want to risk the game tricking him by reverting to the previously saved version again with the goblin alive once more.

He'd had enough. It was time to stop the game once and for all. He leaned down to the computer tower and tried to eject the CD, but the drawer remained firmly shut. In exasperation he slammed his fist down repeatedly on the computer tower but still nothing happened. Then, as an afterthought, he squatted down under the desk and pulled out the plug. The screen went blank and the computer fell silent.

Josh stared in disbelief. Why hadn't he thought of that before? It was so simple. He started to laugh and then he laughed more and wasn't sure if it was from relief or hysteria, but it felt good to have something to laugh about.

The answer had been so obvious yet he'd overlooked it. Take away the power source and the game couldn't run. If it couldn't run then it couldn't unleash any more evil on the world.

Josh felt better than he had in a long time. He kicked the plug away from the socket (just in case), went for a shower and dressed for school.

Downstairs his parents were already having breakfast. Josh made himself some toast and coffee and sat down with them. They were discussing Carl Thurston.

"But if he was attacked in his own bedroom then no one's safe," said his mother.

"We don't know the full story yet," his father tried to reassure her. "For all we know he might have been attacked by someone he knew."

"But there was that man in the street too."

"Maybe whoever it was knew them both or maybe it's just a horrible coincidence."

"Oh, Roger. You're grasping at straws. First there were all the animals dying and now two attacks on people and all this in one week. A coincidence? I don't think so."

"OK then, suppose you're right and no one's safe anywhere. What can we do about it?"

Josh's mother sat silently and fidgeted with her fingernails.

"See, Rachel? There's nothing we can do about it anyway so there's no point in worrying."

"But we can be extra careful."

"Yes, we can. But I can't help but wonder how that poor boy or his family are ever going to get over what happened to him."

"Do you know him well, Josh?" his mother asked.

"No, he's fifteen so he's two years above me at school."

"Do you know who he is?"

"Everyone knows Carl Thurston."

"Why, is he famous?" she asked innocently.

"More like infamous. It's a matter of survival at school to know who he is so that you can avoid him."

"So he's a bully?"

"A big bully. He hangs around with two others and they seem to get a real kick out of terrorising small children."

"Have they ever picked on you?" His mother looked concerned so he chose his words carefully so as not to upset her.

"A couple of times," he said with a shrug of his shoulders. "But they generally leave me alone because I'm not scared of them, so I'm usually fine."

She wasn't convinced. "You tell me straight away if any of them come near you."

"Please, Mum. I'm fine. Really. There are always plenty of teachers around anyway."

"All the same..."

"Mum, don't fuss." But he knew his mother couldn't help it. She always worried about him.

She was going to say something more but his father cut in.

"The boy's fine, Rachel. He's sensible enough to know what to do. But Josh, there've been two attacks here in two days and one was fatal, so make sure you go straight to school and come straight home afterwards. Don't worry your mother unnecessarily. It's not safe anywhere anymore and we must keep the doors and windows locked at all times."

"Yeah, Dad, I know." He didn't correct his father and tell him that there had been three attacks.

*

It was lunchtime at school before the first rumours started to circulate about Carl Thurston being killed, but it seemed that no one wanted to believe it.

After lunch the headmaster called a special assembly. He told them all that Carl Thurston had been attacked and killed while in the hospital. He said that the hospital staff had seen no one, nor had anyone been caught on CC TV either entering or leaving the ward. Obviously this killer was very determined and very elusive and all the children needed to be extra careful and to trust no one.

None of the children could stop talking about it for the rest of the day and on the way home Josh heard many weird and outlandish theories about it.

Some kids thought it was an inside job and that one of the nurses or doctors had killed him. Others thought the killer had come through the window or that a vampire had flown in as a bat. One thing was certain though: this murder had everyone's imagination working overtime.

Josh just hoped that he'd put an end to the killings by removing the plug. He himself had been responsible for every death even though he wanted no part of it. It had all been so unfair.

The game had been feeding off his negative emotions, but he was only human and so couldn't help feeling angry sometimes. But that shouldn't mean that someone had to die. And even when Josh had refused to play, the game had chosen a victim at random and killed anyway. He'd been given no choice or control over his situation.

He tried to look on the positive side, that at least he'd thought of a way to stop the game and at least it was Carl Thurston who'd died and not someone who he really liked. But somehow these thoughts weren't very comforting.

And what about the man who was attacked in the street? He wasn't a bad person as far as Josh knew and Josh hadn't even been angry at him. How could he have been? They'd never even met.

Hopefully though it should all be over. He'd unplugged the computer and without electricity the game couldn't possibly play anymore, either with or without him. Of this he was completely sure.

The game could never force him to play again.

Could it?

Chapter 16

Josh was so glad it was Friday afternoon. It had been such a strange week and he was glad it was over. He hurried home from school but came to an abrupt halt as he rounded the corner of his own street.

It looked as though all of their close neighbours were out and they were standing in a big group talking. Something else must have happened. Josh began to panic. How had anything happened? He'd unplugged the computer so it was harmless.

They all turned towards him as he walked down the street. He quickly scanned the crowd to see if his parents were there. They weren't.

"There he is," said the old woman who lived in the house opposite theirs. Then as Josh approached she said, "I heard about your tragic news. I'm so sorry."

Josh was speechless. What tragic news? What had happened to his family? He could only stare at her in horror. She put a friendly hand on his arm. "I'm sorry, Josh, I just assumed you already knew. It's been on the local news today about your school friend who died."

School friend? They were talking about Carl Thurston. Josh felt relief wash through him.

"Oh sorry," he said. "I just got worried when I saw Mum and Dad weren't here and when you said 'tragic news' I thought you were taking about them."

Everyone laughed nervously.

"Oh Josh, no. They're inside. I'm sorry. I didn't mean to upset you. But you did know about your friend, didn't you?"

"Yes, Mrs Baker. Unfortunately I know everything."

"You just keep yourself safe now," she said.

"Don't worry, I will."

His parents were in the kitchen when he arrived, and as he put down his bag and walked down the hallway he heard them talking.

"Roger, I'm really scared."

"Don't be. Josh is a sensible boy and he doesn't go out alone much anyway."

"But that other boy wasn't out though, was he? First he was attacked in his bedroom and then he was killed in the hospital. In intensive care no less, where they have lots of windows to see into the rooms from the corridors and regular patient checks."

"Then there's no point in worrying, is there? It just goes to show that if something's going to happen then it's simply going to happen and there's nothing you can do to stop it. It's kismet my dear."

"How can you be so blasé about your own son?" His mother was clearly very upset.

"I'm not talking about Josh. I'm saying it could have been anyone. And besides, the guy in the street wasn't a child. All I'm trying to say is that there's no point worrying about things that are out of your control. We'll just have to be extra vigilant about keeping the doors and windows locked and make sure that we never go out alone."

Josh entered the kitchen in time to see his father kiss the top of his mother's head as though he was trying to kiss her worries away. They both looked up as he entered.

"Josh, we heard about what happened to that boy. Even though you did say that he's a mean bully, no one deserves that," his mother said.

"I know. Everyone's been talking about it all day. There was even an extra assembly this afternoon so that the head could tell us about it. And before you say anything, I heard you as I came in. We have to keep the house locked and never go out alone."

"That's right," said his father. "And you can begin this new regime right away by accompanying your mother to the shop."

"What, now?"

"Yes," she told him. "I need a few things for dinner. I'm only going to the corner shop. It's not far."

Josh thought it best not to argue. After all, how could he tell them that *he* was the cause of all the deaths, even the squirrel's, and that the killer was in his bedroom, so locking the outside doors wouldn't help?

Instead he took his bag upstairs to his room and changed out of his uniform. At first he'd worried about going into his room and finding that somehow the computer was on. But he couldn't hear anything as he approached and when he looked inside, the computer was exactly as he'd left it. Did that mean he'd defeated the game? It certainly looked like it. He felt his spirits lift.

He knew his mother was waiting for him downstairs so he changed quickly and the two of them set off to the corner shop at the far end of the street.

Before leaving the house Josh had taken a can of cola out of the fridge and he drank from it as they walked along. It was still a blisteringly hot day and the chilled drink felt good.

When they reached the shop Josh said he'd wait outside with his drink.

"Stand right outside the big window so that I can see you," his mother clucked.

"Yes, Mum."

"And don't move away so I can't see you."

"Yes, Mum."

"And don't be cheeky like your father," she said with a smile before going inside.

Josh stood exactly where he'd been instructed and drank his cola. He tipped his head back and drank thirstily.

As he lowered the can he saw that someone was standing directly in front of him, the end of his nose only inches from Josh's. Startled, he almost choked on his cola. Then he saw that it was Lee Williams. Josh didn't want a confrontation with him in front of his mother, but judging by the sneer on Lee Williams's face, avoiding a confrontation wasn't an option.

Lee Williams glanced behind Josh into the shop and then snorted in disgust.

"Mummy keeping an eye on diddums, is she? Scared the big bad boogie man might get her baby next?"

Josh couldn't think of anything to say and thought it best to say nothing. He daren't take his eyes off Lee Williams for a second, but he knew that somewhere close by would be Adrian Sparks. Perhaps he was in the shop.

"Well, precious little geek boy, I personally hope that you *are* the next victim then it'll be good riddance to bad rubbish."

Josh still didn't speak. Lee Williams, standing a good two inches taller than him, again glanced over his head into the shop.

"I think an even better idea would be if your old lady was the next one, then she couldn't breed any more little geeks like you."

Josh was scared but was also becoming angry. He knew Lee Williams was trying to provoke an angry response but Josh was afraid to let himself react. Even though he knew the computer was unplugged he still carried the embedded fear of becoming angry with someone. So he stood still and hoped that his silence would prevent an altercation.

"Doesn't matter, I suppose, anyway, geek boy. I bet your father thinks she's too ugly to shag anyway."

Josh took a step forward so quickly that Lee Williams took an instinctive step back. Josh could now feel his face burning with anger and he clenched and unclenched his fists.

"Ooo-hoo," laughed Lee Williams. "Come on, geek boy. Do your worst."

The approach of a large television network van interrupted the two boys before anything more could be said. The van parked at the curb a few feet away and several men with video-cams jumped out and began filming in all different directions. They shouted to each other as they worked.

"Get a wide shot from the far end of the street."

"I'll start from here and zoom in close to where it happened."

"Can you get a shot of the store and pan out to include as much as you can get?"

The two boys turned to look at them and then turned back to each other.

"You're lucky this time," said Lee Williams angrily, jabbing his index finger at Josh's face. Then he turned and walked into the shop just as Josh's mother came out.

"Your friend doesn't look too happy," she said, nodding her head in the direction of the shop door.

"He didn't want to be on television," said Josh, looking towards the TV crew.

"Oh no, not more of them. They've been in our street a lot today and I saw on the lunchtime news that they'd also been filming outside your school."

Josh carried the bag of shopping for his mother and the two of them headed home together. His mother kept up a running commentary of everything that had happened that day, the police coming back and the television crews everywhere. But Josh was only half listening; his mind was dwelling on the game once more. Even though he'd unplugged it, he still felt uneasy about it and getting angry with Lee Williams had made him feel worse.

When he got home he went straight up to his room to check the computer. To his relief it was still exactly as he'd left it. Unplugged and silent.

With nothing else to do, Josh spent the rest of the day in front of the television. He channel-hopped to find all the news about the murders. It was on every channel, even CNN. Wow, their small North Nottinghamshire town was on the international news.

After dinner Josh went upstairs feeling relaxed now that the computer was unplugged. It was Friday night so he thought he would spend the weekend chilling in front of the TV or reading.

He stopped abruptly at his bedroom doorway and felt his blood run cold. The computer was on and the game was on the screen. He could see Salvador still in the woods, standing next to the dead goblin right where he'd left him.

He felt an overwhelming urge to turn and run. But run where? Downstairs and never go back up again? Down to his parents and try to convince them that it's a computer game that's killing people? He was trapped and he knew it. There was nothing he could do except go in and play. But how had the computer managed to turn itself on again?

He stood hesitantly for a few minutes. Eventually he stepped forward into his room. Kneeling down in front of the computer desk, he mentally braced himself before looking underneath at the plug. He was worried that the plug was still on the floor. Seeing that would be too scary to handle.

But the computer was plugged in. He felt momentarily thankful. But no one had been upstairs as far as he knew, and even if they had, they wouldn't have stopped to plug in his computer. Nor would they have switched it on. Unfortunately that only left one explanation – the computer had plugged itself back in. But how could it?

Josh's mind reeled with the reality of what he was thinking. Surely there was no way that the plug had moved on its own.

Just exactly what was this game capable of? If it could materialise creatures in order for them to kill, perhaps it materialised one to plug the computer back in. But then again how could the game do anything if the computer was switched off?

Josh didn't want to think about it anymore. It was all too strange. Instead he sat in the chair and looked at the screen. Maybe what he should be concentrating on was the problem in hand, which was the game itself. Obviously he was going to have to play, no matter how the computer had managed to turn itself on.

His most worrying concern was that he'd been angry with Lee Williams. Actually he'd been more than just angry. He'd hated him with every fibre of his being. And somehow the game knew, and somehow it had reactivated itself to finish what Josh's anger had started.

On the screen the dead goblin was slowly fading away. In its place a large pile of food appeared. Josh allowed Salvador to eat it all as his energy level was down to almost nothing. As soon as his energy level was back up to the top he saved the game and then walked Salvador forward through the rest of the woods.

He came across more food as he went and allowed Salvador to collect it and store it in his bag.

The woods eventually thinned and turned into fields. The fields gradually widened as he walked along until they were just wide open grassy spaces. Then large rocks and bushes came into view, and eventually Salvador was at the edge of the ocean.

He turned right and followed the coastline and soon, amongst the rocks, caves could be seen. Some were only small and some looked huge. Josh wanted to take a look inside some of them but the bag contained no means of producing light and the cave interiors were pitch black.

Up ahead he saw that one of the large caves had an intermittent glowing light inside. The light was only dim but through the dark open mouth of the cave it was easy to see. He moved Salvador cautiously forward for a closer look and then saved the game at that point just in case something gruesome jumped out and attacked him.

Again he inched Salvador closer to the mouth of the cave. When he was near enough, Josh swung his viewpoint on the screen around so that he himself could look directly into the cave entrance from behind Salvador.

Josh waited for the light to glow again so that he could get a glimpse of whatever was inside. Salvador moved nervously from one foot to the other as though sensing Josh's apprehension.

Josh was afraid all right. He couldn't imagine what was in the cave and would have preferred to never find out.

The light began to faintly glow again and then brightened. With the interior of the cave illuminated, Josh was able to see the source of the light and his jaw opened involuntarily.

Inside the cave was a dragon. Its mouth was open slightly and Josh could see the flames within.

"A fire-breathing dragon," he whispered, barely aware that he'd spoken.

The dragon wasn't huge as cartoons and books normally depict them. This one was only the size of a large dog and it likewise stood on all fours. But unlike a dog it had scaly skin and glowing red eyes.

As he watched, the dragon closed its mouth and the cave was once more plunged into darkness. Josh waited, knowing that its fiery mouth would open again soon and then he could once again see the dragon. Maybe if he watched it a few times he might be able to figure out a way to defeat it.

Seconds ticked by with nothing happening. Then from within the cave a low guttural growl could be heard, only faintly at first but increasing in volume until there was no doubt that the dragon was angry about something. But what? Josh hadn't seen anything else in the cave with it.

Then the sound stopped.

Josh waited.

Without any warning the dragon blew out its hot breath, throwing flames at least ten inches from its snout. Only this time it wasn't inside the cave or standing on all fours. It had moved to the entrance and was rearing up on its hind legs.

Salvador's face glowed from the close proximity of the dragon's fire. Then the dragon moved swiftly, so fast that Josh didn't have time to react.

The dragon grabbed Salvador's arm with its front feet, which looked more like hands, and breathed fire onto his arm.

Salvador fell to the ground, screaming. He writhed about in pain and tried to lie on his burning arm. But instead of extinguishing the flames, they quickly spread and Salvador's whole body was soon engulfed in fire.

He continued to scream for only two seconds and then he lay still. The fire burnt itself out a few moments later and only a pile of ashes remained.

The whole scene had looked so real and Salvador's screams were heart-wrenching. Josh shuddered and began to tremble and he could feel panic setting in.

He was completely dumbfounded. He couldn't believe that his hero had been defeated so quickly.

He lifted his shaking hand to the keyboard and pressed "Escape" to return to the saved version of the game. Salvador was once again standing near the cave entrance.

But still Josh continued to shake. He was worried that the game would switch itself off again. He didn't want that to happen. He wanted to play again and defeat the dragon so that no one else had to die.

He knew that the enemies in the game were becoming bigger and harder to defeat. The game had begun with only mosquitoes and spiders. Now it was goblins and dragons.

But no matter how difficult the game, or how scared he felt, Josh wanted to carry on. He wanted to play again and defeat the dragon. He wanted to play all night and finish the game – to get it over and done with once and for all.

To complete the game was the only way to end this nightmare situation he was in. But how much further Salvador had to go and how many more enemies he had to defeat, he had no idea. He only knew that he had to play on. The game was in control. The game had been in control right from the beginning, long before he ever knew.

As Salvador once more approached the dragon's cave, Josh looked in his bag to try to find anything appropriate. A super-soaker pump-action squirt gun would have been handy, but he had nothing suitable for putting out fires. He chose a large silver shield instead so he could at least be protected.

Josh wasn't even sure why he was fighting the dragon. Perhaps there was something in the cave that he needed, *or maybe not*, his more logical mind told him. What if the dragon was just some murdering decoy planted to distract him from continuing on his journey? It was definitely a possibility, so Josh turned Salvador to the right and walked him past the cave entrance.

But no sooner had he passed than the same cave appeared again, and again, and again. Obviously the game was going to keep him walking past the same cave until he went in, just like when he tried to walk away from the rats in the basement of the old house.

Carrying the shield, Salvador approached the next cave. Once again he stood at the entrance and saw the dragon breathing fire from within. Then when the dragon's fire went out Josh held up the shield in front of Salvador and waited. And waited. And waited. Nothing at all happened. Perhaps the dragon wasn't going to repeat his earlier actions.

How long did he wait last time before the dragon moved to the front of the cave? He wasn't sure, but he didn't think it took this long.

Or perhaps the dragon would do something different this time because it was a different cave and therefore a different dragon. Or was it? Did walking past identical caves mean they were different caves and different dragons that all looked the same, or was Salvador repeatedly going back to where he started and walking past the original cave over and over again?

A third alternative could be that Salvador had been walking forward but each cave was a clone of the previous one, complete with cantankerous dragon.

Josh shook his head, gave himself a sudden reality check and wondered why he was even worrying about whether the dragon in the cave was the same one or not. He was wasting time and needed to carry on with the game.

Josh lowered the shield, but the dragon, unfortunately, had moved closer to the cave entrance and was waiting. It breathed flames directly into Salvador's face as soon as the shield was down.

Once more Salvador fell to the ground in screams of agony and was quickly consumed by the fire.

Josh stared at the screen in disbelief. For a few minutes he didn't move at all and his mind couldn't think.

The dragon retreated backwards into the cave and the eerie glow from its fiery mouth could be seen once more. A pile of ashes lay on the ground where Salvador had been and a few birds came to pick amongst them before the game winked off.

Josh removed his hands from the keyboard, lowered them into his lap and sat back in his chair. He tried to make sense of what had happened and figure out what it meant. Was Lee Williams going to die? Was a dragon going to appear and breathe fire on him? Surely not.

All the other attacks had been unwitnessed and the attackers small. A fire-breathing dragon was something else. Surely that couldn't remain unseen and even if it could its fiery breath would catch everyone's attention.

But there'd been no trace of the other attackers so maybe they'd never existed at all. Maybe the attacks happened spontaneously with no actual attacker. But that was ridiculous.

Josh was getting himself more and more confused. The creatures must have existed for a short while otherwise the man in the street must have split wide open, his intestines falling out right there in the road. And Carl Thurston's throat must have exploded out of his neck, and the cat must have rolled itself up in spider's webs and the dog must have just disintegrated. It all seemed an even more preposterous idea than nonexistent creatures attacking them.

But then again, this whole situation seemed completely preposterous and if he told someone about it they'd never believe him. He could imagine himself locked away in a mental asylum and a nurse saying, "Yes, doctor, this is the boy who thought his computer game was so real that all the animations were capable of murder. It's ludicrous, I know, but he *is* crazy."

Only Josh knew he wasn't crazy, but he still found it hard to believe that Lee Williams was going to be burnt to death by a fire-breathing dragon.

He wished he could go and warn him, but that was impossible, so he just had to leave him to his own fate.

Chapter 17

It was a warm and humid Friday night. Lee Williams was stood at the bottom of his garden smoking his last cigarette of the day. There was no more school until Monday morning. Hooray, he thought miserably. He hated school and always had. It was worse now without Carl and gross the way he'd died. No, murdered, he reminded himself. Someone had murdered his best friend. He still had Adie to hang out with but it just wouldn't be the same anymore.

It was hard to cope with what had happened to Carl. He still didn't believe it. There had to be a mistake. Maybe it was too many over-exaggerated stories. That had to be it. How could anyone have their eyes poked out and then their throat ripped out all in the same day? And how come there were no clues as to who did it?

The police had taken him and Adie to the police station after school and questioned them for hours. They both had alibis for both times Carl was attacked, and anyway, Carl was a mate. Still the police seemed to think that they must know something about what had happened or who had done it.

He and Adie had, of course, blamed the geek kid at school. It was after arguing with him that Carl had been attacked. But the police weren't interested in the geek kid. They seemed to already know him from his uncle dying a few weeks ago and animals being found dead in his garden. Well it all seemed pretty suspicious really that every weird thing that had happened lately was all centred around that little geek.

But the police couldn't have cared less even though he and Adie had pointed out their suspicions over and over again. How could the police hope to solve this crime if they were unwilling to interrogate the chief suspect? Their reluctance just didn't make sense.

He drew deeply on his cigarette as he tried to figure it all out. But it was late and he felt too tired to think of it anymore.

One thing he did need to think about though was making sure he was safe indoors. Poor Carl had been attacked in his own room and then again in the hospital. Boy, if someone wasn't safe in hospital then they weren't safe anywhere.

Goodness knew the whole thing had spooked his mother. She'd gone on and on about locking doors and not speaking to strangers. Christ, it was like being five years old again the way she kept going on.

"I'm not stupid you know," he'd told her. But all that remark got him was a rollicking from his father.

"Lee, how dare you speak to your mother like that? She's worried about you and rightly so after what happened. You just watch your mouth."

"I was only saying..."

"Well don't say. Just keep your mouth shut and do what you're told for a change."

He'd skulked off to his room to stay out of their way after that.

Later, when he heard his parents going to bed, he quietly crept downstairs and came outside for a cigarette.

He felt a pang of guilt when he left the kitchen door unlocked. His mother wasn't the only one worrying about personal safety. Good grief, who wouldn't worry about safety after two murders in as many days.

But still, it was unlikely that anyone would sneak around the back of their house to see if the door was unlocked at the exact time that he was out having a cigarette, wouldn't it? Well he hoped so.

The house wasn't visible from the bottom of the garden where he was standing. In fact, with the high fence on two sides and several large bushes around him, nothing was visible at all. The large copper beech tree spreading out above him meant he couldn't even see the sky.

He was over one hundred feet away from the house too so it was very private and secluded. He couldn't see anyone, they couldn't see him and that was the way he liked it.

He drew on his cigarette again and exhaled the smoke through his nose. But as he did so he heard a noise. The sound had been very subtle so he held his breath to listen.

Nothing. Everything around him was still; not even a slight breeze to disturb the leaves on this warm humid night.

He decided it must have been his own breath he'd heard and to prove it he drew on his cigarette and again exhaled the smoke through his nostrils.

Once more he heard the other sound and he stopped breathing immediately. But this time the other noise continued.

It was the sound of a foot being placed slowly on the ground. There was also another almost inaudible yet worrying sound. It sounded as though something was sniffing the air as though picking up a scent.

He suddenly wished it wasn't so dark.

His mouth became dry and he felt the quickening beat of his heart pulsating against the inside of his ribs. He'd read and seen in movies how people were supposed to feel when they were really scared, but nothing could ever describe how he was feeling right now and although he would never admit it to anyone, not even to himself, he was terrified.

He looked around but couldn't see anything except the dark silhouettes of the tall bushes surrounding him. He looked towards the narrow s-shaped gap that he'd walked through to get in between the bushes, but it was just blackness there now.

Then to his horror he saw what looked like two red glowing eyes in the cavernous blackness of the deep shadows and he heard the quiet sniffing sound again. The eyes were only visible fleetingly, but it was enough to make him momentarily doubt the strength of his bladder muscles.

Then just as quickly as he nearly lost control of his bladder, he regained full consciousness of reality.

God, that had scared him. His heart was now beating so fast and so loud that it drowned out any other noise that he might hear. He had never felt such intense fear before. Something was out there with him but he didn't know what it was. He would have been less afraid if he thought there was a person out there.

Of course it's a person, he tried to reassure himself. *What else would it be? It's probably just some jerk messing around and trying to scare me which is a pretty sick thing to do after everything that's happened lately.*

A hysterical laugh threatened to issue from his throat but he fought against it. He was still so afraid of whoever or whatever was out there. No matter how many times he tried to convince himself that there was nothing to be afraid of, he just didn't believe it.

All he could think of was that he didn't want to be there right now. He wanted to be somewhere light and safe, preferably back in his own room with the light on, the TV on and his duvet covering his body for that extra safe and comforting feeling.

He desperately wanted to be back inside, but to get there he'd have to pass by his tormentor.

Then he heard the slow footsteps again, only this time they sounded louder and closer.

Lee stood immobilised. His rapid, heavy breathing blew the ash off his forgotten cigarette which he still held in between his fingers near his lips. In his other hand he unconsciously clutched his cheap cigarette lighter and held it tightly to his chest.

As he stared into the blackness, the two bushes before him began to shake and a large, dark animal emerged from between them. It moved slowly towards him, sniffing the air to follow his scent.

Although it was difficult to see in the dark, Lee thought the animal looked like some kind of large lizard, but it was larger than any lizard he'd ever seen. It was the size of a large dog.

A shudder rippled up his spine as the animal slowly approached. His bladder finally gave way but he was not aware of the warm liquid which ran down his legs, soaking his jeans and shoes.

While he was still trying to take in the reality of what he was seeing, the creature's eyes began to glow a hot fiery red. They became as bright as hot coals, and then the glow faded.

At the same time it raised itself onto its hind legs, making itself as tall as he was.

Lee wanted to run but he was transfixed and the high wall enclosing him on two sides made him feel cornered with nowhere to go.

The creature didn't move once it was erect, it just stood and stared. Its close proximity and stillness were somehow more worrying than if it had been swinging its head around and screaming.

The waiting was unnerving.

Lee lowered his hand, which was still clutching the cigarette, to his side as slowly as he could. The movement was so slow that it seemed to be several minutes before his hand was hanging by his side.

He then slowly brought his other hand out, away from his chest. Moving his hands had never felt so nerve-wracking before. He was so tense that even if the creature had just said "boo" in a quiet voice, Lee would have screamed.

He wanted to get a better look at the creature but it was too dark to see properly. At the moment it looked like a dragon standing before him, but it couldn't be. Dragons didn't exist except in children's stories.

But dinosaurs are real, his tormented mind tried to tell him. But he also knew that dinosaurs weren't alive anymore. Anyway, what would a dinosaur be doing in Nottinghamshire in his back garden?

This absurd thought made him want to giggle like a drunk. But his thoughts quickly sobered as he caught a quick snapshot of his reality of standing face to face with a dragon.

With his arm now fully outstretched and almost touching the dragon's face, he held up the plastic lighter. But his hand was shaking and the lighter trembled erratically. He spun the flint wheel and the lighter lit the first time. It didn't provide much light and before he could take a proper look, the dragon opened its mouth and his extended arm was quickly engulfed in flames.

The searing pain was more than his mind could cope with.

His brain ceased all conscious thought.

The dragon's fire only lasted a split second but it was hot enough to burn the skin from his arm, melt the lighter into his hand and cause it to explode.

He stood there for a few minutes in an almost comatose state. Then the pain partially penetrated his consciousness.

His head moved slowly as he looked down at his outstretched blackened arm, then he looked up into the dragon's red glowing eyes. His mind could not completely comprehend the dragon, the pain or the whole nightmare he was in.

The dragon took a deep breath as the two of them continued their brief eye contact. As it exhaled, flames consumed Lee's head and he fell to the ground, all the while still holding out the remains of his cigarette lighter.

He didn't think to lower his arm because his mind held no thoughts at all anymore. It had completely shut down, unable to cope with the pain and the horror.

Then his heart arrested as the flames swallowed up his body.

Chapter 18

Josh had slept fitfully that night. His dreams were of running through different landscapes in the game. He dreamt that something was after him, but he didn't know what. All he knew was that if he didn't keep running he'd die. But without having played the whole game he had no idea where he was running to. Every now and then he'd stop and rest, but soon he'd become aware once more that he was still being pursued so would have to run again.

The next morning he woke up feeling tired and sluggish. As he came fully conscious he remembered playing the game the night before.

He sat up, rubbed his eyes and swung his legs out of bed. He padded barefooted across the carpet then bent down and looked under his desk. The computer plug was still on the floor where he'd left it. Even though the computer had somehow become plugged in again the day before, he still hadn't been able to go to bed unless he unplugged it again. He felt sure that it couldn't plug itself back in if he was in the room with it. It was probably someone else who'd plugged it back in anyway. He hoped.

Sounds from outside told him that his parents must be having their breakfast outside on the patio.

Josh pulled back his heavy curtains and the sudden sunlight that flooded the room made him wince and close his eyes. Well it was certainly another warm summer's day. He could already feel the warmth from the sun where it touched his skin through the window.

Looking at his clock he saw it was only 7.30 which was about 3 hours earlier than he usually woke up on a Saturday morning.

Twenty minutes later he was showered and dressed and went outside to join his parents. Their plates were already empty but they were lingering over their coffee.

"Well, well, well," said his father with a smile. "Did you wet the bed Josh? I thought that would be the only thing to get you out of bed so early."

Josh didn't appreciate his father's attempt at humour and simply turned around and went back into the kitchen.

"Roger don't tease him like that," he heard his mother say.

"Get us another coffee while you're in there, will you Josh?" his father called. Then to his mother he said, "Oh stop being such a worry-wart Rachel. He can take it. He's a big boy now."

"He's only just gotten up. Give him a chance."

"Never. Chances are for wimps," said his father and laughed.

Josh loved his parents always being so happy together. If it wasn't for the game he'd enjoy the moment, but after being defeated by the dragon in the game and then having a nightmare about playing, he was nervous.

The only thing that did cheer him up was the computer being unplugged. He had high hopes that even if someone else had been killed, the game couldn't hurt anyone else if he, or anyone else, didn't plug the computer back in. He just wished he could be sure.

Josh decided not to dwell on everything that had happened and just hope that it was the end of it. No doubt he'd find out soon if anyone had been burnt by a dragon.

But with any luck his unplugging the machine had prevented it.

What he'd really like to do was get rid of the computer and the game. But what would he tell his parents? He'd have to come up with a really good reason to throw it in the bin. If he didn't then his mother would insist on taking it to the charity shop because she was dead against wasting things if they could be of use to someone else. So for now simply leaving it unplugged would have to do and then he'd wait and see what happened.

Josh finished making the coffees, made some toast for himself too and rejoined his parents out on the patio.

"We're going into town this morning Josh. Do you want to come?" his mother asked.

"Depends what you're going for."

"Well it's the farmers' market today and it only comes once a month so we don't want to miss it."

"Is that all?"

"No there's the normal market as well so we thought we'd just have a look around seeing as it's such a lovely day."

"No thanks. I feel like just chilling out in front of the TV."

"But it's so nice outside. Why would you want to waste it in here?"

"Because the only good programs for kids on TV are on this morning. So just like you wanting to catch the Saturday market, I want to catch the Saturday TV shows."

Josh's mother opened her mouth as if to speak and then snapped it shut again.

His father laughed. "Huh, he's got you there Rachel."

"Oh don't you start. You don't like him watching too much TV either."

"Well I don't think it will hurt just for one morning."

"I guess not, as long as the doors stay locked."

"Yes Josh," his father said. "That's most important after everything that's happened around here lately. It's not safe anymore and I don't want you talking to any reporters either."

"Reporters?" Josh didn't understand what they had to do with anything.

"Yeah, there seems to be quite a few of them around still. They never stay long, just long enough to do their bit on camera. But they pester people for statements all the time and I've even seen some knocking door-to-door trying to get a quote."

"Well don't open the door to anyone when you're on your own," his mother cut in. "It doesn't matter who they are, you just don't answer the door at all."

"Yes Josh," his father finished for her. "When we're out the doors stay locked until we get back. Do you understand?"

"Yes Dad. Of course I do."

"Good. We shouldn't be too long anyway."

"OK."

His mother tried not to fuss too much about him being alone as they left later that morning, but she didn't do a very good job.

Josh fully intended to stay slumped in front of the TV while they were gone and that's exactly what he did. He sat with the remote control and channel-hopped repeatedly to find his favourite programs. It felt good to relax and forget about the game for a while.

A couple of hours passed before he heard a key turning in the front door lock.

"Josh?" his mother called anxiously.

"What?" he called back without even moving an inch.

His mother looked at him as she passed the living room but didn't say anything. Josh could tell that she was agitated.

He got up and followed them into the kitchen where they put down their shopping bags.

"What's up?" he asked innocently.

His parents shared a worried glance at each other.

"Sit down Josh," said his mother and they all sat down at the table.

"Do you know a boy called Lee Williams?"

"Yeah sure. He was the one talking to me outside the shop yesterday."

The colour visibly drained from her face. "Oh, that was him."

Josh picked up on the past tense of her words immediately. "Was?"

She started to fidget with her fingernails.

"I'm sorry Josh. He had some sort of accident last night and died."

"How?" Josh knew they were going to say that he'd been burnt.

"No one knows for sure," answered his father. "He went into his garden for a cigarette and somehow he set fire to himself with his cigarette lighter."

"So smoking really is bad for you," Josh said with an attempt at humour that didn't go down very well.

"Some people are saying that it wasn't a cigarette lighter," said his mother. "They think it was a case of spontaneous combustion because nothing around him was burnt yet he was..."

"A pile of ashes?" Josh finished for her.

"Yes, just about. Apparently the police are baffled. There were also animal tracks but they don't know what kind, but the tracks begin and end without coming from anywhere or going anywhere."

"That could be just idle talk," said his father. "In fact, a lot of it could be. Who knows?"

All three sat in silence, each with their own quiet contemplations; except Josh. His mind reeled with the reality of what was happening. He felt so guilty for causing another death but he was powerless to stop it.

For as long as he could that day, Josh avoided going back to his room because he couldn't stand seeing the computer. Even when it was switched off he felt as though the blank screen was watching him.

But he knew he'd eventually have to go in there, so he waited until his father went upstairs later in the afternoon and followed him up. He knew it wouldn't make any difference if someone else was upstairs once he was in his room, but there was a certain comfort in not being completely alone.

He climbed the stairs reluctantly, listening all the time. As far as he could tell his room was silent which meant the computer was off.

When he entered his room he was relieved to see that he was right. He began to breathe normally again, unaware until he did so that he had been holding his breath. He picked a book from his bookshelf, lay on his bed and began to read.

Soon he was engrossed in the story. As he read he relaxed more. He was in his room and the computer was switched off. Heaven.

But he knew he'd thought this too soon when he heard the "start" button click and the computer tower hum into life. He felt his heart drop in despair and he began to tremble.

How had the computer turned itself on? He'd unplugged it, hadn't he?

He swung his legs off the bed and bent down to look under the table. The computer was plugged in again.

His heart thumped loudly in his chest.

When had the computer been plugged in again? Was it before he came in or while he was lying on the bed? God, he wished he'd checked the plug when he'd first come in. It was worrying to think of things moving while he was in the room, but what worried him more was that the computer knew he was there. It must have been waiting for him.

Josh looked from the plug to the computer screen and back again. He knew that the game wanted him to play, but he just wanted to crawl under the table and pull the plug out. No matter how powerful the game was, it still needed electricity to run. Why else would the computer have plugged itself back in again?

But Josh also knew from experience that the game was also capable of playing while he wasn't there. At least when he played himself he had a chance of winning, but if he let the game play on its own then ultimately the game would win.

Maybe he should get some scissors and cut the plug off so that the game couldn't play at all? It was a good idea and Josh knew he should do it but he was afraid. He was very afraid. Just the thought of defying the game made him shudder. He hated his own cowardice, but couldn't fight it.

He knew the game was capable of many evil things, and he was just plain scared.

With great reluctance he obediently sat down once more to play the game. Salvador was on the screen and was outside the dragon's cave again. Josh had no idea yet how he was going to defeat it.

He took out the shield again and held it in front of Salvador only this time he was determined not to lower it. How he was going to kill the dragon with the shield permanently raised he had no idea. He only knew that to lower it meant certain death.

Salvador took a few more steps nearer to the entrance to the cave and stopped. So did the glow of the dragon's breath. Now he knew for sure, after the last time, that the dragon had moved closer and was only a few feet away. Salvador stood there for a very long time but Josh didn't know what else to do.

Perhaps the dragon would make the first move. But what if it didn't?

Perhaps there was something that Salvador could use. Josh leaned closer to the screen and looked around the outside of the cave, but he saw nothing that could be of any use.

He studied Salvador for a few seconds, standing quietly behind his shield, and then he moved his viewpoint in closer to get a better look at the shield.

He noticed it had a few small words and pictures engraved on it, even on the inside. Was it fireproof? Well the dragon must think so because he hadn't tried to burn it. But what if it did? Would the metal become too hot to handle? He hoped not.

Then he noticed three letters on the middle of the shield. He leaned closer to the screen, with his nose almost touching, for a better look. Yes, it was definitely what he thought. The letters were H2O.

Water! That would probably be the only thing that could defeat a fire-breathing dragon. But how?

Josh felt excited even though he wasn't sure what to do. Did the shield turn to water if the dragon breathed on it? Is that why it didn't? Or was there some way to turn the shield to water and throw it at the dragon?

Just out of idle curiosity he moved the mouse until the cursor was over the letters.

Bingo! Once over the letters the cursor turned into a pointing finger. Josh clicked the mouse and the pointing finger pressed on the letters.

A strong jet of water issued from the front of the shield and sprayed directly into the cave.

From inside came the loud trumpeting of the dragon, sounding just like an angry dinosaur. As the water continued to gush forth, there was a loud 'thud' from within the cave and he knew that the dragon had fallen. Obviously it couldn't survive without its fire.

The water gushing from the shield began to slow until it was just a trickle and then it stopped. Salvador lowered the shield.

Josh saved the game to ensure that the dragon could not come back and then sat back triumphantly in his chair. It was a relief to have finally beaten the dragon but it was bad that someone else had died first, even if it was only Lee Williams. But the smile on his face still remained.

He pressed the "Escape" key to turn off the game but nothing happened. His smile disappeared. He pressed it again several times and groaned in despair. Then he tried to turn the computer off at the tower, but, unsurprisingly, that didn't work either.

This was bad. The game was becoming more dominant. Josh was being given no choice but to play on.

In his mind he saw himself growl as he abruptly stood up and swiped the monitor and keyboard off the table. Then he bent down and wrenched the tower out from under the desk before hurling it to the floor where it disembowelled itself, sending pieces of motherboard and compact disk flying across the room in every direction.

But in the frustration of reality he meekly put his hand on the keyboard and prayed that he'd have the speed and strategy to outsmart the next enemy.

Back in the game he walked Salvador into the cave. He wasn't sure what he would find in there but he knew there must be a reason for needing to defeat the dragon. Perhaps it was hiding something.

The cave was pitch black inside and he had no way to illuminate it. But as Salvador ventured further forward he saw a light in the distance. As he walked nearer the light grew bigger and brighter until he could see that it was another entrance.

He made Salvador run to reach it and once outside he stopped to survey his new surroundings.

This side of the cave was on the edge of another village. It only looked small but it was very similar to the previous one.

Josh walked Salvador through the milling villagers. Some of them spoke to him but they didn't say anything of importance.

Just like in the previous village the people seemed so real and it was too easy to just stay and watch them, but Josh knew he had to keep his mind on what he was doing and look out for the next enemy.

Salvador strode mindfully through the crowds with his head turning this way and that, stopping to listen whenever someone spoke to him. Sometimes he even turned around and walked backwards when someone called to him from behind.

Maybe it's just as well that Salvador never speaks, thought Josh, *because sometimes he seems real enough already.*

Just then a strange little limping man shambled up to Salvador.

"Whoa lad. Wait a minute."

Salvador stood still.

"You've got to be careful where you wander around here," the little man continued as he fumbled in his shoulder bag. "There's danger in these parts to be sure.

"Here take this," he said, producing a quite modern looking 21st century torch which looked quite out of keeping in the old-fashioned village. Josh smiled at the irony of being given a torch AFTER he'd passed through the dark cave.

Salvador took the torch and put it in his bag.

"Be on your way now and remember to fear death." The little man moved to one side to allow Salvador to pass.

Josh walked Salvador on, fleetingly wondering why the little man said to fear death when surely it came to everyone sooner or later so why fear it?

After a while he came to the edge of the village and the beginning of some woods. Josh felt sick and tired of going through different woods. If this game didn't pose such a threat in his real life, he would've found it quite boring by now and stopped playing. But he didn't have the option of not playing and that thought kept him miserable and moving.

If he hadn't seen any woods in the game before he would have thought these looked dark and dangerous. But by now the woods were a sight all too common and so didn't look as threatening as they did at the beginning of the game.

But Josh also knew that the woods concealed danger. He made Salvador take out his long sword and hold it in front of himself as he walked amongst the turning, morphing trees. He'd chosen the long sword in the hope of keeping whatever was waiting in there at a distance.

The worried expression on Salvador's face and the way he twitched nervously as he looked to left and right told Josh that he was frightened.

Josh had never seen a nervous computer graphic before and didn't hold out much hope of victory if Salvador was already scared.

The woods became darker and denser but there seemed to be no sign of an enemy. If something did suddenly appear, Josh suspected that the so-far-mute Salvador might actually shout, he looked so jumpy.

Soon the trees began to thin and the whole atmosphere lightened. Salvador began to look less concerned, but Josh was still wary. Surely there had to be something waiting for them in the woods.

Then another thought occurred to him. Perhaps they were trapped in the woods and something was waiting at the other side to prevent them from coming out.

Salvador had lowered his sword as his tension eased, but Josh made him raise it again.

Salvador glanced down at the sword as it rose and then looked directly at Josh with a questioning look as if to ask, "why?"

Josh jumped back in surprise and his spine collided with the back of his chair, making it tilt backwards which gave Josh another scare and he quickly grabbed the edge of his desk to stop himself falling any further.

His heart was pounding and her nerves were taut, but Salvador, unconcerned or unknowing of the panic he'd created, quietly turned and looked ahead again.

Josh sat dumbfounded for a few seconds. Never before had Salvador looked Josh in the eye or indicated in any way that he was aware of his presence.

But then again, thought Josh, Salvador's never been so afraid either.

In the beginning Salvador had acted like any other character in a computer game; unemotional. But then he became progressively more nervous and now it seemed he knew Josh was there too and knew that he was controlling his movements. This made the whole situation even freakier.

Josh put his hands back onto the keyboard and walked Salvador out of the woods. But it felt unnerving now that he knew that Salvador was aware of what he was doing. Salvador was a puppet in a dangerous place and Josh controlled his strings and his destiny. It was a responsibility he loathed.

Onward Salvador walked, both he and Josh feeling twitchy, and jumping at every sound. But still nothing happened.

Then within seconds they were completely out in the open with no trees before them. Salvador lowered his sword and this time Josh didn't stop him. Somehow being out in the sunshine made them feel easier.

Not far in the distance were some hills. Josh wondered if it was up there that the next enemy lay in wait. If he was right and each one was becoming stronger and more evil, then he wondered what would be next after the dragon.

It seemed easy to walk Salvador across the open expanse of fields to the hills. Too easy. It gave Josh a false sense of security so he made Salvador put away his sword and run. He looked like a well-trained athlete as he ran. His arms pumped in complete synchronisation with his long striding legs.

It didn't take him long to reach the foot of the hills and as Josh scanned back around the open fields, he saw there was nothing in pursuit.

The whole running incident reminded Josh of when he was very young and the fear he had if he woke in the night and needed to go to the toilet. It meant he had to get out of bed and switch on the light by pressing the switch by the door.

To do that he had to cross the bedroom in the dark. In his child's mind, crossing the open expanse of darkness meant that every bogeyman and demon in the whole world would try to grab him before he could reach the switch and flood the room with light. Of course, to a child, light meant safety because he was only afraid of what he couldn't see.

To make the journey safer he would leap out of bed and bolt across the room as fast as he could. That way the scary things had less time to catch him.

It was a similar situation with Salvador. To cross the open field it was safer to run and cut the journey time in half, therefore, halving the chances of being caught by anything waiting to leap out at him.

But whether or not there'd been anything out there it didn't matter now. He was safe and the hills weren't very high and so shouldn't be too difficult to cross. That was, of course, unless something was waiting up there for him.

Boy was this game turning him into a pessimist. He just couldn't get his mind out of the 'worst-case-scenario' way of thinking.

Well he was about to find out if there was anything up there. He gave Salvador a small knife to carry and sent him up one of the hills.

It was more of a very steep slope than a hill. Probably what the people in the north of England called a moor. The ground was grassy with large rocks poking through so Josh had to be careful where Salvador walked.

On the way up nothing at all happened. Nothing jumped out at him and nothing tried to follow.

What a strange game this was, thought Josh. At the moment it was more like a stroll in the country than a hero's dangerous quest.

As Salvador crested the hill, Josh lifted his knife, ready for whatever lay at the other side.

But what he saw puzzled him rather than frightened him.

At the foot of the other side of the hill was another village and beyond it, in the distance was what looked like a rocky field. It looked as though Salvador had a long journey rather than a dangerous one.

As Salvador descended to the village Josh could see people milling around and going about their daily business, much like he had previously seen in the last villages. Nothing at all looked scary or threatening. And once

Salvador was walking amongst them, Josh discovered he was right. The villagers greeted Salvador as he passed by, but other than that they ignored him.

So what was the purpose of his being there?

Josh let Salvador visit a couple of stores which were there but there was nothing to buy that Salvador didn't already have so he didn't purchase anything.

Puzzled, Josh carried on moving Salvador through the village and headed to the rocky field beyond. The village path lead past all the houses and ended at a set of large iron gates.

The gates were open and Josh now saw that he'd been mistaken. The rocks he'd seen from a distance weren't rocks at all. They were gravestones and the field he'd seen was a cemetery.

This, thought Josh, *must be it*. This must be where Salvador would meet his next enemy.

But what would it be? Josh could only think that it would be a ghost. He looked at the small knife in Salvador's hand and knew it would be useless if it was.

He put the knife back into Salvador's bag and glanced through the other weapons he carried, knowing already that if a ghost was waiting for him then there was nothing that could defeat it.

Salvador stood outside the cemetery gates nervously moving from one leg to the other while Josh tried to think what to do. But it was useless. Josh couldn't think of anything that could kill a ghost, if kill was the right word.

There was always a chance that he was wrong and that it wasn't a ghost lying in wait for him. But he couldn't imagine what else he would find in a cemetery. Unless of course, he was completely wrong about the whole situation and there was nothing at all in there.

The more he thought about it the more he was sure that he was right. Salvador had already passed through two villages and crossed over an open field and over some hills with nothing at all happening. So there was a good chance that he could pass safely through a graveyard too.

On three sides, the cemetery was enclosed by woods with the village on the fourth side behind Salvador. Maybe that was the clue. Maybe the woods were the next place of danger, since this was Salvador's only option of where to go next.

Josh thought it over for a few more minutes and then finally walked Salvador through the gates. *After all*, he reasoned, *where else can he go?*

There were several paths leading in different directions but Salvador walked down the path which led directly forward from the gates and was soon surrounded by gravestones.

Josh stopped him going any further as a feeling of foreboding swept over him.

Something felt wrong. Something felt very wrong.

Then it hit him. In the village it had been sunny and the chatter of all the people there had seemed quite loud and Josh had still been able to hear them as Salvador stood outside the gates.

Now it was quiet. A complete silence had fallen over the graveyard and the sky now looked overcast as though a storm was brewing.

How quickly the atmosphere had changed.

As Josh contemplated the situation and wondered what to do next, a mist began to form around the base of all the gravestones. It rose to only about six inches but quickly spread out until it covered the entire ground and nothing could be seen through it, not even Salvador's feet.

Salvador gave a small squeak of terror, and although it could barely be heard, even in the silence of the graveyard, it startled Josh as though it had been a loud boom.

Josh had the feeling that this was where he would come face to face with his next adversary. He also thought that perhaps he'd been wrong about there being no reason to pass through the last village. Perhaps there was something there that he needed but he just hadn't seen it.

One thing he did know for sure was that he had to get Salvador out of there as quickly as possible and get him back to the village. He didn't have a clue what he'd have to go back for but maybe he could try to speak to the villagers and find out. It must be their cemetery so hopefully they could not only tell him what was in there, but how to defeat it.

But, then again, if they knew how to defeat it then why hadn't they already done it themselves? How could they bury their dead in a place where a creature was waiting to kill them? Or perhaps whatever was in there never bothered them, or perhaps this wasn't where they buried their dead.

But there were graves weren't there?

Josh didn't have time to try to figure it out now. All he knew was that he had to get Salvador out of there fast and the village was the best place to go if for no other reason than that it was safe there.

He turned Salvador around to run back to the gates, and then as an afterthought, he saved the game at that point. Salvador had come so far since he last saved the game and if something were to chase him now it might catch him before he got to the gates, or worse still, it might be waiting for him at the gates and then he'd have no chance of escaping.

But just as this thought crossed his mind he realized that Salvador was in an even worse situation. Nothing was going to leap out at him before he reached the gates, nor would there be something lying in wait when he got there.

The gates were gone.

Because of the ankle-deep mist Josh couldn't see the path. Salvador stood surrounded by gravestones with the woods beyond the fence no matter which way he turned.

He moved Salvador forward in gloomy resignation, knowing that the direction didn't matter anymore. He would meet his next enemy no matter which way he went. The game was in control again. The game was always in control.

Salvador walked and walked but no matter how far he went he made no progress. The edge of the cemetery remained just as far away as it had always been. Josh tried several different directions but it made no difference and soon he wasn't even sure where the gates had been.

After a few more tense minutes he heard a sound. At the moment it was far off but it was getting closer.

He shared a worried look with Salvador. Whatever was out there seemed too heavy-footed to be a ghost. But it was certainly footsteps of some kind. Slow, heavy footsteps.

It was impossible to tell where the noise was coming from, but it was beginning to sound like an upright two-legged creature.

He turned Salvador around and around to try to discover the source of the noise, but so far nothing was stirring.

One thing Josh was sure of though, was that wherever it was it was big and solid and would be upon Salvador soon.

They both stayed motionless and waited.

The waiting, although short, seemed prolonged.

Then Josh, moving slowly as though afraid that whatever was coming might see him, looked in Salvador's bag for a weapon and chose a long knife.

Now the footsteps were close. He turned Salvador around, and then he saw it.

Its skin was grey and deathlike and its clothes were filthy with earth from the grave. Its shirt was hanging open and on its chest were large wounds, which had been crudely stitched up, and Josh knew, from the homicide shows that he'd seen on TV, that they were from an autopsy.

The creature was a zombie. One of the living dead. Its eyes were rolled up and only the whites showed. Josh wondered if it could see without its pupils, but it seemed to know exactly where it was going.

As the zombie made its slow approach Josh wondered why this was happening at all. Up until now the game had worked purely from Josh's negative emotions. Even when he'd gotten angry at the computer and refused to play, the game had played on its own and then killed a stranger. But this time he hadn't refused to play. He'd been reluctant and the computer had forced him to, but he hadn't even thought about not playing.

Nor had he been angry with anyone and Lee Williams and Carl Thurston were already dead.

Suddenly he knew the answer. Adrian Sparks would be the next to die. Last week he'd been angry at all three of them when they picked on him near the school gates. That must be why the game wanted to play on, to wreak its warped idea of revenge on the remaining school bully.

As much as he disliked Adrian Sparks, Josh had had enough of death and was tired of having to shoulder the responsibility for the demise of the game's chosen victims.

He just couldn't let the game win again, so he decided to do the only thing he could think of to keep Salvador safe. He let Salvador make a run for it. The zombie was slow and it seemed to be alone. So he turned Salvador in the opposite direction and ran.

But he'd only gone a few steps when he abruptly stopped. The zombie was still coming towards him.

He turned him around several times but no matter which way he looked, the zombie was always right in front of Salvador and coming closer. There seemed to be no way out.

Josh was scared. The game was cheating and wouldn't allow Salvador to leave the cemetery. The game wanted to win and Josh had the feeling it would. But he had to try.

He held Salvador still until the zombie came within striking distance. While he waited, he couldn't be certain, but he thought he saw Salvador swallow hard. Josh hoped that wasn't what he'd seen because knowing that Salvador was nervous too made Josh even more worried.

The waiting was soon over despite the zombie's seemingly slow progress.

Josh raised Salvador's hand and brought the long knife blade down hard on the zombie's shoulder. But the zombie didn't even flinch. It took one more step closer, and using its already outstretched arms, it pushed Salvador in the chest making him fall flat on his back with a heavy thump.

The zombie was strong and it didn't stop coming. No matter how fast Josh stood Salvador on his feet again, the zombie would push him back down.

Over and over it happened with Salvador constantly retreating. But to where? And how long was this going to go on?

Salvador's energy line in the corner of the screen was diminishing but Josh couldn't see what he could do to stop what was happening.

Then just when Josh thought the whole situation was hopeless, he got a break. It was only a second or less of time between Salvador standing up and the zombie reaching him again but Josh seized the opportunity.

He thrust Salvador's hand forward which held the knife, stabbing the zombie in the chest as he did so. Again and again he repeated the action with Salvador grunting with the force of each thrust.

But to Josh's dismay, the stabbing had no effect and the zombie didn't even bleed.

He'd expected blood to come pouring out and the zombie to clasp its chest in agony before falling to the ground and dying. It always happened that easily and dramatically in the movies, especially when it was the good guy doing all the attacking. The good guys always won in the movies and the bad guys died quickly.

But this wasn't a movie. This was an evil game possessed in some way that Josh couldn't quite figure out. Maybe it was something that Uncle Neville had added to the game without realising the harm it would unleash on the world. Or perhaps he'd put it in on purpose, knowing exactly how deviant the game would become. But Josh didn't really believe that his uncle would do something so bad. The game had, after all, killed his uncle. Of this he was now certain.

But whatever had happened to make the game so hellish, it didn't really matter right now. Salvador was in trouble, and if Josh's earlier reckoning was right, then so was Adrian Sparks.

The zombie was still standing and seemed quite unaware that it had been stabbed repeatedly. Josh briefly wondered what to do next. How was he going to kill something that was already dead?

The split second that it took him to think this was all the time he had before the zombie pushed Salvador hard in the chest once more and sent him sprawling to the ground. Josh reacted instinctively and raised Salvador back to his feet as fast as he could. But the zombie was fast. Too fast.

As Salvador rose into a sitting position, the zombie took one step forward, swinging its leg up quickly as it did so. Its foot caught Salvador squarely under the chin and lifted him about two feet off the ground.

Salvador's body swung up like a rag doll, his feet flying higher than his head and then he body-slammed to the ground.

Josh could no longer see him because of the ground-level mist, but when the zombie raised its foot and brought it stamping back down, Josh knew from the muffled scream that it was grinding Salvador's head into the dirt.

The zombie swung its other leg forward and kicked Salvador hard. Salvador screamed loudly and the kicking continued. Although the mist still covered over exactly what was happening, Josh could feel Salvador's pain from his screams.

Then as the zombie brought its foot forward for the final time, Josh heard a loud crack. Salvador instantly fell silent.

The zombie bent down and lifted Salvador up from the mist. Josh could tell by the unnatural angle of his head to his body that his neck was broken.

Looking Josh straight in the eye the zombie attempted to grin. Then the game quickly switched off and as the screen turned black, Josh felt the dread rise from the pit of his stomach.

Chapter 19

Adrian Sparks was afraid. He was afraid because this week his two best friends had died. No, not died, murdered. They had both been horribly murdered. One had been attacked in his own bed and then murdered in the hospital. The other had been burnt to death in his own back garden.

The police thought the burning might have been an accident, but he didn't think so at all. How could anyone burn themselves to death accidentally with a cigarette lighter? It just didn't make sense unless he'd dowsed himself in petrol first and he'd never have done that.

Accident? Huh!

Carl and Lee's parents were in a terrible state because of it all. His own Mum and Dad had tried to quiz him over what had happened but it just made him angry. How the hell was he supposed to know what'd happened? He hadn't even been there at the time.

Well to hell with them and their questions. He had more important things to worry about, like who was going to be next? Unfortunately he thought he already knew the answer to that. He was going to be next.

It was all too much of a coincidence. The three of them always hung out together and now only he remained. Someone had murdered his two mates and now he felt sure that whoever it was would come after him too.

What was most worrying was the fact that he knew he wasn't safe anywhere. After Carl had been attacked in his own bedroom, it seemed that no one was safe in their own beds.

Since Carl had been attacked, before going to bed Adrian checked his room to make sure that he was definitely alone before he turned out the light every night.

Tonight was no exception. He opened his wardrobe and checked inside, checked the built-in cupboard in the corner of the room and lastly looked under his bed. If anyone had seen him doing this he would have pretended he had lost something and would never have admitted what he was really doing. He'd even put a book under his bed so that, if he was caught searching, he could pretend that was what he was looking for.

Damn. It just wasn't fair. He hated feeling scared all the time. Whenever he went out, he kept looking over his shoulder to make sure no one was following him after that guy got his guts ripped out in the street.

Then if that wasn't bad enough, Carl was attacked in his bed and again in the hospital. Geez, how the hell can anyone get murdered in hospital?

He'd felt terrified after that. What happened to Carl was like something out of a horror movie.

And then, Christ, if all that wasn't bad enough, Lee had been burnt alive. He'd heard it rumoured that Lee's charred skeleton had been found still standing, but he wasn't sure if that was just talk. It seemed that it only took a matter of hours after a death before rumours started to fly.

His face began to grimace and he felt tears threatening as he thought about his two friends, but he cleared his throat and shook his head before it went any further. He just didn't want to have a major crying fit about it. God how pathetic would he look getting up tomorrow with red, swollen cry-baby eyes? No, there was certainly not going to be any crying right now.

But in the privacy of his own bedroom he allowed himself to be afraid. He couldn't have avoided it anyway because he was scared shitless.

He turned on his television before turning out the light and getting into bed. He used the remote control to flick through the channels but there was nothing that he particularly wanted to watch. But he was reluctant to turn it off and plunge the room into darkness. He felt much safer when he could see, even though he knew it was illogical. If someone was going to come in and kill him, they probably wouldn't care if the light was on or not.

Did Carl have his light on when he was attacked? He had no idea.

He used the remote control to look through the channels again but he didn't think he could concentrate on anything anyway.

It had been a long day and he was tired. The police had briefly questioned him about Lee's death. Previously they'd questioned him about Carl's murder. As if he could have had anything to do with it or known anything about it. If he'd known it was going to happen he would have stopped it somehow.

But who in the hell could do something so vile? Was there really some psychopath wandering around unnoticed? And how was this weirdo so smart that he could sneak in and out of places with no one ever seeing him?

Or was it a her?

Maybe that's why no one suspects her? No one ever thinks a woman's going to do them any harm. People always notice a strange man lurking around somewhere but no one pays much attention to women. Or maybe the killer was a child? People usually ignore kids most of the time.

Perhaps it was that little snot-bag ginger geek kid after all. Everything seemed to be happening around him. First his neighbour's dog was eaten, then someone was killed almost right in front of his house and now, after he, Carl and Lee had tried to give him a good hiding, Carl and Lee are dead too. Hmm.

He shrugged his shoulders and laughed at his own thoughts.

No, that little shit couldn't hurt anyone.

But then another thought struck him. What if someone else was killing people FOR the geek kid? That was feasible.

Then he smirked at how ridiculous he was being. Who'd care so much for the geek kid that they'd be willing to commit murder for him? Come to think of it, who'd care about the geek kid at all? Well whether he had anything to do with it or not he would give the geek kid a good hiding next time he saw him anyway, just to be on the safe side. After all, it was the geek kid who'd got them in trouble in the first place, so he owed him a good beating.

After a while his thoughts just rambled on from one subject to another. He was really tired and wanted to sleep but he felt edgy about turning the TV off. There was such a feeling of comfort just lying there in the flickering glow of the screen.

The rest of his family were all in bed and the house was quiet, except for the low volume of his television.

Soon he was way too tired to be afraid, so he pressed the power button on the remote control and the television winked off.

He put the remote control on his bedside table and it landed with a loud clatter in the now quiet room. It was very dark in there due to his heavy blackout curtains at the window. Usually he loved sleeping in a dark room but tonight the darkness was more of a threat than a comfort.

He'd hoped that he'd fall straight to sleep and then wake in the morning with the sun squeezing around the edge of the curtains to show him that he'd survived the night.

But this didn't happen. Instead he felt restless and tossed and turned. He knew that he'd never get to sleep if he didn't keep still so he tried to resist the urge to move, but it was no good. The minute he wasn't concentrating on not moving, he changed to a different position. It was no use. He was too tense and couldn't relax. His ears were alert and straining to hear even the quietest of sounds.

Damn. If he didn't get to sleep soon then this was going to be a very long and nerve-wracking night. He threw himself onto his back in annoyance. What could he do to help himself sleep?

He remembered once reading in a magazine (it was his mother's that he'd just picked up one day out of boredom) that slow breathing could slow down your heartbeat. The magazine article was about stress and it said that if you closed your eyes and concentrated on slow deep breaths, then your rapid heartbeat would return to normal and the stress would go.

Well right now he needed to slow down his heartbeat because he was sure it was pumping at a great rate and keeping him awake.

So he put his arms by his sides, closed his eyes and concentrated on his breathing. At first it was so rapid that he wondered if he'd ever be able to control it at all. No wonder he couldn't sleep; he was breathing so fast he was almost panting.

After a few minutes his breathing slowed. He tried to breathe in and out as slowly as he could. First he breathed in for a count of five and then out for a count of five, then six and then seven.

Ah, that felt good. Now he was much more relaxed and able to sleep.

But then something interrupted his concentration. What was it?

He held his breath to listen but there was nothing now. Had he heard something? No, he didn't think so. What was it then? Something just didn't seem right.

He opened his eyes but couldn't see very much in the darkness, only the vague shapes of his furniture.

He let himself breathe again. Then all of a sudden he knew what was wrong. There was a strange smell in the room. A sort of earthy smell. But it smelt foul, somehow dirty. Was there such a thing as dirty dirt? He doubted it but it still smelled of rotten earth.

Suddenly the smell was gone. Had he just imagined it through all his deep breathing? But then the smell returned as quickly as it had vanished. Only this time it was accompanied with what he'd been dreading. A noise within his room.

Something had moved very slowly and very quietly but he'd definitely heard it.

Even though he was too scared to move, his body went into fight or flight mode. His heart rate increased, his mouth went dry and he felt sweat pop out through all the pores of his skin. He could hear his blood rushing past his ears.

He lay there like a frightened child. He didn't want to move because that would alert whatever it was to his presence. He strained his ears to listen for any more external noises but could only hear his own internal panic.

This situation was bad. It was very bad. It was the worst.

The smell, which up until now had been faint, became stronger.

Damn it! He couldn't hear anything and the room was so dark that he couldn't see anything either, not until whatever it was got up close and then it would be too late.

He needed to see. He felt helpless in the dark. He needed to flood the room with light and then, as imaginary bogey men do in a child's mind, whatever was there would retreat back into the shadows.

He put out a shaking hand towards his bedside lamp, but in his haste he knocked it over. Still shaking, he reached over to pick it up quickly, but before he had a chance to switch it on, something grabbed him by the front of his T-shirt and pulled him up into a sitting position.

He let out a scream that wasn't loud enough to be heard outside the room, and at the same time felt warm urine saturate his boxer shorts and mattress.

After that everything happened so fast and yet strangely in slow motion at the same time, while his fear kept him immobile.

Up close in the darkness he could see that a large, bare-chested man held him but it was the man's eyes that kept him spellbound. The eyes were upturned and he could only see the whites. This was the worst and scariest thing he'd ever seen.

Being up close to the man, he now realized where the awful smell was coming from.

Who the hell was this guy? What was he doing in his bedroom? And what was he going to do next?

Adrian wanted to scream but his throat remained shut tight.

He wanted to fight and run and get away. But he couldn't. He could never have explained why but his body just wouldn't move and he couldn't tear his gaze away from those upturned eyes.

The man had picked him up so easily that he must be very strong.

Adrian continued to stare transfixed as part of his mind began to shut itself off from this strange and terrifying reality he'd suddenly found himself in.

The man slowly brought up his hand and pushed his palm into Adrian's face. But before applying too much pressure he let go of Adrian's T-shirt and put his hand on his back.

Then he pressed hard in both directions, pushing Adrian's back forward and his head back. Adrian could feel the immense pressure on his face and body but was too shocked and traumatised to react.

There was a loud snap and Adrian felt his head jolt fiercely back. The hands released him. His neck felt strange and uncomfortable and there was something in front of his face. What was it? Then he realized that it was his poster on the wall above his bed. He also realized that he was looking at it upside down.

In that last split second of his life he knew that his neck was broken and that his head was hanging down his back. He wondered why he felt no pain, but he didn't live long enough to even begin to work it out.

He also died unaware that the nape of his neck was protruding grotesquely through his throat. But in the

morning when his mother came in, she would be very aware
of this.

Chapter 20

Josh's family spent Sunday at home, his parents listening carefully to the local news on the radio. At lunchtime it was announced that there had been a suspicious death of a local boy but no details were yet revealed.

Josh felt that he already knew what the news would be. Adrian Sparks had died from a broken neck. Where or how it had happened he didn't know but he did know what had done it.

He spent the morning listening to his parents voicing their concerns to each other. They were extremely worried about there being four deaths in four days and three of them children – children whom Josh had known. They were obviously worried about Josh, about how these deaths were mentally affecting him as well as how safe he was.

The telephone rang several times and his mother talked at length with other parents.

Everyone was worried. Josh was dying to tell his mother about what was really going on. He carried his secret around everywhere he went and it was getting progressively harder to keep. How he longed to show someone the game and explain what was happening.

The game. Oh God, the game. How much longer was this going to go on and how many more people had to die? And if the game was about journeying to The Promised Land, then where the hell was it? So far there'd not been any clues or directions. All he was doing was wandering around and seeing where he ended up. If the game would start giving him a few hints then maybe he could figure a way to get there more quickly so that it could all be over.

Most computer games that involved a hero's quest usually included a map of where they were and where they were supposed to end up. But this game had nothing like that at all. It was so infuriating to have to wander about in the game with no instructions or sense of direction, just hoping and praying that he was getting near the end.

He'd been thinking about the game all morning... well, good grief, how could he think of anything else? *Journey to the Promised Land* had taken over his life by intruding on his personal feelings. The lives of many people seemed to be in his hands and so far he'd let them all down. Well if he couldn't beat the game then he'd just have to keep on trying until he did.

He marched resolutely upstairs determined to win because if he didn't defeat the zombie then more people might die. Playing the game was inevitable because he was never given any choice. All he could do now was play as much as he could and get it over with fast.

He sat in front of the computer, switched it on and waited to see if it would work. The computer tower whirred and clicked into life and the game appeared on the screen.

Josh was grateful that the game worked this time. But then he realized that he didn't want to feel gratitude to this game for anything when what it made him feel most of the time was angry. Angry at being so controlled and manipulated. Angry that he was being used to choose victims when he didn't want any part of it. He felt like a puppet, a marionette made to dance by whoever was pulling his strings. He felt as though he was walking under a heavy cloud of hopelessness. Play on he must, whether he liked it or not, and he really did not like it. He scowled at the computer.

On the screen Salvador was in the graveyard once more. Josh took a look in the bag to find a more appropriate weapon, but could see none. Eventually he chose a sword thinking that at least the blade was long and so could hold the zombie at a distance.

He walked Salvador through the cemetery, swinging the sword in front of him as he went. It made a satisfying 'swish' as it sliced through the air.

It wasn't long before the zombie's slow footsteps could be heard. He turned Salvador around in every direction looking to see where the noise was coming from.

As soon as the zombie came into view he moved Salvador towards it, swinging the sword as he went. He didn't have any sort of plan other than what he was doing now and so he didn't know what he'd do when Salvador reached it. All he wanted to do was to use the sword to keep the zombie away from Salvador.

The zombie was slow so it was always easy to see where it was, so as long as he could keep it at a distance he should be safe for the time being.

The zombie continued its slow pace forward, seemingly oblivious to the swinging sword.

Soon Salvador's sword and the zombie were as close as they could be without contact. He expected the zombie to stop, but it didn't.

As the sword swung from left to right, the zombie stepped into its path and as the sword arced again it sliced off the zombie's head as smoothly as a knife through butter.

The zombie's body collapsed to the ground and its head rolled away out of sight.

Josh stopped swinging the sword. Was that it? Was it really so easy to defeat the zombie? He didn't know that to kill a zombie you had to decapitate it and it was just luck and great timing that he had found out. He thought he would have to play for ages and was worried about another defeat, so the relief he now felt was immense. It seemed as though the game was only interested in committing murder, and once its victim was dead it didn't seem to care what happened in the game.

He put Salvador's sword back in his bag and saw the food in there. He couldn't remember the last time Salvador had eaten to keep up his energy line.

During the first attack from the zombie, Salvador had used up most of his strength fighting and so had become weak and been defeated.

But his time the fight had been brief. Still Salvador's energy line was only half full so Josh let him take some food until he was restored to full life again.

He walked Salvador a few paces away from the zombie, intent on carrying on with the game. First he stopped and set a new virtual bookmark to save the game at that point, but no sooner had he done it when the screen went blank and the computer switched itself off.

Josh slumped back in his chair. Relief at not having to play any more mingled with worry that he would have to play again soon. He felt emotionally drained.

The game remained silent for the rest of the day, but it was no real comfort. Josh constantly worried about the game whether he had to play it or not.

*

On Monday all the talk among the children at school was about the death of Adrian Sparks. Everyone seemed to agree that he'd died from having his neck broken but once again there were many theories circulating.

Some were saying that he was attacked in his bedroom just as Carl Thurston had been. Others said he fell down the stairs, while others said he was beaten up in the street and his neck got broken in the fight.

Even though he had never liked Adrian Sparks or his two friends and their deaths meant he wouldn't be picked on anymore, Josh still felt bad that they were dead. He also felt guilty and worried that someone might suspect that he was to blame. How anyone could possible know the truth, he wasn't sure. It was just a nagging feeling that wouldn't go away.

The talk and speculation about what happened to Adrian Sparks carried on the entire day. Josh sat with a few other boys at break time and tried to steer the conversation onto other things but it didn't work.

"I can't believe all three of them are dead, just like that," said one boy with a snap of his fingers.

"Yeah, but it won't be long till three more take their places," said Josh. "Is there three more as bad as them?"

"They say Sparks' mother had some sort of breakdown. She kinda went gaga after she saw what had happened to him," said another boy.

"Won't it be a lot quieter around here without them though?" asked Josh.

"I heard that it wasn't just his neck that was broken, it was his whole head that had been ripped off," said the first boy.

"Yeah," replied the second boy, sniggering. "Maybe his old lady tripped over it when she came in or kicked it across the room. Can you imagine Sparks' mother kicking him in his face and sending it flying?"

The two boys laughed loud and long as though it was the funniest thing they'd ever heard. Josh made several more attempts to change the subject but they wouldn't budge.

The rest of the day carried on in the same vein and by the end of the day Josh was sick and tired of hearing about it. Knowing the truth made it impossible for him to join in any gossip. He walked home with his head hanging, just thankful that the day was over.

As he turned the corner onto his street he noticed Leonora walking with her two friends a few yards in front of him. They didn't normally walk home in the same direction as Josh so he wasn't expecting to see them. His spirits lifted at the sight of her. How he longed to be walking along with her. He was aware that he wasn't the only boy in the school who thought she was beautiful. Quite a few of them had tried to approach her but she always seemed quite aloof to them. That was one of the reasons why he had been surprised when she came to talk to him at school recently. She didn't usually talk to any boys.

Now here she was on his street. Did she know he lived here? Was she going to his house? He wished, but he doubted it very much.

Leonora and her friends passed by his house and continued further along. Josh stopped at his front gate and watched them. At the end of the street they went into the corner shop.

Although he didn't know why, he felt he had to follow her, so he ran down the street after her. He'd felt so elated to see her so unexpectedly and now that she was here he wanted to see more of her.

As he neared the shop he slowed to a walking pace and tried to look as though he just happened to be going to the shop at the same time.

He stopped outside and peered cautiously through the window, ready to duck out of sight in case she saw him looking. But she and her friends were busy looking through some magazines.

He stood and admired the delicate way her slim hands leafed through the pages making the bracelets jangle on her narrow wrists. He loved her blonde hair and petite figure. She always made him think of the word 'sweet' whenever he saw her. Her two friends, on the other hand, as well as reminding him of the two ugly stepsisters, always made him think of the word 'sour'.

He could never understand why she stayed with those other two. However, he understood perfectly why the other two wanted to be with Leonora. The only way they could get a boy to look their way was to stand near a pretty girl.

He suddenly realized they had seen him watching and they nudged one another and giggled. Josh felt embarrassed and could feel his face blushing. He turned away from the window.

Now what was he going to do? He didn't want to leave or they'd think that he was running away. But if he just stood there, what would he say to them when they came out?

He liked Leonora and he was pretty sure that she liked him. Why else would she have come up and spoken to him at school?

Maybe this was his chance to talk to her. It was usually the boy who asks the girl out, so maybe she was just waiting for him to ask her. Yes, this was his opportunity. She was here, he was here and they weren't at school surrounded by lots of other people, just two others.

Suddenly the shop door opened and there she was, followed closely by the two ugly stepsisters. She smiled at him and her friends smirked but he didn't care. She was there and she was smiling. That must mean that she was happy to see him.

"Hi," he said.

"Hi," she said straight back.

An awkward silence followed. He wasn't sure what to say next.

"Can I talk to you?" It was a difficult to think of something to say. He felt so nervous.

"Sure."

Another awkward pause.

"Can I speak to you alone?" he said glancing at her two friends but without actually looking at them.

"There are no secrets between friends," one of them quickly spat at him.

"I'm not your friend," he spat back.

"We're not leaving, so if you want to say something either be quick or go away."

He looked at Leonora, but she just shrugged.

"I-I just wanted to ask you if you'd, um, well, you know, just hang out with me, maybe, sometime. We could meet up together."

Her friends immediately shrieked with laughter. Josh's nervous blushes turned to burning anger. He glared at the two of them and then looked at Leonora, but to his horror she was looking down at her feet and was laughing too.

"Who does he think he is?" one of her friends squealed.

"I don't think so," said Leonora sarcastically and then the three of them walked away still laughing.

Josh felt so humiliated. Never in his life had he ever approached a girl before. He'd been aware that she might reject his offer but he'd felt certain she'd accept. But never had he imagined that she'd laugh at him.

Now she didn't seem so sweet after all and he could fully understand her friendship with the other two. She was just as sour as they were.

He'd never understood the meaning of the word heartbreak before but now it actually felt as though his heart was turning into a cold stone in his chest. How was it possible that her reaction could hurt him this much?

He stood motionless, his face bright red, and stared hard at the ground.

I won't cry, he told himself. *I won't give her the satisfaction. I won't cry.*

He didn't care that her friends had laughed at him, but when he saw Leonora laughing too he felt so hurt, while at the same time hating her for what she did.

Humiliation, heartbreak and anger. These three emotions raged continually inside him. He wanted to cry and scream at the same time.

How could she do this to him? Suddenly everything became clear. What a fool he'd been. Leonora didn't like him at all. She'd only spoken to him at school to get information out of him. He knew that now. If only he'd realized it sooner he could've saved himself so much embarrassment. She was probably going to laugh at him all the way home.

"God, how I hate you," he said quietly under his breath. But at the same time he knew that what he really hated was the fact that she wasn't interested in him. He also hated the fact that he'd made a fool of himself.

He waited until they'd walked past his house and out of sight before he reluctantly made his way home.

In the kitchen he sat and had a large cold drink while his mother chatted to him. She mostly talked about Adrian Sparks' death, but he didn't say much because he didn't care very much about it. He was too busy trying to get over what had just happened.

Once he calmed down he finished his drink and went to his room to change out of his uniform into something cooler.

The computer sat silently on his desk while he dressed. It had briefly crossed his mind that after being angry with Leonora, the game might choose her as its next victim.

But she was different from the others. He'd been angry with her, yeah, but he still liked her. He didn't think he could ever hate her and even though he'd said it out loud, he hadn't really meant it.

In fact, thinking about it, he could have been misreading her. It was possible that the only reason she acted the way she just did was because her two cantankerous friends (he knew what the word cantankerous meant because his mother used to use it often about his grandmother) were there and they were a bad influence on her. Sure, that must be it because she had always been nice to him when she was on her own.

He slowly put on his shorts and T-shirt as he mulled over this new insight. Yes, he was sure he was right. Leonora hadn't just been nice to him to get information, she was a genuinely nice person, *if* she wasn't around her horrible friends. He was glad he'd figured it out because he didn't want to hate her.

He had his back to the computer as he pulled his T-shirt on and that was when he heard the dreaded click and whirr of it coming to life.

The blood instantly drained from his face and torso and he instantly felt cold despite the fact that it was a blistering hot day.

He turned and looked at the screen. There was Salvador waiting to leave the cemetery. No. This couldn't be happening. He didn't hate Leonora. He just didn't.

He closed his eyes and tried to concentrate as hard as he could to make the game understand that it was wrong.

"I don't hate her. I just was just surprised and hurt. I could never hate her. Pleeease. Oh pleeease. I didn't mean what I said. I'm sorry. I know I shouldn't say things that aren't true. I don't hate her. I could never hate her. Honest, I was just angry at her.

"Just go away and leave her alone. I'm begging you. PLEASE?"

But when he opened his eyes Salvador was still on the screen and he was watching Josh with a look of pity.

Josh wanted to beg more and plead his case but he knew it was useless. The game wanted to play and the game was in control.

He wanted to regress back to childish behaviour, throw himself on the floor and have a loud temper tantrum. He wanted to pound his fists and feet into the floor and scream, "It's not fair! Leave me alone! Leave me alone!"

But he was thirteen years old. Far too old to behave like that anymore, but the temptation was great.

Doing anything other than playing the game was useless. He had to play. He had no choice.

He would have to play harder and more carefully than he'd ever played before because he knew that if he didn't defeat the next enemy in the game, Leonora would die.

Chapter 21

"Bastard. Bastard. Bastard." Josh muttered under his breath as he sat down in front of the computer. Salvador left the cemetery and was walking through another village but the people weren't as friendly. They looked worried when they saw him and all went nervously indoors. It gave Josh a terrible feeling of foreboding. More doors opened and closed as the streets emptied.

"You're not helping, you know," he told Salvador when he noticed the anxious expression on his face too.

As Salvador walked around a bend in the narrow road he passed by a small church. A smiling priest in white vestments beckoned him from the open doorway. Josh stopped and watched. The priest continued smiling and waving for Salvador to come in.

This was different. Never before in the game had anyone wanted Salvador to go to him. It could be a trick. On the other hand, the church could be a place of sanctuary.

Josh sat up straight as another thought suddenly occurred to him.

In this game he had to 'Journey to the Promised Land' and somewhere in The Bible it mentioned something about a Promised Land. There had to be a connection there somewhere, didn't there? Was this church the place that he was trying to reach? Would he find The Promised Land in there?

No, it couldn't be. It was far too easy. Wasn't it? He couldn't decide and tapped his fingertips on the desk while he thought about it some more.

Salvador had recently eaten and so his energy line was complete which meant he had plenty of stamina to fight if going into the church turned out to be the wrong decision.

But what if he couldn't get out again? What if it was a trap?

"But what if it's not?" he whispered to himself.

How he'd love to go into the church and find out that he'd made it to The Promised Land and that the game was over. What bliss that would be.

Earlier in the game, he'd been forced to go into a house and kill some rats. He hadn't wanted to send Salvador in but the game wouldn't let him play on unless he did. However, this time he seemed to have an option so maybe it might be best to just carry on walking and see what was up ahead, although he couldn't help thinking that the church and the priest must be significant in some way.

He walked Salvador along the road a few paces and then changed his mind and backtracked to look at the church again. The priest looked straight at Josh and smiled. Josh cringed. He hated it when the people in the game looked him in the eye. It was so unsettling. He decided to move on even though the silent street was eerily void of people.

Further along the road he came across a pack of large dogs lying at the side of the road. They all turned to look at Salvador as he approached, and although they looked angry, they didn't make any attempt to block his way despite the fact they were as big as Great Danes. Whether or not they were the next enemy Josh wasn't sure but just to be on the safe side he took a knife from the bag, although how one small knife would help against a pack of dogs if they decided to attack, he had no idea.

He quickened Salvador's pace, expecting the dogs to spring into a snapping, snarling frenzy any second. As Salvador passed them they all turned and watched him go by, sniffing the air as he passed, but they made no other move.

At first he was thankful to have passed by so easily, but couldn't help wondering if something worse than a pack of dogs was waiting for Salvador ahead. But he didn't have to wonder for long because he soon came across a derelict old house. He wanted to hurry Salvador past it, but it quickly became clear that the game had other ideas.

The house stood on the left hand side of the road; a large, weathered, timber building. Its windows seemed to malevolently watch Salvador even though they were boarded over.

Before Josh could even begin to wonder about the house, a ghostly apparition glided through the front wall and settled on the road in front of Salvador. Josh's first thought was that the knife Salvador held was now completely useless.

At first the ghost made no move towards him. It seemed to float an inch above the dusty road. Its shape only vaguely resembled human form and it was a transparent misty white except for its two shining eyes.

Josh could only wait to see what the ghost would do. He had no idea how to kill it, if it was possible at all.

The ghost turned and began to move along the road away from Salvador. Then it stopped and lifted an arm and made a beckoning motion.

Reluctantly Josh allowed Salvador to follow. He probably wouldn't have a choice anyway.

Leonora parted from her two friends when she was halfway home from school. They lived in one direction and she lived in another.

"Bye Natalie. Bye Emma. See you tomorrow," she said before turning away.

"See ya."

"Yeah, see ya tomorrow."

Leonora began to walk along the busy main road and then changed her mind as she passed by the end of a back alley between two streets of Victorian houses. If she walked up the alley and through the back streets, she'd be home in half the time. She needed to make up some extra time after hanging around with Natalie and Emma instead of going straight home.

She didn't want to be late because her mother worried about her so much since those three shitheads got killed.

Leonora didn't think she had anything to worry about. Those three jerks deserved what they got and it was probably someone getting their revenge on them anyway. They were always picking on other kids and it was only a matter of time before some crazed psycho-dad got sick of their kid being bullied and decided to put a stop to it.

Yeah, she figured it was something like that. If it was random killings then it was too much of a coincidence that those three got killed one after the other. No, it had to be someone who was specifically after those three.

But she'd been unable to convince her mother of her theory and so her mother continued to worry and issue strict instructions.

"Leonora, come straight home after school. Don't go anywhere else and only walk on the main roads. You'll be safer there with more people around. And for goodness sake don't speak to any strangers. Trust no one. Even if someone asks you the time, just ignore them because you never know."

But she hadn't gone straight home and had even detoured to follow Natalie and Emma to a corner shop.

That's where they'd seen the boy. She knew he liked her because she'd often seen him watching her at school. She thought he was nice too, but he was also a geek and no one liked geeks.

She felt a bit guilty for the way they'd treated him, but what else could she have done with Natalie and Emma there?

She hadn't meant to be cruel to him but if she hadn't gone along with the others they'd never have let her live it down. If Natalie and Emma hadn't been there she probably would have tried to not hurt his feelings. She might have even stayed and talked to him for a while.

But instead she pretended that she disliked him as much as they did. She could tell by the look on his face that he was hurt by her rejection. It would have been better if he had asked her when she was alone, or better still, if he hadn't asked her at all.

She shrugged and turned up the alley. It was narrow but not too long so within a couple of minutes she had emerged from the other end.

Across the road was a church. It was quite small with stained glass gothic windows and it sat to the right in a small walled churchyard full of old leaning gravestones.

As she'd walked along the back alley, she'd seen a woman standing in the churchyard, just inside the low brick wall that surrounded it. As she approached she saw that it was an old woman and she seemed to be watching her.

Now that she was only across the road, her mouth dropped open in surprise when she recognised the old woman. It was her grandmother.

Normally Leonora would have been delighted to see her, but her grandmother had died just over a year ago.

It can't be her, it just can't be, her logical mind tried to tell her, but her eyes told her that it was. She didn't know what to do and so just stood rooted where she was, in shock.

She longed for it to be her grandmother. She wanted to run and throw her arms around her and smell her again. God how she'd missed her.

The woman in the churchyard continued to smile and then raised her arms and mouthed the word 'Leonora'.

Leonora couldn't stand the waiting anymore. It must be her grandmother if she knew her name.

She stepped forward and looked right and left. There was a brief break in the traffic flow so she crossed the road. But when she looked forward again she saw that her grandmother was now standing a few feet further inside the wall. Boy she must have moved fast. But Leonora didn't think about it for more than a split second. All she wanted was to be with her grandmother. How or why her grandmother had come to be there she didn't care anymore. There would be time for questions later. Now she just wanted to be with her, even though she felt slightly afraid.

So many questions without answers tumbled over each other in her mind. Was this a trick? Was she seeing a ghost? Surely it wasn't possible for her grandmother to still be alive, was it?

With tears in her eyes she hurried on. This whole situation reminded her of the story of *The Little Match Girl*. In that story the Little Match Girl had missed her grandmother terribly after she died and then she'd seen her grandmother's ghost when she struck a match in a cold, dark, back alley. Seeing her grandmother's ghost had filled The Little Match Girl's heart with renewed longing to be with her and Leonora now knew how she felt.

As she entered the churchyard her grandmother turned and walked towards the church. Leonora followed, not wanting her grandmother to leave her again, but not understanding why she was walking away.

As though in answer to the unspoken question, her grandmother turned and beckoned for Leonora to follow, and then continued on past the gravestones to the far side of the little church.

Again her grandmother turned, and smiling her sweet smile that Leonora had always loved so much, she raised her hand and beckoned again before turning down the narrow path at the other side of the church.

Briefly Leonora thought that it might be dangerous to be following her dead grandmother. But the thought merely passed through her mind unconsciously and she paid it scant attention. Her grandmother was here and she wanted to be with her so nothing else really mattered.

She was well-read on the subject of ghosts and the supernatural, so she knew that the dead only contacted the living for a reason and once they'd accomplished what they came to do then they would peacefully pass over for ever. So her grandmother must have come back to show her something important so Leonora felt duty-bound to find out what. She also didn't want to lose sight of her because once she'd done what she came to do, she'd vanish.

At the far side of the little church the passageway was narrow and dark, with a high wooden fence on the other side blocking out most of the sunlight. A timber shed with a pitched roof stood at the other end of the passageway, which not only blocked even more light, but also the exit.

Her grandmother was halfway along the side of the church when she turned again and smiled. Any hesitation Leonora felt about following her melted in that tender look and she stepped into the narrow gap.

*

Josh and Salvador followed the ghost to some woods at the edge of the village. The trees were very close together. Their high branches had all intertwined over the years creating an almost solid, leafy canopy which blocked out almost every drop of daylight.

The ghost turned and beckoned once more before disappearing from sight amongst the dark tree trunks.

Josh didn't allow Salvador to follow. There was something very wrong with what was happening. Once the ghost and its brightly shining eyes were swallowed up by the gloom, there was a long pregnant pause. Josh waited because there was nothing else he dared do.

He remembered that he'd once seen a movie about a ghost. In the movie, the ghost couldn't actually harm anyone, but it used its presence to lure its victims to their grizzly deaths. He felt that this ghost was trying to do the same thing.

He looked back up the street for some sort of escape route or something to help him. But the road was straight with nowhere else to go except back to the old house or to the dogs or to the church.

The church! That must be the answer. Churches and graveyards were the sorts of places where ghosts usually hung out, weren't they? And the priest had smiled and looked friendly so maybe he could help.

He took Salvador back to the church, treading wearily passed the sniffing hounds and then hurrying on. He went up to the priest who still smiled and waved. As he approached some options appeared on the screen next to the priest which read:

Burial
Wedding
Sermon
Confession
Exorcism
Forgiveness
Advice

Straight away Josh knew what to do. He clicked the cursor on the word "Exorcism." The computer whirred; the words disappeared from the screen. The priest put his waving hand down, dropped his smile and turned to look at Salvador.

A speech bubble opened near his mouth and the words *"Show me your problem"* appeared within it, one letter at a time as though typed by an invisible hand.

Josh walked Salvador back along the road and the priest obligingly followed. The strange apparition was standing in front of the woods again and still beckoned.

The priest approached the ghost and as it turned to enter the woods he took a small bottle of clear liquid from his pocket and splashed it over the ghost.

The ghost threw up its arms, screaming and wailing. It was such a chilling cry, the hairs stood up on the back of Josh's neck. Steam hissed from its back where the liquid had landed. It seemed to be in so much pain that Josh almost felt sorry for it.

As the steam increased the ghost began to evaporate, still screaming and thrashing the whole time. Soon there was nothing left except a few wisps of steam rising from the ground. Josh moved the cursor over the bottle in the priest's hand and the words *"holy water"* appeared next to it.

Ah, now I get it, thought Josh.

The priest replaced the bottle in the pocket of his robe, smiled at Salvador, and left. Josh watched him walk away and then turned Salvador towards the woods. This must be the way he had to go because there was no other way forward but there was still the problem of what the ghost had been trying to lead him to. He would have to be very careful.

Salvador was just about to enter the woods when Josh stopped him. He leaned closer to the screen. He thought he'd seen one of the trees move, but now he wasn't sure.

As he looked carefully at the tangle of old gnarled trunks and raised roots, he began to see a definite shape amongst them.

He watched carefully until he saw movement again and this time he saw clearly what he was looking at.

In amongst the twisted misshapen trunks and the mass of outcropping roots was a human skeleton. It twitched every few seconds for almost a minute then it slowly untangled itself from the mountain of wood it had lain in.

When it finally raised itself up to its full height it was taller than Salvador. Throughout the game Josh had known that Salvador was tall because he was always stood a good head and shoulders above all the villagers. But now he looked small.

The skeleton must have been what the ghost was trying to lure him to. Well it might be only made of bones but it was obviously alive and potentially dangerous. Potentially? More like no doubt about it.

Josh clicked the cursor over the word "Save" at the bottom of the screen. He didn't trust the skeleton not to leap out and take him by surprise. He hadn't bookmarked the game since the zombie died and he didn't want to have to walk all the way to the woods again.

The skeleton was difficult to see in the darkness between the trees because its bones were dark grey instead of the usual white, but it became easier to see as it advanced into the open.

Before Josh knew what was happening, the skeleton produced a sword from behind its back and stabbed Salvador through the chest.

Salvador staggered backwards and fell to the ground. The skeleton watched Salvador as he choked out his last few breaths and lay still. Bending forward it grasped the sword firmly by the handle, twisted it 45 degrees and pulled up hard.

Salvador's body rose several inches from the ground before the skeleton put its foot on his chest and stamped his limp body back down. The sword pulled free with a sickening slurp. The skeleton held the bloodied sword in the air victoriously and looked at Josh.

Josh slumped back in his chair and closed his eyes. He'd lost again.

Chapter 22

While Josh was engrossed in his on-screen apparition, Leonora was fully engrossed with the ghost of her grandmother. She was still bursting with curiosity to find out just what her grandmother was trying to show her.

Once her eyes adjusted to the gloom at the side of the church, she could see that her grandmother was pointing to the timber shed at the end. On the shed door was a life-sized painting of a skeleton. It seemed like a strange thing to see in a churchyard but it had been very artistically done. Whoever had painted it had used a dark shade of grey and had meticulously painted all the correct shading on even the smallest bones.

But why was she being shown this? Surely her grandmother hadn't come back to show her a painting? There must be something inside the shed that she was supposed to look at. Her grandmother turned and continued to lead the trance-like Leonora to the shed.

When they were nearly at the other end of the passageway her grandmother stopped in front of the door, turned and smiled kindly at her, then looked at the skeleton. Leonora followed her gaze and to her horror she saw that the skeleton wasn't a drawing anymore, if it ever had been. It was now three dimensional and standing in front of the door.

It moved so swiftly and unexpectedly that by the time Leonora had taken a sharp breath in surprise, the skeleton had drawn back its arm and plunged a sword deep into her chest.

She looked questioningly at her grandmother who only smiled sweetly again, before fading away.

As Leonora fell to the ground she felt afraid, very, very afraid and very, very confused. She also felt a hot burning pain in her chest.

The skeleton leaned over her, and smirking, pulled out the sword. As she looked at the evil face, her logical mind briefly wondered how it was possible for a skeleton to do any facial expressions without a proper face, and then she felt warm sticky blood spreading over her body.

Her dying thoughts, as she lay looking at the clear blue sky, were of her grandmother. How could she have betrayed her like that? Her grandmother had always loved her just as the Little Match Girl had always been loved by her grandmother.

Then, too late, she remembered that in the story, the grandmother's ghost had also led the Little Match Girl to her death.

If only she'd remembered that sooner.

*

When Josh opened his eyes the skeleton lowered the sword, stabbed the tip of it into the ground, leaned an elbow on the handle and looked gleefully down at Salvador's body which was now soaked in a pool of blood.

Josh was surprised that the game was still on. Was it going to let him continue playing?

He sat forward and pressed the 'Escape' key. The game reverted back to the point where Salvador was still alive and the skeleton had only just stood up.

But he needed a plan and he needed it quickly because he knew the skeleton would leap out at Salvador within seconds. He looked back along the road thinking that maybe the priest could help him again. But then he saw something even better.

The dogs. They love to eat bones.

They were all still sleeping by the side of the road.

He returned to them and took some food from Salvador's bag. He let Salvador drop some of it on the ground. The dogs woke up and sniffed the air above the food. One by one they stood up and began to eat hungrily. He left a trail of food all the way back to the woods. The dogs followed, eating hungrily along the way. He threw the last piece of food in amongst the trees and then retreated to safety back out on the road.

The dogs continued to follow the food trail past Salvador and into the woods. Josh heard a low guttural growl from one of the dogs, then another and another until the whole pack was alert and angry.

Then without warning they sprang forward as one huge mass. There was a lot of movement and scuffling and two of the dogs yelped. They emerged again, each carrying a different bone. The last dog to emerge was actually carrying a skull in its jaws.

Josh breathed a sigh of relief and clicked on "Save." No sooner had he done this than the screen went blank and the computer switched itself off.

Josh was pleased that he'd managed to defeat the ghost and the skeleton before the game stopped but he didn't know if that meant that Leonora was safe or not.

Although he had eventually won the war with the skeleton, he had lost the first battle, which meant he wasn't entirely positive about Leonora's safety.

He would just have to hope that she would be OK. But he knew from what had gone before that there was little hope.

*

Later that Monday evening the telephone rang at Josh's house. He and his parents were watching television and all three looked at the clock. It was nine thirty. No one usually rang so late.

Josh's mother went into the hallway to answer the phone. After talking quietly for a few minutes she went into the kitchen and filled the kettle with water.

Josh's father went in to join her and he could hear them both speaking quietly and seriously. Josh knew that something was wrong and he was sure he knew what that something was. It was Leonora.

After a while his father reappeared on his own.

"Josh could you come into the kitchen? We need to talk to you."

Josh turned off the television and went into the kitchen. His mother and father were seated at the table, each with a cup of coffee. Another cup was on the table and he sat in front of it. He tried to take a sip but the coffee was still too hot to drink.

His mother looked worried.

"Josh that was my friend Tricia on the phone. A friend of hers has a daughter called Leonora who goes to your school. Do you know her?"

Josh's heart sank. So it was true. Leonora was dead. He'd kept thinking that as long as no one told him that she was dead then there was still a chance that she was alive. But now he knew the awful truth.

"Yeah, she's nice," he said without looking up.

"Well she went missing on the way home from school today. Her mother's been frantic trying to find her, ringing round everyone she knew and the police have been out following every possible route she could've taken home."

"She's dead too then," he said. It was a statement rather than a question.

Josh's mother hung her head sadly as she spoke. "I'm afraid so. She was found in a churchyard and she'd been stabbed in the chest."

There was silence and no one spoke for a while.

It was his father who finally broke the silence. "We've made a decision, Josh. We think that it would be best if you don't go to school for the rest of this week. There's something very strange happening to the kids round here and hopefully soon we'll find out who's doing these things and they'll be stopped. In the meantime it's best if you stay here with your mother while I'm at work. Maybe things will be better by the weekend."

Josh listened quietly. He didn't know what to say. He would prefer to go to school because at least while he was there he didn't have to play the game. But on the other hand, perhaps he could finish it sooner if he was home all day, although the thought of playing more often filled him with dread. He wasn't really sure which was the lesser of the two evils.

"Did you know Leonora very well Josh?" his mother asked quietly.

"Not very," he told her honestly. "But I did speak to her after school today."

His parents glanced at each other, not knowing what else to say. Then the three of them drank their coffee in silence.

Chapter 23

Tuesday dawned bright and sunny the following morning in complete contrast to how Josh felt. He'd gone to his bedroom as soon as he could the night before and cried like a baby. What he was crying about he wasn't completely sure. He was sad about losing Leonora. He was unhappy that he had to keep playing the game. He felt bad about the bullies dying and the stranger in the street. He even felt awful about their canary and the neighbours' dog and the other animals that were found in their garden. The whole situation just sucked and there was nothing he could do about it. If the game was so insistent about living off his bad feelings, then it should destroy itself, because right now he hated the computer and the game more than he'd ever hated anyone in his whole life.

Josh lay on his bed and cried for what seemed like a long time. He hugged his pillow to his face to muffle the sound so that his parents wouldn't hear. Eventually his tears were spent and he slept fitfully on top of his bed covers all night.

The next morning he ate his breakfast in the kitchen and his mother, who'd already eaten, stood near the sink drinking her second cup of coffee. The back door was open and the sun streamed in, cheering up the whole room, but Josh and his mother's attention was gloomily fixed on the small television on the kitchen counter.

There was an extended news item about Leonora and the other four local deaths. The news team had been out filming where Leonora had died, but apart from the fact that she'd been stabbed, the police, once again, could find no evidence that a crime had been committed. They were completely baffled and were asking anyone who knew anything to come forward.

There was also an interview with the parents of the three boys and they were pleading for help in finding whoever had been killing their children. It was disturbing to see murder scenes of places he'd been and photos of people he knew.

As Josh and his mother watched in silence he was wracked with guilt. Everything was because of him but he couldn't tell her.

"Josh you haven't said much about this yet. Are you OK?"

"As OK as I can be, I guess."

"I know it's terrible for a young boy to have to endure so much death around him and I can't even pretend to know how you're feeling."

"It's OK Mum. You don't have to feel bad for me. It's not your fault that all this is happening."

"I know, but I feel so frustrated that there's nothing I can do to stop it."

Josh laughed at the irony of his mother's statement. Here she was saying how bad she felt when it was he himself who was causing it all. How would she cope if she knew the truth? Josh had never felt so frustrated and helpless in all his life and knew he felt a lot worse than his mother.

"Mum there's nothing you can do. There's nothing that anyone can do."

After the breakfast dishes were done, Josh went to his room. The computer sat silently on the desk and for that he was grateful. He needed time to try to think of what to do.

He flopped down onto his bed and lay on his back with his arms behind his head. He was glad he didn't have to go to school because he really didn't think he could face everyone talking about Leonora and giving their opinions about how she must have died.

But who would die next? Perhaps while he stayed home from school no one would die because he wouldn't be able to get angry with anyone.

It was a comforting thought but only for a few seconds because he remembered that once before he hadn't been angry and he hadn't even played the game himself, but someone had still died. The stranger had been killed almost right outside their house.

He was worried about what was going to happen next. It was the 'not knowing' that was the worst.

One thing he was certain of was that the game had to be played to the end and he was the only one who could finish it and stop the deaths. But just how far from the end of the game he was, he didn't know, although he had the uncanny feeling that he'd be finding out very soon.

Chapter 24

Throughout the following week Josh made repeated attempts to play the game, but it remained unresponsive. The computer would turn on when he pressed the "Start" button but he couldn't find the files for the game anywhere on the system nor would the disk player open where the game CD still sat.

He wanted to finish the game as soon as he could so that this living nightmare he was trapped in would be over. He tried everything he could think of to get it started but nothing worked. So he spent the week entering his room with trepidation every time he went upstairs, worried that the game would start on its own when he least expected it.

By the weekend he'd given up. He thought he must have been right and that while he was staying at home and not getting angry at anyone, the game didn't have a victim.

But then out of the blue, there was an unexpected turn of events on Saturday morning.

"Josh can you come downstairs. We need to talk to you," his mother shouted.

Josh was lying on his bed reading and he got up immediately and went downstairs. His parents were sitting at the kitchen table.

"Sit down," his father instructed, and Josh sat.

"Josh we've been quite worried about you recently and we think it's gone on long enough."

Josh didn't know what he meant so he said nothing.

"We've noticed how quiet you've been lately. Even with everything that's been going on around here you still haven't said very much. It seems that all you've been doing is spending a lot of time playing on that old computer in your room."

"No I haven't. Just because it's in my room doesn't mean I've been playing on it all the time."

"Don't answer back. We know you have and sometimes we've even seen the computer on in your room when you're not in there. Obviously it's becoming such an obsession with you that you can't even remember to turn it off when you leave the room.

"Not only that but one morning last week we heard you playing on it as soon as you got out of bed. Now that's a bit too much don't you think?"

Josh didn't know what to say. He had no defence except the truth but they'd never believe him if he told them that the computer was switching itself on.

His mother spoke next.

"Josh we're just worried that you might be getting a bit depressed. First you had to cope with the death of your Uncle Neville and now several of your school friends have died. You're just so quiet and you seem to be spending more and more time with that computer and in particular with that strange-looking game. It has to stop Josh. A computer is no substitute for companionship."

"How can I spend time with anyone if you won't let me out of the house?"

"Don't be so rude to your mother," his father snapped.

"But it's true. The two of you can still leave the house and do whatever you want, but I'm stuck here. I tell you what, I'll cut back on how much I use it," he offered lamely.

"No," his father cut in sternly. "You won't use it at all for the next few days."

"Dad, no, you don't understand. I'm fine."

"No. You'll stay off that computer for this weekend at least."

Josh could feel himself beginning to panic. He had to play the game if it came on. He'd have no choice.

"Look I promise I'll hardly use it at all anymore," he pleaded.

His mother looked sad. "Josh if you find it so difficult just to spend one weekend without playing that game then I think you have a serious addiction."

"No I don't," he said, raising his voice.

"Don't speak to your mother like that."

"Look you've kept me locked up in the house all week. I can't go anywhere. I can't see anyone. And now I'm not allowed to play on the computer either. It doesn't leave me with much to do does it?"

"Josh we're not asking much of you and you WILL do as you're told." His father was becoming angry.

"I always do as you tell me. That's why I've been cooped up in here all week. I can't even go down the road to the shop on my own anymore. You're treating me like a baby."

"It's for your own good," his father shouted.

"No, it's not; it's for *your* own good. You're not worried that I'll die. You're just worried how *you'll* cope if I do."

His mother hung her head. She looked hurt and he was immediately sorry for the way he'd spoken. But they were being unreasonable. The game hadn't even been on for the past few days. They were simply assuming that he was playing it whenever he was in his room.

It was difficult enough for him to cope with the game and all the deaths he was causing, but now his parents' interference was only compounding his problem.

Before they could say anything more he turned and abruptly left the room. He went into the hallway but instead of going upstairs, he went outside, closing the front door quietly behind him.

He didn't know where he was going and it didn't matter. He just needed to get out and get away from the house and walk off his frustration.

He pounded around the streets for nearly half an hour until his temper subsided, then he headed home to face whatever they would say. He knew he would be in trouble for leaving the house and his mother would be worried, but it had felt so nice to be out for a change.

But on his return the house was silent. He walked through looking in every room but no one was there. Panic began to rise in his chest. What if the game had played while he'd been gone? He hadn't considered *that* before he left. Now it was all he could think about.

His face burned and his throat ached with a longing to cry. He needed to find his parents.

He went upstairs but every room was empty. The computer sat mutely on his desk. He glared at it. Had it been on while he was out? Had something indescribably evil killed his parents or chased them out of the house? He needed to know. He needed to find them.

He went back downstairs with a heart-rending dread thumping in his chest with every step.

He looked through the kitchen window and saw his parents in the back garden. Relief washed through him with alacrity and a grin spread over his entire face. His father was mowing the lawn and his mother was weeding one of the flower beds. He'd heard the lawn mower when he came home but thought it was one of the neighbours. Obviously they must have assumed that he'd gone upstairs and they must have gone outside shortly after he'd left because they were both nearly finished.

He went quietly to his room.

But as soon as he entered, he felt his heart leap with fright.

The game was on the screen.

Panic gripped him. He hurled himself under the desk and tugged at the electrical wire to pull the plug out of the socket. But it mustn't have been held together very well, because the plug didn't move but the wiring ripped straight out of it.

Josh sprang to his feet and looked at the now blank computer screen and felt a surge of relief. He let go of the electrical flex and it dropped to the floor.

There. He'd done it. The game was gone. No electricity meant no game.

Or did it?

As he watched, the scene of Salvador standing in front of the woods began to fade-in on the screen. It became brighter and brighter and within seconds it was completely restored.

The computer, however, hadn't come back on and was still silent – but the game, the damn game, had managed to work on its own.

Josh was horrified. He wanted to smash the computer into pieces. He wanted to open his window and hurl the computer to the ground. He wanted to swipe it off the desk and jump up and down on it while screaming and swearing and completely venting his anger.

But in reality he would do none of these things because he feared that any retaliation against the computer or the game might make things worse. How could he play the game and defeat the next enemies if the computer was broken? Somehow he had the feeling that the game could, and would, continue playing no matter what he did to try to stop it.

And now he had been angry with his parents. It had never occurred to him that he might become angry with them. But somehow he instinctively knew that the game had manipulated the argument. They had, after all, argued about the game.

Now the game had responded to his negative emotions which meant that his parents' lives rested literally in his hands. As he felt this weighty responsibility pressing firmly and heavily on his shoulders he had to force himself not to cry.

Downstairs he heard movement and voices. His parents were back inside the house.

Josh couldn't bring himself to play the game. But the game must have known because on the screen Salvador began to walk through the woods so Josh knew instantly that not playing was not an option.

Reluctantly he sat down and took control of the game.

Chapter 25

The woods where Salvador was walking were only small but they were full of food, so Josh allowed Salvador to eat some to revive his energy level and he put the rest in Salvador's bag in case of future shortages.

Suddenly, in the game, he heard gunshots – lots of them. He held Salvador still and listened. The noise seemed to be coming from further up ahead. It occurred to Josh how strange it was that even though he was playing a 2-dimensional game through a glass screen, it was still possible to tell the direction of any noises. It was such a realistic game, but then he supposed he knew only too well just how realistic it could be.

As he walked Salvador cautiously forwards, the gunshots grew louder. Near the end of the woods he saw flashes of light and heard whistling noises. He came out into the open and saw another village and realized that it wasn't gunfire he could hear but fireworks. The villagers looked as though they'd been having some kind of celebration. There were tables of food out in the streets and banners were festooned across the roads.

A crowd of people stood looking at the lights exploding in the sky. Josh thought they must be crazy because it wasn't dark and so the fireworks, what could be seen of them, had little brilliance.

He briefly wondered if there were such things as fireworks here in the village. All the old-fashioned people and their simple wooden houses suggested that they were living in a time warp of about 300 years ago. Most of their clothes looked as though they were made of brown sackcloth, the roads were dry and dusty. There were horses with saddles and carts instead of cars, and pigs, chickens and other farm animals ran freely everywhere.

So where did the fireworks come from?

Josh supposed that they did have gunpowder in those days so maybe it was possible that they'd learned how to make fireworks. He smiled briefly at his own attempt at futile logic. It was a game. The people weren't real. They lived in a fantasy world where anything was possible. But then again, he corrected himself, they didn't actually *live* at all, no matter how real it looked on the screen. He had no idea why the villagers were celebrating and thought it prudent not to linger here too long.

He was cautious as Salvador passed through the village, alert for anything that might leap out unexpectedly. His hands were shaking. He was afraid of the game and he was afraid even more for his parents' safety. But nothing happened on his journey through the village, and somehow that made him feel worse.

Salvador was now past all the houses. He looked back. The fireworks had finished and all the people were back at the tables of food. So far, so good.

When he turned around again to continue, he saw something lying in the road up ahead. It looked like a pile of sticks. Josh was unsure of what to do. He was almost certain that there'd been nothing in the road before, but now there were sticks – ordinarily sticks were not threatening, but this game wasn't ordinary.

Josh had no option but to proceed because there was nowhere else to go. He edged Salvador closer, pausing in between each small step, like a bride walking down a church aisle on her wedding day.

The sticks didn't move despite Josh worrying that they would suddenly rise up and morph into another skeleton or something worse.

On closer inspection Josh could see that what he thought were sticks had wicks. They weren't sticks at all but unused firecrackers.

Salvador picked them up, and then Josh immediately let them fall to the ground again. He'd picked them up with the intention of putting them in the bag in case he needed them in future. But then he'd had second thoughts. What if it was a trick and somehow they exploded in the backpack and killed Salvador?

Maybe that's what the game had in mind, or maybe it was making him more paranoid and nervous on purpose, so he'd lose the game and his parents would die. And then what? Would it kill him too? He hoped he would never find out.

His concern at the moment was to keep his parents safe. He had to play the game carefully and cautiously and he hoped his trembling hands wouldn't inhibit his ability to play.

The road soon ended at the edge of an open field and across the other side was a hill, a barrier with unknown dangers lurking on the other side. It would be quicker to walk around the hill rather than over it, but Josh decided to be cautious and go to the top to see what might be waiting at the other side. He didn't want to be taken by surprise again.

The hill wasn't very steep but it was very stony and rocky. Several times on the way up Salvador's foot slipped on the small stones, creating a mini avalanche.

Halfway up was a large outcrop of rock. Salvador put his hands up, gripped the edge and pulled himself up. Josh was amazed to see a small cottage on top that hadn't been visible from the bottom of the hill. He could only see the front section of the cottage; the rest of it was built into the hillside.

It was made of logs and had a small window next to a small door. Whoever owned it must have been very short but the cottage had a deserted look about it as though it had stood empty for a long time, so the tiny owner must be long gone.

Josh was still anxious to see what lay on the other side of the hill so he continued on, taking Salvador around the little cottage.

But he'd only gone a few steps past when the door opened and a troll-like creature emerged and sprang towards Salvador. It was very small and thin, about the size of a young child, but it was old and wizened and extremely ugly. Its dry and wispy white hair was brushed back from its face and hung down to its hips. It was completely naked and seemed to have no sexual genitalia of any kind and its skin was a streaky, washed-out grey colour.

He also noticed that it had no weapon.

Josh quickly chose a small knife from Salvador's bag and when the troll was near enough Salvador began to swing the knife out in front of him from left to right and kicked out repeatedly with one foot at the same time.

But the troll seemed very adept at ducking and diving and so he missed it every time. It ducked backwards, sideways, forwards and even jumped quickly enough, while continually backing away, to avoid being kicked.

This ineffective attack continued for quite some time until Salvador's energy level was almost depleted.

As they fought their way back to the door of the troll's house, Josh decided to try a new tactic. As he kicked out at the troll he also punched with Salvador's empty hand and to his amazement and delight it worked. The troll jumped up to avoid being kicked and got punched in the face instead.

The punch landed in the middle of the troll's face and it fell backwards through the door and into the house.

Josh let out a slow breath, satisfied that he'd beaten the troll, but within seconds the troll re-emerged with a small brown box in one hand. It put its other hand into the box, pulled out a tiny gun and aimed it at Salvador's chest.

Shocked, and moving on pure instinct, Josh pressed the "Escape" key. The game stopped and returned to the previously saved version while Salvador was still in the woods. He was thankful and somewhat surprised that pressing the "Escape" key worked. He'd expected the game to be unresponsive to any attempt not to play, but he'd simply panicked and pressed it anyway.

The troll creature had moved fast. Too fast. Josh hadn't had enough time to think of how to react and he'd *never* thought that the troll would have a gun. When the troll first appeared, Josh thought that it ran at Salvador to try to bite him or something because it had no visible weapon. But is that what trolls did? Did they bite?

He tried to remember anything that he knew about trolls. Josh had gathered a whole host of information on a lot of different subjects because he was such an avid reader. One thing he did remember was that trolls were well-known for stealing from people's homes. That must be how it acquired a gun.

Thud!

Josh froze. The noise seemed to come from his parents' bedroom.

Bump!

He listened, his heart racing. Then from a distance he heard his parents.

"Rachel?"

"Coming."

They were downstairs. Josh was scared. If it wasn't them in the bedroom then it must be...

He heard drawers being opened and things being dropped on the floor.

He had to work fast before his parents heard it too. He didn't want them coming up to investigate.

"Josh, what are you dropping up there?" his mother called from the bottom of the stairs.

Before he had time to even begin to think what to say, he heard the troll scamper across the landing like a monkey and then he heard his mother's blood-curdling scream.

Josh felt his heart sink faster than an elevator with a snapped cable.

He heard the troll run down the stairs and his mother's hasty footsteps in retreat.

He stood up and went towards the door. He had to go and help them. But what could he do? He hesitated with his hand on the door handle. This would be his first face-to-face encounter with one of the enemies from within the game.

Half of him wanted to charge out to the rescue while the other half was afraid and wanted to stay where it was safe. He hated himself for such cowardice. But if he left the room he would be just as defenceless against the troll as they were, and if he stayed where he was the troll would probably seek him out eventually anyway.

The best thing would be to kill the troll in the game and then the other would disappear, hopefully before it had a chance to do any harm. He wished he knew more about trolls.

Not long ago at school, his class had learnt about myths and legends. He remembered trolls being part of what was discussed but no matter how hard he tried to think of what was said about them, his mind was a blank. God, he wished he'd paid more attention in class that day. He'd remembered that trolls stole because the day before the lesson, one of his classmates had been arrested by the police for trying to shoplift. After the lesson another boy called him a troll for trying to steal and everyone had laughed uproariously as though it was the funniest joke in the world. But the name stuck. From that day forward the boy was only known as Troll, much to his dislike.

Now he could hear movement from downstairs but his frazzled mind couldn't register what the noise was.

He had to sit back down and play the game. He had to get rid of the troll in the house, and getting rid of its digital doppelgänger was the only way.

After taking one slow, deep breath, he sat down. Salvador was already walking through the woods. Josh took control of the game again and made Salvador run as fast as he could.

Salvador pumped his arms back and forth vigorously as he sprinted through the trees. A couple of times he stumbled but managed to keep his balance.

As he raced to the end of the woods and heard the fireworks he didn't slow down. He kept going and sped through the village. Passing the unused firecrackers on the road brought back his memory of what he knew about trolls.

They had a weakness. Noise! They were very afraid of loud noises because the Greek God, Thor, used to throw hammers of thunder at them.

He turned Salvador back to collect the firecrackers and took them up the hill.

Once again the troll came out of its house and approached Salvador. Its face held an expression of sneering glee at seeing its victim once again.

Josh had to use all his concentration to keep his mind on the game because he could hear noises from downstairs in his house and was desperate to know what was happening.

His father was shouting and his mother was screaming. There was much thumping and banging as though things were being thrown. Hearing all this was disturbing, but the most hideous sound of all was the underlying cackling laugh of the troll. It was upsetting enough that his parents were downstairs fighting for their lives, but to know that the troll was laughing in their faces the whole time was worse. Josh doubted, however, that his parents cared either way right now. But he did.

As the troll on the screen came nearer to Salvador, Josh saw that it was already carrying the gun. That was not how it had approached him before. The game was cheating, trying to trick him, but Josh was one step ahead.

Salvador lit the first firecracker and threw it just as the troll aimed the gun.

The firecracker landed at its feet and exploded, throwing the troll backwards in a screaming maniacal fit. Josh threw another cracker and another until the troll's screams were silent and it lay still. Salvador cautiously took a closer look.

The troll appeared to be dead although it didn't look injured so whether it had died from fright or injury Josh didn't know. Nor did he care.

He quickly saved the game and then listened carefully to what was happening downstairs. Nothing. He couldn't hear anything and that worried him.

Was the troll gone? Were his parents still alive? Had it hurt them?

He didn't know, nor did he have time to find out because on the screen he could see some sort of movement. Outside the troll's house something was emerging out of the ground. At first it was only one thing but then another and another appeared until there were eight of them.

He watched in amazement. First heads appeared, then necks, then shoulders. As soon as they rose fully out of the ground he could see they were dwarfs. Eight dwarfs. They rose up eerily, coming through the ground without disturbing it.

All of them were naked, except that each wore a pair of brown ankle boots, and like the troll, they appeared to have no genitalia. Their heads looked too large for their thick, squat bodies. Their arms seemed too short and Josh doubted they could touch the back of their own heads.

Each dwarf had ten thick, stumpy fingers and two chubby, bowed legs. But it was their faces that looked most disturbing. They had blood red lips that were so thin, their closed mouths looked like nothing more than a red slash across their faces.

Their noses were large, thin and misshapen, with quite a pointed tip. They all had long orange hair with a fringe hanging above their black eyes. There was no other colour to their eyeballs except black; no whites and no coloured irises. They were the most soulless eyes that Josh had ever seen.

Once the mutant dwarfs were fully out and standing on top of the ground, they all looked as one at the dead troll. Then they looked angrily at Salvador, their lips turning up at one corner in a snarl.

Despite the dwarfs being so small, Salvador was outnumbered and Josh doubted he could fight them off if they all attacked him at once. The dwarfs all raised their right arms in unison. Each chubby little hand was holding an axe.

From downstairs he heard his mother cry, "Oh my God! Please! No!" and he knew that the dwarfs were already in the house and the dwarfs on the screen must be working in almost complete synchronisation with their evil twins downstairs.

Josh was so startled when he heard his mother that he physically jumped and knocked the mouse off the desk. It hung from its wire and tapped against the wall as it swung to and fro. He scrambled quickly to get it, his hands severely shaking.

It took him several attempts to get a proper grip on the mouse and place it back on the mouse pad, all the time worrying that Salvador would be killed while he wasn't watching the game.

When he looked back at the screen both Salvador and the dwarfs were all looking straight at him as though waiting for his attention before they carried on. One of the dwarfs even raised a questioning eyebrow at him as if to say, "Are you quite finished?"

But Josh wasn't finished and he got such a fright at seeing them all looking at him from inside the game that he gave a small involuntary scream and jumped again, nearly knocking the mouse off the desk once more. Luckily he managed to grab it in time, but he burst into tears.

He felt so flustered and so helpless. He knew that crying was only going to make his task harder but he couldn't help it. Tears streamed down his face.

He tried to control his crying and wiped the palm of his hand over his eyes until he could see the computer screen clearly again. Then he sniffed loudly, wiped his hand under his nose then wiped the snot on his hand on the side of his shorts.

In the game, all eyes were still on Josh. One of the dwarfs folded its arms impatiently and another looked at the back of its wrist as though seeing an imaginary watch. A third dwarf yawned and looked bored. The game's arrogance was worrying.

Josh had never been so scared in his life. He longed to go down and join his parents and try to help them but he knew that leaving the game would likely cause their deaths. They mustn't die. He mustn't let it happen. His heart was breaking at the thought of losing them. It was sickening to think that they were downstairs with the mutant, black-eyed dwarfs.

But right now he dared not take his eyes off the screen. The dwarfs were now turning and edging closer to Salvador. Josh felt sweat trickle down the side of his face. These weren't mythical creatures like goblins and trolls with inherent weaknesses. These were small angry people with sharp weapons and Salvador was outnumbered. Josh tried hard to think of what to do, but could come up with nothing.

He was just a thirteen-year-old boy and he couldn't save his parents.

Josh wept silently.

Chapter 26

From downstairs Josh heard his mother screaming and then she began to shout. He couldn't hear what she was saying because she sounded quite hysterical but he felt her fear.

Her utter panic jolted him into action. He wiped away his tears and took a hard look at the situation on the screen. He looked at the dwarfs, the dead troll and Salvador. Then without giving it a second thought, he made Salvador pick up the gun from the dead troll and open fire on the dwarfs.

One by one they dropped like flies. Josh was so pleased with his actions and so surprised that he began to laugh. It wasn't a good kind of laugh because he was still crying at the same time. But he couldn't help it. Killing the dwarfs had been so simple and the answer had been there all the time.

His laughter quickly became long and hard. He couldn't ever remember laughing so loudly before.

Then just as rapidly his laughter subsided and his crying increased. He knew he was making a ridiculous noise at the same time, but he was unable to stop.

He sat slumped in his chair with his hands in his lap. His shoulders jerked up and down as he cried. He felt mentally and emotionally drained.

He didn't want to play the game anymore. He wanted to be left alone to live his own life again, but more than anything else, he wanted his mother. He needed to be with her desperately right now. But at the moment he didn't even know if she was dead or alive and he was making so much noise that he couldn't hear anything but himself.

He tried to calm down and stop crying, but it was difficult. After some effort he was crying silently again. He listened. There was no sound from downstairs.

He saved the game and moved Salvador past the dead dwarfs. Lying next to each of them was a vial of brightly coloured liquid and a small shield. That was strange. All the dwarfs had had before were axes, but now they were gone and there were vials and shields instead. He clicked the cursor on one of the vials and Salvador picked it up. The liquid looked like it might be magical because it changed colour constantly every few seconds from blue, to green, to pink, to yellow.

He opened the vial, expecting it to make a loud noise or explode or smoke or something, but nothing happened. There wasn't even the slightest fizz and the colour-changing liquid just continued to swirl around inside the vial. Josh frowned.

He tilted the vial and poured a drop of liquid onto one of the dwarfs. The drop landed on the dwarf's chest and sizzled like an egg dropped into a hot frying pan. The sizzling quickly turned to a cracking sound as the dwarf's appearance began to change. Its skin slowly began to change to a rough sandy colour, beginning at the point where the liquid had landed and spreading over its entire body. Even the black eyes changed to the same light colour.

The whole process of change happened quickly and when it finished the dwarf lay there looking like a statue that had fallen over.

"Stone," Josh whispered to himself. "It's turned to stone." The liquid wasn't so disappointing after all.

He stored the vial in Salvador's bag. He had a feeling that this liquid would come in very handy in the game at some future point. Why else would it have been left for him?

He took another vial of liquid from another dwarf and poured a drop onto it. But the liquid missed its intended target and fell onto a shield instead. The liquid sizzled again but this time it disappeared, leaving the shield untouched. Josh waited to see if there was some sort of delayed reaction. He let another drop fall onto the shield. Again the sizzling, hissing sound came and a tiny, almost invisible, puff of smoke rose from the shield, but then nothing.

Josh was thoughtful for a few seconds, and then he poured the whole contents of the vial onto the shield.

Again there was the sizzling hiss, and a quite visible puff of smoke rose, but most of the liquid ran off the shield as though it was waterproof.

Or magic-proof, thought Josh.

The liquid that ran off the shield had been absorbed into the ground around it with no adverse affect.

Josh looked at the scene in front of him and made his own deductions. The magic liquid was harmful to dwarfs or living creatures, harmless to the earth and couldn't touch the shields.

Just for one last test, Josh turned the vial upside down and let Salvador hold it there until the last final drop trickled out and fell onto another dwarf.

This time it landed on the dwarf's face. After the sizzling sound and wisp of smoke, the dwarf's face began to twitch. At first Josh thought it was coming back to life, but the twitching changed to movement under its skin. Its face looked as though someone was trying to push their knuckles out through its flesh.

The knuckle shapes then became still and blossomed as warts on the outside of its face. Then the rest of its body began to twist and morph for a few seconds leaving the dwarf looking like a hideous toad-like creature.

Josh grimaced. The clarity of the game never ceased to amaze him. Even though he was only watching the events taking place through a 15-inch computer screen, every detail was as clear as if he'd seen it in person.

But then it was no wonder that what he was seeing seemed so real. It was real. All this could happen to his parents if he wasn't careful. He had to concentrate on the game. He had to be vigilant. He also needed to try to look ahead and be ready for anything that might happen. But what was the meaning of everything he was seeing?

The dwarfs were not only offering magic potions but also, it seemed, magic deflecting shields. That had to mean that the next enemy must have powerful magic and be very dangerous.

Josh didn't feel good about this. He thought of his Uncle Neville. Had he gotten this far in the game? Uncle Neville had died from seemingly un-fatal injuries, namely his broken ankles. If one of the creatures so far had killed him he would have had fatal stab wounds or a broken neck or his intestines would have been removed.

But Uncle Neville had not been injured in any death-inducing way. So was it magic that had killed him? That would be one explanation as to how the game had murdered him without leaving any evidence.

And if the next enemy HAD defeated Uncle Neville, how could Josh even hope to win? Uncle Neville was a grown-up who was so smart that he'd invented the game. Josh was a thirteen-year-old boy whose computer knowledge was limited.

The big question was, why was the game the way it was and so capable of evil? Uncle Neville had said that the game contained his secret ingredient, but Josh had no clue what that meant, and probably never would.

It was obvious that Uncle Neville had been trying to make the game as life-like as possible because he'd certainly achieved it. It was also abundantly clear that it had gotten out of control.

Up until now Josh's mind had been filled with scenarios of what he'd do once the game was finished. In every case he had always seen himself as the victor. Now he wasn't so sure. With magic now included, he needed to keep all his wits about him and not let the game trick him or any sounds downstairs distract him. It all seemed so simple in theory, but he knew that in practice it would be almost impossible.

He sat up straight and tried to get his mind back on everything that was happening in the game.

He let Salvador keep hold of the vial and he picked up a shield for safety before carrying on to the brow of the hill. Once at the top, he stopped and looked around. The other side of the hill sloped down gradually and looked very similar to the side he'd just walked up, but without the little cottage. The flat land at the bottom stretched out for miles before him. Most of the ground looked stony and dry. In the distance an enormous dark castle loomed in an otherwise barren land.

Although the castle was distant, Josh knew he would be forced to go there because there was nothing else to see.

Reluctantly he started Salvador on his long journey down the hill, still holding the shield in front of him with one hand and holding out an open vial in the other.

But the journey to the castle, which he thought would be long, took no time at all. Once Salvador was at the bottom of the hill, the castle seemed to slide towards him with every step he took. It was so strange the way it was happening that at first Josh thought it was an optical illusion, but within a few steps Salvador was standing in front of the castle.

The sky rapidly darkened, huge black clouds hung low overhead and eerie noises screeched around him from every direction. Salvador turned to Josh with eyes wide with terror. It seemed cruel to make him carry on but Josh wasn't going to let the game try to put him off, so he took another deep breath and carried on.

The castle was an extremely large and intimidating structure and Salvador was dwarfed by its size. There was a drawbridge over a small moat around the castle, and the dark arched doorway beyond, which must have been over ten feet high, looked gloomy and forbidding.

Josh felt a lone tear well in his left eye and run down his cheek. His lips trembled with the beginning a fresh bout of crying but he fought hard to hold it all back. He didn't want to cry again. To beat the game he had to give it all his concentration. There was no time for self-pity.

He studied the picture on the screen and inwardly he acknowledged his feelings of dread while at the same time knowing he couldn't allow them to dominate his actions.

Salvador went warily through the doorway looking left to right all the time. Once inside he was in an enclosed empty courtyard. The floor was covered in thick sawdust. Cannons, sandbags and other paraphernalia that Josh didn't recognise were scattered around untidily as though the people who had been there had left abruptly, dropping things as they went.

There were several small doors to either side and at the other end was what looked like the main door into the castle itself. It had to be the main door because it stood alone, was much larger than the other doors and was lavishly decorated with ornate carvings of soldiers victorious in battle.

Salvador walked to the door. Josh was surprised because he wasn't controlling him. He knew Salvador had to go through the door sooner or later so it didn't really make any difference if the game made it happen sooner.

Salvador put his hand to the door, pushed it open and went through.

The door closed behind him with a loud slam. The screen faded to black and then another scene faded back in. Josh could now see Salvador at the other side of the door. He was in a dark room. There was a window, or what must have been just a hole in the castle wall, but not much light filtered through from the dark sky outside.

The interior walls looked to be made of the same dark grey stones as the exterior walls and the floor looked like bare earth that had been trodden hard and flat. There was a small wooden table in one corner of the room and a wooden stool in another. On the opposite wall was another door.

There seemed to be no one around but still he held up the shield as he moved Salvador from one room to the next.

There were dozens of rooms. Each one was different in size and shape but they all had depressing dark stone walls and only one other door. There wasn't much furniture in any of the rooms, just a few tables and chairs, and it was hard to tell what any of the rooms were used for. Josh could feel his heart thudding in his chest every time he opened a door, afraid of what might be waiting in the next room. As Salvador ventured further into the castle, Josh felt as though he was being swallowed up alive.

He didn't know where his next enemy would be. What would live in a castle? A knight? A king?

As Salvador put his hand on the next door, there was a spark and a crackling sound. Salvador withdrew his hand and looked at Josh.

"I don't want to go in there," screamed Josh. *"I don't want to. I don't want to. I DON'T WANT TO!"* But his protests were hopeless.

The game wanted to play.

Without any help from Josh, Salvador jumped up, kicked open the door and entered the claustrophobic interior of the next room. It was similar to all the others and contained only an old wooden table in one corner. There was a small gothic window on the far wall and next to it stood a figure in a long black hooded robe.

Salvador and Josh exchanged a worried look and then looked back at the hooded figure. It slowly raised one arm and pointed its hand up at ceiling. A lightning bolt flashed from its fingertips up to the ceiling where it burst into a shower of sparks that fell all over the room.

"A wizard," said Josh. Although he'd only whispered the words he startled himself with how loud it sounded in his quiet bedroom.

The huge wizard stood motionless and mute, its hands by its sides and its face hidden within the blackness of the large hood. Josh kept Salvador still, expecting the wizard to make the first move.

Minutes ticked by. Salvador shifted his weight from one leg to the other as he waited. Josh wondered why the wizard wasn't moving. Perhaps it wasn't a wizard after all.

He put his hand on the mouse and moved the cursor over the hooded figure. The words *Fear me and die* appeared on the screen. He moved the cursor away from the wizard and the words disappeared. As they faded a thought occurred to Josh. Were the words instructions for two things that he was supposed to do? Was he supposed to be afraid and then die? Or maybe it was a warning that if he *feared* the wizard he *would* die.

I am afraid though, thought Josh.

Salvador was still holding the magic liquid and the shield so maybe now was the time to use them.

Josh pressed the arrow and shift key on the computer keyboard and Salvador lifted the shield until it was in front of his chest. He felt confident that this would give Salvador some protection. If the wizard had a magic wand for casting spells, Josh was sure the shield could deflect it just as it had done with the magic liquid.

He pressed the arrow key and on the screen Salvador walked towards the wizard. He walked stiffly. Josh was tense.

Outside the castle the sky grew quietly darker along with the interior of the wizard's room.

Thunder rumbled and lightning flashed. The room momentarily lit up brightly with the lightning and in that split second Josh could see that the wizard's eyes were completely red, except for the small, shiny, black pupils.

He shuddered at the sight and felt slightly unnerved. The wizard looked like the epitome of evil.

Despite the amount of noise coming from the computer speakers, Josh became aware of movement and shouting downstairs in his house. His parents were still alive. He felt a surge of relief even though they were in danger.

He returned his attention to the screen because above all the noise of the storm outside the castle, he could hear the wizard mumbling and, too late, he realized that the wizard was chanting.

Josh tried to move Salvador and throw the magic liquid in the wizard's face, but Salvador didn't respond. Josh hit the keys again and again but there was still no response from Salvador. In desperation he slammed the palms of his hands onto the keyboard hitting every key at once, but his effort was in vain. Salvador didn't budge. His shield had afforded him no protection against a chanted spell.

The wizard turned to look Josh in the eye and then bent backwards and laughed. Josh pounded his fists on the keyboard to try to move Salvador, but he seemed completely paralysed.

Suddenly he became aware that downstairs all movement and shouting had ceased too and only the wizard's taunting laughter could be heard from both places.

Josh slumped his shoulders. He felt helpless. His parents were doomed. Salvador couldn't fight an evil wizard if he couldn't move, and neither could they.

He looked at Salvador's strength line. It was almost on nil. No wonder it had been so easy to paralyse Salvador. Josh had forgotten to feed him after using so much energy to walk over the hill and defeat the dwarfs and the troll. How could he have been so stupid as to bring Salvador all that way without feeding him?

Now his parents were in trouble and there was nothing he could do to help them. Josh had never felt so wretched.

On the screen the wizard turned his attention back to Salvador.

"Well," the wizard said in a very deep, throaty voice. "How does it feel to be a failure? How does it feel to know that you're going to die a very slow and excruciatingly painful death and there is nothing you can do about it?"

Again it started its evil laughter, and then abruptly stopped as though a sudden thought had occurred to it.

"I know," it said to Salvador, taking a step closer. "To make things more interesting, I'll give you an even chance to escape your imminent torture."

Josh sat forward to listen. Could this be his way out of this predicament? Was the game really going to give him an even chance to win? Josh knew this would be his last chance to save his parents.

"Are you ready?" the wizard asked Salvador and waited, as though expecting a reply. "What's the matter? Cat got your tongue?"

Josh could hear the sarcasm in the wizard's voice and he felt instantly disheartened. He wasn't going to be given a chance to save his parents after all. The game was just playing with him by getting his hopes up and then dashing them.

On the screen the wizard stepped even closer to Salvador and stood with its hands on its hips. It bent forwards to look Salvador straight in the eye, head cocked arrogantly to one side. Salvador couldn't move and probably couldn't speak either, as he hadn't done so throughout the whole game. By the wizard's sarcastic tone of voice, it already knew this anyway. Josh could see now that the wizard would use

Salvador's muteness as an excuse not to give him an even chance.

But then he said something else that made Josh reconsider.

"Well, I'll just take your stony silence as a yes. So you *are* ready."

Josh was pleasantly surprised. Maybe the game wasn't playing a trick on him after all.

"Hands up all those who don't want to die," instructed the wizard.

The frozen Salvador remained still.

"Go on, hold your hand high in the air if you want to live." There was a pause. "No one? OK, back to the original plan of torture and death it is," and the wizard set off with raucous laughter at its own attempt at humour.

Josh felt cheated. He didn't know what to do.

When the wizard's laughter subsided, a noise could be heard from downstairs. It was only a quiet sound but Josh definitely heard it. He listened carefully then he realized what it was. It was his mother quietly weeping.

He burst into tears. He wanted to help his mother and couldn't bear to hear her being so sad and frightened. But he didn't know what to do. He felt that there must be a way to defeat the evil wizard, but he just didn't know how.

In panic and sheer desperation he started banging his hands on all the keys on the keyboard again, but still nothing happened.

He slammed his hand repeatedly on the 'Escape' key to try to make the game disappear from the screen, but it remained exactly where it was. Then he pressed the 'Eject' key on the disk drive again and again, but the game's disk remained firmly locked in place.

The situation was hopeless. He could see no way out.

His parents were going to die and he was helpless to stop it.

"Check mate," he said quietly to himself, and wept.

Chapter 27

"Josh."

The word was only a whisper but he heard it quite clearly and it seemed to be coming from the computer. The voice sounded very familiar.

Josh wiped his eyes and looked at the screen. Salvador was still paralysed and the wizard was slowly circling him like a wild animal getting ready to pounce on its prey. He couldn't see where the voice was coming from. Was it Salvador? No, Salvador couldn't talk.

"Josh."

He heard it again. It sounded far away. Was it someone outside the castle? But it was a whisper, not someone shouting, so he wasn't sure. But he was now sure that he knew the voice and had heard it many times before.

Then he remembered whose voice it was and a shiver went up his spine. It was Uncle Neville. Fresh tears began only this time they were tears of happiness.

"Uncle Neville?" he asked.

There was no response.

"Oh Uncle Neville if that's you please help me, please." Josh took a big sniff to try to clear his runny nose and he swiped at the tears on his cheeks.

"Eat," came the whispered voice again.

"Eat?" Josh didn't understand.

"Eat!" The voice was louder, but still a whisper, and the word was a command.

Uncle Neville had come back from the grave to help him. He knew what Josh had forgotten. But it was too late. Salvador was paralysed and unable to eat.

Is that what had happened to Uncle Neville? Had he forgotten to feed his hero too? But what good was the advice now?

Josh moved as though on automatic pilot. Uncle Neville said *eat* so that was what he must let Salvador do.

He put his hand on the keyboard and tried to move Salvador but he was still unresponsive. Now what? How was he going to get the food? Then the logical answer struck him like a lightning bolt. He should get to the food in the bag the same way he always did. He put his hand on the mouse and moved the cursor over the bag. He clicked the mouse. The contents in the bag appeared. So far so good.

He moved the mouse over the food and clicked. It worked! The food disappeared from the bag and Salvador's strength line increased. Josh hurriedly clicked on all the food until the strength line was complete.

He closed the bag and quickly pressed the key that controlled Salvador's arm that held the vial.

To his amazement it worked. Salvador's arm shot forward and the liquid splashed over the wizard, who was taken completely by surprise.

He had expected the wizard to interfere and not allow him to retrieve the food, but he'd done nothing. Then he'd expected him to react as Salvador's strength line increased or certainly when it was full. Maybe the wizard was only aware of what was happening on the immediate screen and so had no knowledge of what was happening elsewhere.

Up until now the game seemed to know Josh's every thought and intention so he didn't understand. But then again, he didn't really care why it had happened, only that it had.

The wizard began to scream. Josh watched as it raised its arms and shouted, cursing the sky. Outside the castle a storm began to rage so fiercely that the castle walls shook.

Outside his own bedroom, the sky blackened and an angry, lashing storm began, identical in ferocity to the digital one before him.

On the screen the wizard still screamed and cursed, whipping up the storm into a further frenzy. Through the crescendo of all the noise around him, Josh could hear nothing else. He desperately wanted to know what was happening inside his own house but his eyes were riveted to the scene before him.

The wizard swayed from side to side as it screamed. The swaying soon turned to writhing and then the screaming ceased.

The fingertips on its raised arms changed colour from tanned flesh to sandy-white. The wizard watched the changing hand with terrified, bulging eyes. The colour continued to expand quickly over its hands and down its arms. Even its robe changed. Once the colour reached its shoulders it spread up its neck and engulfed its whole head before travelling down its chest and over its whole body.

Then there was silence. A deafening silence.

The storms ceased and the skies, both on the computer and in the real world, lightened with surprising speed.

The wizard didn't move at all; not even its chest rose and fell as it breathed. It was stone. The liquid in the vial had turned it to stone. The twisted look of agony on its face had been petrified forever.

Josh saved the game.

From downstairs there was no noise at all now, only a heavy silence. He was desperate to go down and see if his parents were all right but he daren't leave the game alone. Who knew what it might do if left on its own? It was best to finish it.

He turned Salvador around and left the wizard's room. He retraced his path through the castle. He felt uneasy, expecting the game to trick him again at any moment. Maybe another enemy would appear, or the way out would change and become a maze of rooms that he couldn't navigate, leaving Salvador trapped in the castle forever. Every time Salvador went through a door, Josh dreaded what might be in there. But each time the rooms were just as he'd seen them before without even the slightest change.

Eventually Salvador emerged into the courtyard and there was a side door with an engraved wooden sign on it which said 'EXIT'. That door had not been there before, Josh was sure of it, but he was glad to see it now.

He opened the door cautiously and found that it opened straight out to the rear of the castle which seemed strange because he didn't think castles had back doors and even if they did the door, at least from the inside, had opened on the left hand side of the castle, not the back. It didn't make sense but it made things easy for him and he wasn't about to look a gift horse in the mouth.

Outside the back of the castle there was a road leading a short way into the distance, and three long roads leading in different directions forked from the other end. He walked Salvador along the short road to the junction with the other three. There were three wooden street signs at the crossroad, one pointing to each road, but he wasn't sure what the signs meant.

The road to the left led away into some mountains and there was a picture on the road sign of a beautiful house. The road in the centre led into some distant caves and there was a picture of gold and diamonds on the sign. The third road to the right led to sandy dunes and the road sign showed a picture of fruit and vegetables falling out of a hollow horn.

Josh contemplated the signs and the roads. Obviously he was supposed to make a decision as to where to go. So this was how the game was going to trick him. Never before in the game had he had any choice of where to go. Forward had been the only way.

Now he was forced to choose his own fate, or more correctly, the fate of his parents.

He was too mentally exhausted to think. Did the game know this? Is that why it was forcing him to choose? Or was it just coincidence?

He didn't know. Nor was it important. What was important was making the right decision. The wrong one, he knew, meant death.

He looked at all the signs again. His choices seemed to be a beautiful house in the mountains, gold and jewels in a cave or fruit and vegetables in the desert.

Why would he want any of these? His tired mind couldn't understand the choices.

Josh sat back in his chair and tried to concentrate. There was still no sound from downstairs. Were his parents all right? Had the wizard hurt them or were they still paralysed?

"Think, Josh, think," he told himself, trying to focus his mind back on the task facing him.

The first road into the mountains looked tempting and the sign with the beautiful house could mean home, and that would mean safety. How he longed for safety. But whose house was it and why was it in the mountains? Did the house mean safety for Salvador or for Josh and his parents? And safety from what? Were there more enemies over there? Josh's head spun with all the possibilities of what the sign could mean.

The second road to the caves could be the right one because the sign showing gold and diamonds meant the caves must be gold and diamond mines and he could become rich enough to buy anything he ever wanted. But again, what did it mean? Richness in life or in the game? Anyway why riches? His main priority now was to finish the game and escape the living hell he and his family were presently in.

Maybe riches were symbolic for whatever he wanted in life, so if he wanted safety he could have it. But wasn't that what the house in the mountains represented? He wasn't sure.

The third road was even more puzzling. The sign showed food but the road went into some sand dunes so it looked like a desert. There was no food in a desert. This had to be the game trying to trick him. Perhaps it wanted him to choose this road by showing a picture of food, especially after he was nearly defeated because he forgot to feed Salvador and keep up his strength.

But the food he picked up in the game to feed Salvador was just white lumps. It was supposed to represent 'manna' like in the Bible when the people were sent manna from heaven and they ate a white substance from the ground.

So why was the sign showing proper food and why falling from a big horn? Maybe just to tempt him. But why the horn?

He remembered that he'd seen that picture before, engraved on the front of the old Town Hall in the town where they lived. One day he asked his mother about it and she had said it was called *Cornucopia* or *The Horn of Plenty,* and that it was symbolic of a promise of an abundance of everything.

But apart from sand there wasn't plenty of anything in a desert.

Still, something was trying to gel in his mind. Something to do with the desert and the *Horn of Plenty*. The desert and the *Horn of Plenty*. The desert and the *Horn of Plenty*.

In the Bible the Israelites had been led through the desert for many days until they came to the Land of Plenty which was also called *The Promised Land*.

That was it! Josh almost jumped out of his chair in excitement.

He'd figured it out. The Horn of Plenty would lead through the desert to The Promised Land and that was what this game was all about. *The Journey to the Promised Land*. But something inside him still niggled and made him feel that there could still be danger ahead.

Josh looked at the three choices again and decided to stick with his decision.

Salvador turned to Josh with a questioning look on his face.

"I know, I know," he told his digital partner. "You want to get going and get to *The Promised Land* too, don't you? But I've got to be careful. I don't want to make the wrong choice."

Salvador lifted an eyebrow and pointed his finger at his chest and then at Josh.

"Oh, I get it. *We* don't want to make the wrong choice. OK, then, which way do you think *we* should go?"

Salvador turned and pointed to the road leading to the desert.

"You want to go that way too?"

Salvador nodded and pointed hard at the road again. Josh followed the direction of his finger and saw a tiny speck of white further along the road. He walked Salvador to the spot and saw that it was a lump of food. Salvador smiled at Josh, picked up the food and ate it.

Josh smiled too and gave a small laugh. He wasn't controlling Salvador anymore, he was moving of his own free will and Josh had never actually seen him eat before. He'd usually just click on the food and it would disappear and Salvador's energy line would grow, so it was only ever *assumed* that he'd eaten without actually seeing him do it.

Now Salvador could not only eat but could move freely. He ran along the road, picking up food and eating it as he went. The further he went the more food there was on the ground, making Josh sure that they'd chosen the right direction. It was manna from heaven, helping them to *The Promised Land.*

Eventually Salvador crested the dunes and on the other side the land spread out far before him, changing as it went along from white sand to green grass. Josh could see trees in the distance and birds flying.

Salvador ran towards it all as fast as he could. Soon Josh could see and hear animals too and before he knew it, Salvador was there in amongst it all and it was beautiful. A real Garden of Eden.

The word "*Congratulations*" came up across the screen in large red letters and then the game switched off.

Josh sat there in the quiet stillness.

It was over. He'd played and he'd won.

He'd spent so long waiting to reach this moment but somehow the blank screen and heavy silence felt like a huge anticlimax. After all he and Salvador had been through, this was it. Nothing. Even though he was victorious, he felt cheated. The game was finished, but his worry wasn't over yet. He still didn't know what had happened to his parents.

He got up slowly and left the bedroom, apprehensive and afraid.

All was quiet around him as he descended the stairs. He wasn't sure what to expect but he knew he wouldn't be entering an Eden as Salvador had done.

The first thing that struck him when he reached the bottom of the stairs was how neat and clean the house still was. He was expecting it to be in complete disarray but it was as though nothing had happened.

He wasn't sure where his parents were, if indeed they were still there at all. He looked in the neat and tidy living room first but they weren't there. Then he looked into the equally neat sitting room.

Finally he looked in the kitchen. Again everything was exceptionally neat and tidy only this time his parents *were* there. He let out a heavy sigh of relief.

They were both sitting at the table with their heads face down on their folded arms. Although they weren't moving, Josh knew they were still alive as their backs rose and fell with their even breathing.

He stood and cried like a baby. Never before had he ever cried as much as he had today, but then again, he'd never before had a day like today and never wanted to again. He stood with his arms hanging limply at his sides and cried for a long time.

He longed to run up and hug his mother. His need for physical contact was never as great as it was right now. He wanted them to wake up. He *needed* them to wake up. But he was also scared of what would happen when they did.

Although they seemed physically unharmed he couldn't help but wonder what the day's terrible events had done to their minds.

When they woke up it would probably be questions, questions, questions. They would want to know about everything that had happened.

Perhaps it was time to tell the truth and unburden everything that he'd been keeping to himself.

Would his parents understand? Or would his mother never get over the shock?

One thing he did know for sure was that after today their lives would never be the same again.

Chapter 28

Josh stood in the kitchen and watched his parents sleeping until his tears abated. He wondered how he would even begin to explain the game to them.

Then he had a terrible thought. What if they wanted to turn it on? He must never let them do that. Just to make sure he decided to get rid of the game and the computer before they woke up.

But what if they never wake up? What if they're under some sort of sleeping spell from the wizard? These questions worried him but he didn't have time to think about it. He had to get rid of the game once and for all.

He marched resolutely back upstairs, went into his room and picked up the computer tower. With the game disk still in it he carried it downstairs and out into the garden. He dropped it ungracefully on the ground near the bin. It hit the ground with a loud crack. He went back and brought the rest of it out piece by piece.

He walked to the garage to look for a hammer and brought out the biggest one he could find. It was so heavy that he needed two hands to carry it but he didn't care. The heavier the better.

He swung the hammer down onto the computer tower again and again. Breaking it was slow work with having to lift such a heavy hammer but he enjoyed every second of it. He couldn't remember anything he'd ever done giving him such a feeling of satisfaction. He took out his anger on the computer and it felt good. He worked himself into a frenzy with the hammer.

When the tower was in lots of broken pieces he started on the keyboard, then the monitor and finally the mouse.

He swung the hammer as high as possible every time before bringing it down with as much force as he could manage. Plastic, metal and glass flew in every direction until the job was done and Josh had worked off his anger and hate. When he stopped and saw all the broken pieces around him, he felt gleeful.

He calmly returned the hammer to the garage, picked up all the scattered pieces, and threw them all in the bin.

As he closed the lid a huge smile spread across his face. He couldn't stop it and he didn't want to.

"Josh have you gone mad?"

The voice behind him made him jump but he was so happy to hear it.

"Dad. You're OK."

His parents exchanged a questioning look.

"Of course I'm OK. Why shouldn't I be?"

"No reason," Josh lied. "Is everything all right?"

"Of course everything's all right. What's wrong with you?"

"Me?"

"Yes you," his mother said with a smile. "You look like you've seen a ghost."

"Haven't you?" Josh asked them sincerely.

His father gave a small nervous laugh. "Josh is something bothering you? Have you been up to something we should know about?"

Josh just stood and stared, opened mouthed, not knowing what to say.

"Josh, what is it?" His mother looked slightly worried.

"Nothing," Josh lied again. "I've just had my mind on other things today, that's all." Then he smiled to try to lighten the mood. "Chill out. It's nothing."

"Was that pieces of your computer that you put in the bin?" asked his father.

"Yep."

"Well that's a bit extreme isn't it? We only asked you to cut down on your computer time, not destroy it."

Josh was flabbergasted. His parents obviously had no recollection about what had happened. He didn't understand why but once again he didn't want to look a gift horse in the mouth. It was much better if he didn't have to explain everything, and better if they didn't remember, so he went along with them as best he could and tried to pretend everything was normal.

Inside he was bursting with happiness, but daren't show it. He felt so light and unburdened that he thought he could float if he tried.

The game was gone. It was never going to play again. Everyone was safe and now their lives could get back to normal again.

It was just a pity that he couldn't share his feeling of elation with his parents. It was another secret that he had to hide, but by now he should be good at keeping secrets.

*

The next morning Josh woke early. It felt wonderful to be in his room without the ominous presence of the computer constantly hanging over him like the sword of Damocles.

He lay there for quite a while enjoying his new freedom. He was so lucky his Uncle Neville had come to his rescue yesterday.

"Oh Uncle Neville. How did you ever make something so evil?"

It had been wonderful to hear his voice again but it made Josh miss his uncle all over again. Well today was Sunday and he had no plans so he thought he would go to the cemetery and sit by Uncle Neville's grave for a while.

Later that morning his father went with him and walked around inspecting the inscriptions on the other headstones while Josh sat down.

After making sure his father was far enough away and couldn't hear him, Josh began to speak.

"Uncle Neville, I know you're there and I know that it was you who helped me yesterday. Not so long ago I couldn't understand why you would have such an evil game but you didn't mean to did you? And I bet that it got you in the end didn't it? It nearly got me too but I guess you know that already."

He paused, feeling his chest tightening and his jaws began to ache with the strain of needing to cry again, so he gave up and let the tears flow.

"Oh Uncle Neville, I've missed you so much. It's been so horrible around here and it was so hard for me, you know?" Josh cried and talked and cried some more for quite some time. He poured out all the details of what the game had done and how frightened he'd been.

"But you saved me and Mum and Dad. I thought we were all going to die. Oh God, I was so scared."

Josh hung his head and his shoulders shook with every sob.

His father watched him discretely from a distance, his heart breaking for his son.

After a while his tears stopped and Josh sat quietly, staring at the ground. Then he stood and walked over to his father, silently took his hand and the two of them left the cemetery together in silence.

It had been a long time since the two of them had held hands and his father was surprised and touched. He squeezed Josh's hand and smiled down at him. Josh looked up and smiled at his father.

Josh felt happy for the first time in weeks.

Chapter 29

Epilogue

Mike O'Grady wheeled the Harrisons' bin to the curb ready for the bin wagon. He'd been emptying bins in the town for over ten years now. He loved his job and the nice weather made it seem so much easier.

He'd heard something rattling as he'd moved the bin so he opened the lid for a peek inside. It was a computer, complete with monitor and keyboard and someone had smashed it all up. What a shame.

Then he saw that there was a disk still in what was left of the disk drive so he took the disk drive out for a closer look. Although the disk drive was broken, the disk still looked in good condition.

The wagon pulled up near him and he placed the bin on the lift at the back and hit the "start" button. As the mechanism lifted the bin and emptied it he gave the broken disk drive to the driver.

"Keep that for me will you!" he shouted and then went back on with his work.

During his break he took a small screwdriver out of his pocket and took the drive apart. He removed the disk and looked it over.

Journey to the Promised Land. It must be a game.

Later that day, when his fourteen-year-old son arrived home from school, he gave him the disk.

"Here Stephen. I found this in an old computer that someone had thrown out."

"Cool," said Stephen and checked the disk for scratches.

"It looks all right," his father told him. "I think it must be a game but I don't know if it works or not."

"There's only one way to find out," said Stephen, and took it to his bedroom.

He didn't actually hold out much hope of the game working because his computer was old and some of the newer games wouldn't even install properly, let alone play, and this one must be new because he'd never heard of a game called *Journey to the Promised Land* before.

He turned on his computer, put the CD into the disk drive and waited for the installation instruction to come on. But to his surprise and delight the game simply appeared immediately without needing to install it at all.

Cool! That certainly made life easier.

He clicked the mouse over the words "New Game." On the screen he saw a man standing on the edge of an old-fashioned village. He was amazed at how realistic the picture was. It was like looking at a real scene. There were a lot of eerie noises coming from the speakers which sent a shiver down his spine.

Cool, thought Stephen. *This is going to be fun.*

End.

© 2007